In memory of: Dinu and Jay

Both were called away prematurely before the match was over. I have 'batted' solo having changed the format, per force, from 'test match' to 'single wicket'. To paraphrase Robert Frost - we shall meet again... not yet though, for '...I have promises to keep and miles to go before I sleep....'

CONTENTS

The Ivory Towers   1

The Talking Newspaper   60

Green Fingers   107

Cold Dish   146

Sisterly Love   188

PCB   236

Mojo Charms   302

The Ivory Towers

The Kenya Airways local flight from Nairobi landed at Moi International Airport Mombasa, as scheduled. Alec Dunlop, BVetMed, MRCVS, made his way through baggage collection and into the arrivals lounge, scanning the placards and the waiting drivers for the hotel shuttle service. The Orange Coral Hotel was a short thirty five minute drive away – a family run hotel renowned for its seafood cuisine and its array of water sports, especially scuba diving. The hotel had been recommended by his colleagues in Nairobi.

Alec was on a short break after a gruelling stint with the wildlife capture and translocation unit of the Wildlife Conservation Dept. The unit tranquilised and translocated wildlife for various purposes – routine tracking and monitoring, treatment of injured animals, capture and relocation from one habitat to another or movement to specialist treatment centres. He had taken a sabbatical from the Royal Veterinary College and had been seconded to various wildlife specialised units to gain an overview of wildlife conservation. A far cry from the small animal practice that he had in South London and his position as a visiting lecturer in small animal medicine at the prestigious Royal

College in Camden. Whilst he enjoyed the challenges of imparting clinical skills to final year BVetMed students, the opportunity to practise wildlife medicine, albeit for a few months, had always been a dream.

In his early forties, Alec had reached a stage in his career when professional apathy sets in; the 'been there, done that' scenario. The dream foray into wildlife medicine and conservation work would be the perfect antidote to professional complacency and an excuse to return to Kenya where he had spent his early, formative years. His father had a long and illustrious tenure as a Home Office civil servant who had been seconded to work in the East African Railways and Harbours head office in Nairobi – years before Kenya's independence in December 1963.

Alec's childhood memories of Nairobi and the beach holidays in Mombasa were as faded as the sepia tinged photographs in the family album. There were no photographs of their last vacation in Mombasa – his mother had died in a horrific car crash on the way to Mombasa, at a notorious accident black spot just before the town of Voi. Alec had blotted out the painful memory of that fateful day. His father had brought Alec back to the UK soon after the tragedy; a disruptive phase in both their lives. 'Bwana' (Swahili for boss or master) Dunlop, an ebullient soul, had been reduced to an empty shell. Alec, with the resilience of youth had survived the tragedy; seemingly without any emotional scars. Dunlop senior never quite came to terms with the guilt that hounded him for the rest of his life, for relinquishing the wheel to his wife just minutes before the crash.

On the recommendation of a colleague, Alec enlisted as a volunteer with a UK registered charity involved in the conservation and protection of elephants and its habitats in Kenya. Its charters also embraced measures to control poaching and the illegal ivory trade. His secondment for six months to the Kenyan branch of the charity had taken a while to clear immigration and licensing requirements – a period of six months with the wildlife department had been approved. The translocation unit and the demanding work done by the local vets fascinated him and he was eagerly looking forward to the assignments in Laikipia and in the Nairobi National Park.

The persistent lack of rain in the Laikipia region had intensified the drought cycle. Scarcity of water was a factor that triggered human-elephant conflict and needed immediate resolution. Whilst the other game had been controlled and managed by the game wardens, the Laikipia elephants had gained undue notoriety. Rogue elephants, especially the ones exhibiting 'musth', as a result of higher testosterone levels, had become a nuisance, breaking through the electric fences and encroaching on to human habitats in search of water and foliage. These unruly episodes of aggression were sometimes used as an excuse by the farmers to succumb to poachers' inducements. The equilibrium between wildlife and human habitats was also dependent on tribal machinations between the Samburu, the Pokot and the Turkana tribes – all jockeying for the control of the pastoral lands and grazing rights.

Alec's insights into the tribal rivalries and Kenyan politics were primarily based on his father's reminiscences. He was certain that although Kenya had moved on since independence, the old internecine conflicts between the tribal 'troika' still held sway. The poachers exploited all these nuances to their benefit – playing one against the other in elaborate games of chess with real ivory as the currency of discord, decimation and destruction.

Alec had just assisted the wildlife capture unit to relocate a few rogue elephants further towards Mount Kenya. The use of the Dan-Inject Dart system to tranquilise-immobilise the elephants with etorphine and then promote full mobility-recovery with the antagonist, diprenorphine, was the standard drug regimen followed in most game parks. He found the whole process fascinating, especially the logistics of sedating elephants – the adherence to stringent protocols presented extreme physiological challenges. All the clinical protocols had to be executed quickly to avoid complications – a few extra minutes of prostration or a delay in reversing the tranquilising phase could compromise cardiac and pulmonary functions. Fatalities, though rare, did occur.

For the time being the danger of marauding wildlife had abated. The repairs to the fencing had somewhat mitigated the problem. Once animals stray from designated national parks and reserves, monitoring them becomes difficult and these animals then become easy targets for organised gangs of poachers.

Just before Alec's return to Nairobi, the game wardens received word that poachers had been spotted on the western plains of Laikipia. There were indications that this was the same network of poachers who had shot down a renowned bull elephant – a shattered tracking collar had been found identifying the tusker as 'Rafiki' (friend). The game wardens had been monitoring Rafiki and knew that his massive tusks would make him prone to a fatal outcome; their surveillance efforts in monitoring and protecting the pachyderm had been in vain.

The game wardens, some of them armed, set off in the direction of the last reported sightings of a small herd of elephants. The tracking team, on reverting to their records, knew that the herd was vulnerable because of the presence of pregnant females and young calves. The tusks were there for the taking and the conservation taskforce was fearful of further casualties – Laikipia's fast diminishing elephant population was at imminent risk.

The team reached the western edge of the target area and saw empty cartridge shells strewn all over a copse of Acacia trees. A blood trail indicated that the elephant herd had not escaped unhurt; some, if not all, had been wounded. No carcasses were found, which was unusual as the poachers had AK-47s and could have mowed down any number of elephants. Quite possibly the poachers, due to time constraints, were targeting a particular elephant for its longer tusks. It could also be a hit and run operation – the poachers trying to maximise its ivory harvest as the gang retreated towards the Somali border. There was virtual immunity for the poachers once they fled deep into the war torn Somali territory – the anti-poaching taskforce knew that this was a deliberate strategy followed by the poachers; a war of attrition with the odds heavily against the authorities.

It was almost a couple of hours before sunset when the game wardens came upon a comatose bull elephant; shot at point blank range. The gaping wounds, where the tusks had been hacked off, were still bloody and smothered by swarms of bluebottles. The slashed carotid artery still pulsating with arterial blood, spurting out with each feeble heart beat – the poacher's panga (machete) had made short work of the thick layers of skin, subcutaneous fat and muscle. A nearby 'manyatta' (a Samburu or Maasai enclosure with mud walled huts) had been used as a makeshift abattoir – its expanse of ochre soil stained and damp with pools of coagulated blood. The bluebottles were engaged in a frenzy of egg-laying on the exposed flesh – within a day the rotting flesh would be seething with maggots.

One of the armed wardens shot twice into the frontal and the temporal lobes of the comatose elephant to perform instant euthanasia. The shots reverberated in the abandoned manyatta; the acoustic impact amplified by the surrounding walls.

The group split up, with Alec following the two seasoned and experienced game wardens. They had only one Heckler & Koch G3 rifle between them; a wholly inadequate piece of armament against the AK-47 armed poachers. Alec felt inhibited without any arms, not that he would have known how to use one. He had only ever used a dart gun to tranquilise a gazelle, which was just a few days ago. Engaging with professional poachers was a different ball game and Alec realised that he was out of his depth in this deadly conflict. His apprehension grew as he viewed the golden orb sinking into the horizon; nightfall not yet imminent but preying on his mind.

Within the hour, with the sun fast receding and silhouetting the Acacia trees, they were ambushed by a four man splinter group of poachers. Before Alec could react, a short burst of fire felled both the game wardens. Alec was transfixed as he saw two men emerge from the thick undergrowth shouldering a pair of tusks, with blood still dripping off the ivory surfaces. The third poacher had a blood soaked 'panga' in his left hand and an AK-47 in his right. He quickly nudged the two immobile game wardens and approached Alec, still keeping him in the line of fire. Alec instinctively raised his arms in silent supplication.

For a split second, the poacher raised his AK-47 and took aim as if to mow Alec down. A quick command from behind Alec compelled the gunman to pause and look to the leader, the fourth poacher.

The tribes are all pastoralists and value their cattle as their most prized assets. The respect accorded to the 'daktari' vets for their curative powers was on par with the respect given to tribal medicine men; vets treated and cured cattle. The leader's keen powers of observation probably averted another killing. Alec's life hung in the balance momentarily and was saved by the slenderest of threads – the bright red, highly visible rubber tubing of his stethoscope.

'Waccha, hiyu na daktari' (leave him alone, he's a doctor), the fourth poacher, dressed as a Samburu warrior shouted across from behind Alec. The authority implied in the terse command was palpable. The AK-47 was lowered and the third poacher's tacit submission was mirrored in his eyes and by his body language. The trio presented a morbid sight – the bleeding pair of tusks straddling the shoulders of the two poachers and the third poacher armed with an AK-47 and a blood-soaked panga.

The six foot tall Samburu with short braided colourfully beaded hair, the leader of the pack, was unarmed. He quickly frisked Alec and took away his wallet, which contained about five hundred pounds. As the Samburu looked up and snarled, Alec noticed the missing two lower incisors, traditionally removed to ameliorate the symptoms of lockjaw (tetanus) if it ever struck – prophylaxis in abeyance! The braided hair and the face were both smeared with red ochre. His torso was bare; the lower half draped flamboyantly in a bright orange cloth. Half his left ear lobe was missing. The Samburu looked ferocious in the fading daylight; the snarl distorting the ochre hued face. Alec shuddered as the frisson of fear flashed across his face and avoided making eye contact despite realising that the Samburu had probably saved his life.

The leader shouted a few more commands and the group retreated into the bush. The Samburu turned around and threw Alec's empty wallet back at him. It was all over in a few minutes, although for Alec, it had seemed like an eternity. Alec ran towards the prone men and his cursory scrutiny told him that he would not need his stethoscope to confirm death. With his hands shaking, Alec retrieved a walkie-talkie and placed a Mayday call to the base camp. Alec and the two dead game wardens were picked up by a camouflaged Toyota Cruiser within the hour. A sombre mood descended on the base camp; the cloud of death settling like an ominous shroud.

The four poachers with their haul of bloodied ivory tusks were about a mile away from their agreed rendezvous point, continuing on their retreat towards the Somali border. The Samburu slowed down and, at the pretence of wiping out the spoor, deliberately fell back a few yards. The other three were intent on getting to their parked Toyota Cruiser and hardly noticed the Samburu's covert move.

He withdrew his Smith & Wesson 686 gun from the hidden thigh holster and in one fluid motion shot his three colleagues. The Samburu's height meant that the trajectory of all three shots was downwards; either piercing the heart or the lungs or rupturing the descending aorta. Death was instantaneous. As he got closer, he shot them again; a textbook perfect execution. He frisked all three and pocketed all their cash, the car keys, and a dog eared diary that the third poacher had. As he quickly counted his haul, the Samburu's parched lips stretched into a wide smile – the British Sterling would fetch a small fortune on the back streets of Mogadishu. Before pocketing the diary he flicked through and frowned – the first few pages appeared to be blank.

The Samburu, without so much as a backward glance, continued towards the parked car, which carried false 'GK' number plates and was the same make and model as used by the national parks. He retrieved the Toyota, hidden amongst the thick shrubs near an abandoned manyatta. Within minutes he double backed to where the three bodies lay, to collect the tusks and the single AK-47. The three bodies were left behind for the scavengers; the hyenas and the vultures would make short work of the corpses. Before he started his journey towards the Somali border, he wiped clean the 686 and the thigh holster and placed both on the passenger seat; wrapped in an oil rag found in the car.

An hour into the journey, the Samburu pulled off the dirt track into the bush and found a series of termite mounds; some as tall as the smaller Acacia trees. After giving the gun and holster a final clean, he hoisted himself onto the bonnet of the Toyota and dropped the gun and the holster separately into two of the largest mounds – even the local tribesmen kept away from the huge ochre structures as they frequently sheltered cobras and scorpions.

The disposal well away from the scene of the brutal executions meant that the final vestiges of his traitorous act would lay buried in the makeshift tombs for eternity. He spotted the circling vultures in the distance – nature's carrion disposal had begun and once the hyenas got wind of the rotting bodies, all evidence of death would be erased in a few days. He got into the Toyota, nonchalantly humming a popular Swahili melody as he sped towards the border.

After a fretful night, Alec was picked up at dawn by the twin engine Cessna for his short flight to Wilson airport, situated on the outskirts of Nairobi. He was scheduled to fly to Mombasa that evening. Whilst Alec would soon bury the memory of the trauma; for the Kenyans, the destruction of their ecosystems was monumental. The economic and human impact of the illicit ivory trade was already mushrooming into an epic African tragedy. The fallout for the human race was yet to be quantified, but the omens for the survival of wildlife, especially the pachyderms, were not sanguine at all.

Alec's Mombasa stay did little to lessen the trauma of the Laikipia incident. His mind kept harking back to that fateful afternoon, especially as he sat on the peaceful beach listening to the soft distinctive sounds of the Indian Ocean. The stark contrast of the brutality of that hot afternoon amidst the Acacia trees and his present serene setting on the beach felt surreal. He made a conscious effort to block the images of the mutilated elephant carcass and the dead game wardens as he returned to his hotel.

After a couple of days of rest and recreation at the Orange Coral Hotel, Alec visited Mombasa's old town and Fort Jesus – both sites had an emotional and nostalgic effect on him; probably because both locations reminded him of his father. He recollected his father's discourses about the historical impact of the Portuguese, the Omani Arabs and lastly the British, who in 1895 declared Kenya a protectorate of the British Empire.

Visiting Fort Jesus, which was built by the Portuguese in 1593, reminded Alec again about his father's two favourite obsessions – archaeology and Greek mythology. Standing on the parapets, looking out to sea, brought back discourses his father was in the habit of launching into with the gusto of the cognoscenti – the countless journeys that Indian and Arab traders, in their small dhows, would have made trading spices, ivory and gold.

It had all started with Vasco da Gama's exploratory expedition in 1497. The Portuguese explorer's fortuitous discovery of the sea route to India, past the Cape of Good Hope, Mozambique and Mombasa, opened up the Eastern trade routes. Alec wondered whether a sizeable portion of the illicit ivory traversed, more or less, the same traditional sea routes of yesteryears –

from Mombasa to Dubai, Somalia, India and beyond; the traditional dhows still operating with almost total impunity.

The old town was within walking distance of Fort Jesus. As he approached, with its disproportionate number of curio shops, and the harbour, the smell of rotting and drying fish wafted across from the seafront; the small dhows and boats simmering in the sun, the old town, with its crisscrossing narrow lanes, was abuzz with tourists, hawkers and a motley crowd of Indian, Arab and European residents; many of them British and German expats. The buibui (an East African garment for Muslim women with a veil that could be flipped back over the head) clad Muslim ladies intermingling with sari clad Indian housewives out doing their daily shopping and chores.

The tourists were eminently visible because of their sartorial exhibition of various designer brands and the plethora of expensive cameras and zoom lenses; opulence on show for the pickpockets weaving their way towards their targets with a clinical and laser focused detachment. These cloistered lanes were fertile hunting grounds for these petty criminals – siding up to their victims with pre-planned precision, just as a mamba would slither, guided by the thermal images, towards its ingenuous rodent prey.

Alec paused and watched with fascination as the coffee sellers with their shiny brass kettles and the distinctive patterned ceramic cups meandered through the crowded lanes – it was almost an art, the way the coffee sellers managed to produce a symphony of tinkling sounds just by the rhythmic clicking of the ceramic cups.

Alec could not but indulge in savouring the scalding black Arabic coffee ('kahawa') and the sweet fried dough like pastry ('mandazi'). This was turning out to be quite a 'walk down memory lane', Alec pondered, as he retraced his way back to the taxi ranks near Fort Jesus.

A day later, Alec caught up with his old friend, Musa, who was a wildlife photographer and cameraman. Musa had prospered as a cinematographer and, rumour had it, that he had profited handsomely from his Hollywood film contracts – two blockbusters shot entirely in Kenya were the making of his international reputation and his fortune. His Hollywood fame attracted more work and led to lucrative contracts – wildlife photoshoots, books and advertising films. He had become a minor celebrity.

He had the look of opulence; the Range Rover Discovery and the bejewelled bullion appearance. A stark contrast to Musa's cash strapped time in London whilst studying cinematography at the National Film & Television School. Alec had bailed him out on a number of occasions with small loans until his remittances arrived from Mombasa – the family had licences to run boutiques in a couple of major beach hotels. The pair had remained friends ever since – they had shared digs in London whilst studying.

Alec had caught a taxi from the Orange Coral to Musa's studio near the Mackinnon Market on Nehru Road. He was pleasantly greeted by Ava Patel, Musa's office manager who supervised the many artisan workmen who produced most of the props for Musa's film and advertising assignments. She was Musa's girl Friday – managing his business affairs whilst he was out on shoots; mostly within East Africa and occasionally overseas.

Alec was bowled over by the alluring vision of a devastatingly attractive thirty five year old who exhibited traits of the racial mix that was so prevalent on the Kenyan coast – an Indian, Omani/Arab and Portuguese amalgamation that serendipitously creates a stunning cocktail; a classical and sculptured look. Alec was enthralled by the sheer stunning symmetry of her features; a Nubian queen reincarnated. He had met her once many years ago when Musa had stopped over in London on his way to Hollywood – it had been Ava's first overseas trip.

'Hi. Good to see you after all these years. My, you have grown into a heart stopper!' Alec gushed still trying to re-configure the image that he had of her as a slip of a girl; the caterpillar had magnificently metamorphosed into an enchanting Monarch butterfly.

'Alec! What a pleasant surprise.' Ava blushed profusely as she tried to ignore the compliments; nothing that she had not heard before. They had not seen each other since their brief encounter in London many years ago. 'Hope you did not get stuck in the traffic? Where are you staying?' she enquired. Musa had informed her about Alec's imminent arrival for their lunch meeting.

'At the Orange Coral, the hotel shuttle uses the priority pre-paid toll lane so we did not have to queue up.' The bridge crossing from Bamburi beach into town was notorious for the bottlenecks and its interminable queues. Alec almost retorted that if this was traffic then the M25 in the UK would probably qualify as a parking lot.

'Are you with us for a while?' Ava queried, making small talk whilst Musa attended to a few routine calls.

'Yes. I head back to London after doing a stint

at the Animal Orphanage and the National Park. There's also an anti-poaching conference that I've been invited to attend. Hopefully it will give me an overview of the illicit ivory trade. Are you joining us for lunch?' Alec asked wishfully. He did not want to relinquish the exquisite apparition that was in front of him.

'No such luck, no rest for the wicked. I have loads to do, enjoy your lunch. Hopefully, we'll meet before you leave?' Ava remarked casually.

Alec and Musa left shortly thereafter with Ava's words still ringing in Alec's ears. He just could not believe his eyes; her maturing into such an awesome beauty.

The lunch at the restaurant gave them ample time to catch up on old times – they were meeting after a long lapse. Whilst the food was delicious, the spicy taste was something that his palate was not accustomed to – his favourite Indian restaurant in South London paled into insipid insignificance in comparison. The authentic North Indian cuisine with nuances of Punjabi, Sikh and Gujarati tastes resulted in a fusion of flavours that was quite unique and delectable – the recipes had evolved over decades of Indian presence in East Africa.

The homemade garlic and chilli gravy that the restaurant was famed for took its toll on Alec's unsuspecting palate – Musa took pity on his friend and plied him with double helpings of Indian 'faludo' and 'kulfi' on the way back – the Blue Room was well known for its ice cream and Indian desserts. They parted at Alec's hotel – Musa promising Alec one final bit of sightseeing before his return to Nairobi.

Alec was just about to have an early night when Ava called from the lobby. He was so taken by surprise that he floundered for a moment, then quickly brushed his teeth, acutely conscious of the lingering garlic and onion aftertaste, and slapped on some aftershave before going down to reception. He spotted her across the lobby, casually dressed in designer denims and a white cotton embroidered top. Despite the lack of makeup she looked ravishing.

'Gosh, I barely recognized you without the work overalls that you had on this morning.'

'Thought I'd wear something unobtrusive – this town is still very conservative, so have to be careful that I don't draw attention,' Ava whispered in a conspiratorial tone. Reading the quizzical look on Alec's face, she continued, 'Fancy a nightcap?'

'Why not, let's go down to the poolside bar,' Alec offered.

'No, let's walk down to the beach, there's a night spot that serves exquisite cocktails and amongst the cosmopolitan mix we won't stick out like two sore thumbs.'

'One sore old thumb, you mean? I am easily that, you hardly qualify with your age and looks.' Alec was away again, plying her with compliments, which she seemed to take in her stride; signs that she was used to male attention and more than adept at fending for herself.

The bar was packed with a very mixed crowd of Europeans and locals, predominantly younger couples. There was a sprinkling of traditionally dressed buibui clad females. Most of these women were diners, as were some tourists, seated around a dance floor, festooned with pulsating strobe lights. A live band with a lead singer was already warming up for the late night session.

After a few drinks, she led him to the dance floor, despite Alec's protestations about having more than two left feet. He was more worried about his dance routine which was disjointed at the best of times. Although he could easily be mistaken for a much younger man than he actually was, her youthful appearance accentuated his age. He felt like a relic especially as Ava and the young jet set around him seemed to move in total synch to the music. However, they had polished off a bottle of red so an alcohol fuelled bravado and the tangible frisson of excitement, generated by the chemistry between them, blunted his inhibitions – he could have danced all night.

After a while, realizing Alec's discomfort, they switched to a slow dance as she cuddled up to him. Despite their age disparities and much to Alec's relief, they were hardly noticed in the cosmopolitan ambience of dancing couples and revellers. There were a few older couples dancing at their own pace which reassured Alec; it had been a while since he last stepped onto a dance floor with someone as pretty as Ava.

As they danced, the couple lost all track of time especially as the singer crooned 'Malaika' (angel), an international love song that had catapulted Miriam Makeba, a South African exile, to universal fame.

'That's Makeba, isn't it? I recognise the tune', Alec said. The Swahili melody lamented the pathos of unrequited love. The Swahili lyrics were lost on Alec but he danced, as best as he could, to the catchy tune. It afforded him the opportunity to hold Ava close and tight. She didn't seem to mind as she synchronised her movements to his slow tempo.

'Well before my time!' exclaimed Ava cheekily. 'Yes, well done – that is a Makeba hit. Right in your timeline, my friend.' She continued the ribbing about his age and played 'young' to lighten the mood. Levity was needed not silence she reminded herself.

Alec ignored the 'barb' about his age and refused to rise to the bait.

Ava expounded, 'Makeba sang 'Malaika' as a duet with Harry Belafonte at the Independence day celebrations on 12th Dec 1963 when 'Mzee' Jomo Kenyatta became the first Prime Minister of independent Kenya.'

'Actually, my dad attended the boisterous celebrations at Uhuru Park on that momentous day. He had also met Mr. Kenyatta at a graduation ceremony –my dad used to be a visiting lecturer at the Railway School in Nairobi. In fact, there's a group photograph of dad, Mr. Kenyatta and other lecturers in the family album.'

Briefly, in the fleeting hours of their nocturnal tryst, 'Malaika' became their song. Alec was flattered by the attention she showered on him – it had been almost two years since his turbulent break-up with a childhood sweetheart. The parting had been acrimonious and he had kept his distance from women until that night when he was swept off his feet. It could be a toxic mix – wine, women and song.

When the seven am wake-up call came through from reception, Alec reluctantly got up

– his head felt sore and he then realized that the other side of the double bed was vacant. The short note on the rumpled pillow caught his eye.

'I had a wonderful night. You did well, 'mzee' (old man), despite the red wine! Got to get back to my flat and then to work. Hopefully, we'll catch up before you leave for Nairobi. Kwaheri (goodbye) for now.' The note was signed as 'kidege' (little bird) – Alec noticed with a wry smile that she had appropriated the little bird epithet from the 'Malaika' song.

He was smiling prodigiously as he jumped into the shower still reflecting on the night's events, not least her tongue-in-cheek reference to their age difference. He had heard Makeba in a live concert many years ago and knew the lyrics vaguely; the melody always reminded him of Kenya.

Alec, softly whistling the melody felt the nostalgia sweep over him – he hadn't realized how profoundly he missed his birth country despite spending almost his entire life in Britain. He had always wondered the path his life would have taken had his mother survived the accident or not had one in the first instance – his parents probably would have stayed back in Kenya and retired on a dairy farm somewhere in Naivasha, a market town located on the shores of Lake Naivasha. His father had had a dream of having a herd of Jersey or Holstein-Friesian cattle and being the gentleman dairy farmer.

The azure blue waters of the Indian Ocean, shimmering in the distance, reminded him, again and again, of the trauma that his father had left behind when he quit Kenya, with Alec in tow, after his mother's tragic and premature death in the car accident. The memory quickly transformed his mood as he dressed to keep his appointment with Musa – the promised sight-seeing tour.

By the time Alec met up with Musa, he had recovered his equilibrium and poise. They visited another landmark that stands on Moi Avenue – the dual carriageway adorned by two pairs of massive elephant tusks; straddling the busy carriageway. The Mombasa tusks probably defined Kenya on the tourist trail just as the Big Ben highlighted London and Britain – iconic structures.

The replica tusks had been erected in 1956 to commemorate Princess Margaret's visit to Mombasa. Initially made of canvas and sisal, the tusks were later replaced by aluminium ones to save on maintenance and refurbishing costs. Musa took a few shots of Alec; dwarfed by the giant replica tusks in the background. Alec had seen smaller versions of replica tusks at Musa's studio; props used in the film trade. The local craftsmen were extremely talented and skilful – from a distance, but for the size, the ivory props looked every bit real.

They spent a quiet evening at the Orange Coral – Alec had invited Musa and Ava as his guests for dinner. It had been a pleasant evening as they dined at the poolside restaurant – with the roar of the waves as they cascaded onto the pristine sandy beach; the palm fringes silhouetted against the milky white moonlight.

'Well, I guess all good things come to an end,' Alec toasted his two guests with the last of his wine. Looking at Ava, his tone had a wishful ring to it.

'Remind me, when do you return to London?' Musa enquired. Ava was quieter than usual as the evening and the dinner drew to an end.

'I am shadowing Doctor Pinto at the Animal Orphanage for a while and we are both attending a conference. I fly back in roughly a month's time. If either of you are in Nairobi, do please call me – I'm at the Hilton.' Alec said the last bit looking fondly at Ava; Musa had missed the glow on Ava's face as she shyly averted her eyes from Alec's ardent gaze. Alec knew that Musa was always jetting off to photo shoots, so the invitation was implicitly for her; more in hope than anything else. The last couple of days had flown by and he was quite taken by this alluring

Aphrodite.

Musa went off to collect the Range Rover and as he drove up to the front of the hotel, Ava slipped Alec a note and dashed off with a cheery wave.

The note had her address and telephone number with a post script – 'come to the flat for a nightcap. PPS: I live on my own, 'mzee' Alec.'

Alec was still clutching the note as he descended from the cab at an address in the old town – he could hear the faint sounds of late night revellers on the harbour front. He had managed to buy an excellent bottle of Merlot from the wine bar at the hotel and as he rang the bell, Alec thought about the 'Malaika' melody and hoped it would invoke the same magical feelings as the previous night; 'mzee' notwithstanding, the 'kidege' was in for a repeat performance.

Alec returned from his sojourn in Mombasa to join Dr Pinto at the veterinary clinic. The Nairobi Animal Orphanage, inaugurated in 1964, was initially used to house and treat orphaned wildlife before releasing the animals into the wild. Over the years it had evolved into a shelter for treating and rehabilitating abandoned and injured wildlife. The Orphanage, as it had come to be known, was sited near the entrance to the Nairobi National Park and had a fully-fledged veterinary clinic attached to it. It was at the clinic that Alec hoped to 'shadow' the attending veterinarian, Dr Pinto, before returning to the UK.

Before the end of his stay in Kenya, Alec accompanied Dr Pinto to a pan African conference convened by the wildlife department. The central theme was the illicit ivory trade and the impact that poaching was having on elephant populations. Alec was astounded when one of the guest speakers, presenting a paper on the illicit ivory trade, revealed the stark statistics of the systematic and organized killing of elephants. The disturbing and shocking revelation was that Africa had only 350,000 to 400,000 elephants left; down from 1.3 million – if unconfirmed census reports were to be believed.

A hush descended in the conference hall as the dire statistic brought home the gravity of the situation and the realization that the world would soon lose all its African elephants; an abject indictment of human avarice and callousness. The conference passed several resolutions to curb the decimation of African elephants – more interaction with the various tribes by providing financial incentives, arming the wardens with the latest equipment and public education and awareness; all good soundbites that would soon be buried under reams of conference reports. Inertia and lethargy would soon replace the initial enthusiasm; well-meaning words and phrases that rarely translate into prompt or concrete action.

The 'elephant in the room' had indeed been the lack of global legislation to ban ivory sales – without this important measure, everything else was just cosmetic tinkering.

The various official and NGO agencies discussed the recent announcement to burn the hoard of ivory confiscated from poachers in the Laikipia region. Kenya had, in the past, burnt seized ivory at periodic intervals – the first bold and pioneering instance was in 1989; an act of aggression against the poachers. This throwing down of the gauntlet was emulated repeatedly by other nations.

On this fundraising event, the burning of the confiscated ivory was delegated to the business community and the corporate sponsors – it was envisioned that the business sector would be better placed to optimise the fundraising rather than the wildlife department or the government.

A few days later, the seized ivory was set ablaze on a specially cleared plot in the national park. The ivory was arranged in a conical pattern with wooden logs piled around to form two towers. The confiscated ivory gleamed through the gaps in the concentric layers of wood.

Amidst tight security, the guest of honour, an international business tycoon, lit the aviation fuel doused timber logs. Whilst the world press was absent from this smaller event, the Kenyan press gave it the full treatment in terms of publicity. Alec, accompanied by Dr Pinto and other colleagues, took full part and stayed back to enjoy the almost festive mood. Earlier in the day, Alec was pleasantly surprised to get a call from Musa – apparently, he had been contracted by a charity to film the entire day's proceeding, with a view to producing a short documentary film – to promote public awareness about poaching and ivory smuggling. Musa's pro bono services elicited generous offers from some Hollywood producers – substantial donations and a promise to finance further such films on conservation.

As ivory takes an inordinately long time to burn completely, the committee of corporate leaders had outsourced the entire process to a pyrotechnist – an off-shore company registered in Panama had won the contract following a well-advertised international tendering exercise.

The pyres were left burning for hours whilst

the charity event and the partying continued. Chilled Kenyan beer and 'nyama choma' (barbequed meat) sustained the attendees late into the night. The strong whiff of barbequed meat and burning fuel masked the industrial fumes of plastic and tyre manufacturers located in the surrounding industrial areas.

After a good few hours, the party fizzled out. The MP, his entourage and other dignitaries were whisked away in a gleaming convoy of Mercedes Benz and BMW limousines; the police escorts orchestrating the journey home. The ashes from the burning piles of embers would be collected and marketed as souvenirs to raise money for the charity – clumps of ash sealed in replica tusks or in glass cubes to be used as paperweights. The money raised by marketing all such merchandise was going to be ploughed back into the coffers of the conservation department for various projects.

Fortunately, as the private security personnel guarding the site were busy escorting the dignitaries out, some of the game wardens stood in as interim sentries. As they all knew Dr Pinto, he inveigled a small sample of the ashes and debris for Alec as a souvenir of the event – a sterile 30ml container, filled with the ashes was handed over as he left.

As Alec had made a generous donation, Dr

Pinto also put his name down on the list of donors who would receive the commemorative souvenirs – 'ivory towers encased in glass cube' paperweights. These mementoes had been specially designed and prepared by Musa's studio in Mombasa – to be delivered to the Orphanage before Alec's departure.

A month later, Alec caught a connecting Emirates flight from Dubai into Heathrow. With several flights landing at almost the same time, it took a while to collect his baggage and proceed through the 'green channel' towards the arrivals lounge. Heathrow was buzzing with returning residents and tourists.

It was well past midnight and Alec, despite his nonchalance, was agitated at the gloomy thought of returning to the backlog of work. The HM Revenue & Customs officer scanning the throng of passengers entering the green channel spotted the anxiety flagged by Alec's body language and pulled him over. Alec hauled his single suitcase on to the examining counter and unlocked the Gucci suitcase.

The officer was in the process of concluding his search when his probing fingers felt the bulge in a pair of pyjamas. When the officer held aloft the 30ml specimen bottle filled with greyish white debris, his arching eyebrows seemed to say it all. Alec had forgotten all about the souvenir paperweights, the replica ivory towers and the 30ml sterile container – all loosely wrapped in clothing to avoid breakage.

'A memento of my visit to Kenya,' Alec responded to the arched eyebrow. 'Laikipia to be precise. It's a souvenir of the symbolic burning of confiscated ivory.' The word ivory made the officer do a double take and he glanced at Alec's expensive suitcase and his three piece crumpled Armani suit.

'Sir, if I may, what is your current occupation?' Before Alec could respond, the officer, waving the C902A declaration form continued, 'I assume you have read this through?' The officer was alluding to the Customs declaration form. The arched eyebrow was defying gravity by now and the attendant expression of disbelief and dismissal on the younger man's face did not go unnoticed. Alec's ire almost exploded.

Alec's brusque words were regretted as soon as they slipped out, 'Veterinary Surgeon and, I am well aware of HMRC regulations, including the more stringent protocols of CITES (Convention on International Trade in Endangered Species). Better than you could ever fathom! The ashes represent ivory that was burnt at a very high temperature, so there is absolutely no chance of any contagion. The sample is virtually sterile. Please take my qualified word for it'. Alec's temper got the better of him as he reached into the breast pocket of his crumpled suit and flashed his Royal Veterinary College staff ID at the, by now, surly officer. The abrupt reply and Alec's 'posh' accent struck a raw nerve and the officer's brow creased with overt irritation.

The irate officer excused himself and sought his supervisor, more to recover from the rising bile in his mouth. A quick discussion with the attending supervisor did not go the way the officer had anticipated. He was advised to curtail the matter by retaining the material, pending further forensic investigation. The officer, duly mortified, advised Alec accordingly and after completing the paperwork, handed over a copy of the confiscation note to Alec, who, without a word, repacked his suitcase and proceeded towards the arrivals lounge. The officer watched Alec's progress through Customs with palpable dismay – he had hoped to exact his revenge for the vet's supercilious demeanour.

Alec had forgotten all about the HMRC investigation until he received a fairly detailed report from a CITES approved forensic lab. He quickly skimmed through the fairly technical report and the words 'no evidence of any ivory' stuck in his mind. He stuffed the report in his briefcase with a mental note to read the report later on. It wasn't until the weekend that he managed to scrutinise the report.

The findings were summarised as: 'Spectrophotometry performed on the ashes & debris revealed the presence of bovine bone and cartilage with traces of polyester resin'. It further elaborated that despite the fact that high temperatures would have denatured any DNA present, PCR (polymerase chain reaction) sequencing was done to assist detection of even minute traces of DNA. The test for nucleotides (DNA base units) came up positive. However, the DNA was confirmed to be of bovine origin. The DNA result matched the spectroscopic findings. 'No evidence of any elephant ivory' was the overriding conclusion.

As the findings sunk in, he went through the digital photographs of his tour. His intuition told him that he was missing something but could not put a finger on it. He reviewed the Moi Avenue shots of the giant replica tusks. Something about the tusks... Musa had said something about the tusks that eluded him. The more he tried, the more it receded into the recesses of his mind. He decided to let it be, as he was sure that the elusive clue would resurface in due course.

It was, much later on, whilst watching TV that it popped into his head, out of the blue. Musa had elaborated that the tusks on Moi Avenue were made of fabricated aluminium to mimic real ivory. Replicas! That was it; the tusks burnt on the day in Nairobi were replicas, not real! The conspirators had burnt plastic or resin props and cattle bones to create an illusion; a charade.

He recalled the two twin towers with the 'ivory' in the middle. Alec quickly deduced that the bulk of 'ivory' burnt on the day was cattle bones – piled in the middle, to make up the mass. The outer layers of the towers that covered and hid the bulk of cattle bones were resin or plastic tusks. The plastic tusks had been artificially stained with dung, mud or tea leaves to impart that 'aged' and genuine look to the 'ivory' – a ploy frequently used by the sellers of fake ivory to hoodwink tourists. The fake ivory and the bovine bones were further sequestered by the logs of wood encircling the conical mass in the middle. To the casual eye, the burning towers represented ivory going up in smoke!

'Quite a clever ruse created for a smoke and mirrors effect'. Alec muttered to himself.

Alec surmised that the real ivory had been switched at some stage and the conspirators had stage managed the entire show. It was quite apparent and obvious that this was an elaborate and well planned conspiracy. Whether a retrospective investigation, after a time lag of months, could unearth anything conclusive was a matter for the forensic teams – fortunately the day's proceedings were well documented including Musa's film, which might furnish visual evidence. The authorities had their work cut out for them – the corporate sector who had organized the event would become the focus of the scrutiny especially the international tendering process.

The real ivory was probably stored in a warehouse somewhere on the coast or already shipped out to the lucrative markets in the Far East. Alec's mind was in overdrive at his stunning and inadvertent discovery. If he hadn't taken the souvenirs and if he had not been stopped at Heathrow by HMRC, the theft would have gone unnoticed.

He could only think of Dr Pinto as his immediate link. He dialled the Orphanage in Nairobi and was informed that the vet was on his clinical rounds and would not be back for another hour or so. It was 6pm in Nairobi. Alec, without further deliberation, left a message for Dr Pinto: 'Urgent, suggest you contact me ASAP. The sample of ashes that you gave me as a souvenir does not contain any ivory'.

The assistant in the lab at the Orphanage

promised to pass on the message and put the phone down. He was working late and was alone in the lab – after making sure no one was about, he dialled an unlisted number in Mombasa. The curio shop owner listened to the message intently as it was repeated verbatim – the tinkling of ceramic cups could be heard in the background. Before he left, the assistant also made a call to his contact in downtown Nairobi; within minutes a series of 'cascading' calls and moves, a domino routine to avoid an audit trail, led to the spice bazaar in Dubai, where the trail ended – for now.

The Dubai trader wrote down a coded message in Urdu and Hindi – his nicotine stained stubby fingers producing a spidery scrawl on a piece of nutmeg stained paper. He stuffed the small note into his money belt – on his way home the note would be deposited at a designated drop off point. He was content to carry out the orders on a 'need to know' basis and would be paid in cash each time a message was delivered successfully – all he knew was that the message was picked up by a courier and delivered to someone, somewhere.

Meanwhile, the curio shop owner, on receiving the call from the Orphanage, dashed out and drove across town to a warehouse near Kilindini harbour. Unknown to him, he was followed by an unmarked police car. A taxi, with a buibui clad figure in the back, joined the two car entourage in front – the Indian driver, his curiosity piqued, kept glancing in the rear view mirror at the veiled female passenger. He noticed that the buibui looked expensive and was a designer brand that had become popular in recent months, especially with the younger jet set types – the figure hugging contours and the elaborate embroidery on the veil and the upper torso were in stark contrast to the floppy shapeless mass produced ones. His eyes were drawn to the rhythmic rise and fall of the bodice with each breath and the fragrance of her Chanel perfume filled the enclosed environs of the cab – the Parisian scent was a welcome change from the normal Persian 'attar' (perfume) that most traditionally dressed females wore.

The driver was admonished swiftly in accented Swahili to keep his eyes on the road and to follow the target car. The young driver, mindful of the strict guidance issued by his employer with regards to single female passengers, looked away guiltily, concentrated on the two cars ahead and steadfastly kept his gaze on the road.

The officers and the female taxi passenger watched from their respective parked cars as the curio shop owner knocked discretely on the roller shutters of a warehouse. An Arab emerged from a side door and the two had an animated discussion. The curio shop owner seemed agitated, going by his gesticulations and demeanour. He left abruptly, visibly annoyed, as the Arab shrugging his shoulders in a gesture of indifference returned to his air-conditioned office on the mezzanine floor of the warehouse – he could see from his vantage point that, as his irate colleague drove off, a car followed him. He failed to spot the stationary taxi parked in the shade of an outdoor café.

The buibui clad figure noticed the Arab move away from the window, paid off the driver and quickly exited the cab. She walked swiftly towards the warehouse and looked back once to ensure that the cab had driven away. As she knocked on the warehouse door, she flipped back her face veil over her head; exposing a heavily made up face – a ploy to deter an accurate description or to distract. She wanted the Arab to recognise her so that she could gain entry.

When the Arab answered the door again with some irritation and before he could reprimand the caller for intrusion, the female shot him twice through the heart. As the Arab slumped backwards onto the cement floor she stepped closer and shot him through the temple. After a cursory check for a carotid artery pulse, a programmed reflex that she knew was redundant – going by the dilated pupils – she veiled herself before emerging into the sultry heat. She pulled the door shut behind her.

The gun disappeared in the folds of her buibui as she swiftly walked to the next block where she flagged down a passing taxi; the cool interiors of the taxi came as a respite from the blazing temperature outside. She ended the journey half way through and paid off the driver near the mosque, which she entered and mingled with the other worshippers. After a short stay, she joined the throng of exiting worshippers and caught a taxi to take her home – she was dropped off some distance from her street; preferring to walk the last stretch.

She was gone before the back-up police arrived and found the Arab in a pool of blood – the two gun-shot wounds to the chest easily demarcated by their entry through the white shirt; both had pierced the heart causing instantaneous death. The point of entry of the third shot at the temple was partly covered by the Arab's henna dyed hair and clotted blood.

The lab assistant in Nairobi watched the 'breaking news' broadcast about the police investigation in Mombasa with trepidation – he never returned to his job at the orphanage. He caught the earliest train to Mombasa and made his way to Lamu and eventually caught a dhow to Dubai and presented himself to his masters.

A few days holed up in downtown Dubai had frayed his nerves to breaking point, so when he received instructions to join an out of town belly dancing show, popular with the tourists, his spirits soared. He intended to collect his payment in dollars and catch the next flight back to Zanzibar. He was steered towards a tent away from the belly dancing extravaganza – the tourists were totally absorbed in the mesmerizing dance routine and the entry of another tourist to a tent farther away went unnoticed.

The lamb kebabs and the sherbet that he was offered were polished off with gusto; the heavy garlic taste masking any after taste of the lashings of barbiturates that the kebabs were laced with. His body was fished out of the Dubai Creek the very next day by the Sea Rescue department of Dubai Police. The police received several calls from passengers of the 'abras' (water taxis) that plied the creek. The corpse lay in the mortuary as an unclaimed 'John Doe', as no identification was found on him.

Alec, unaware of the drama unfolding half way across the world, sat in his study working on his lecture on canine leptospirosis for his final year students. He had yet to receive a call from Nairobi. Alec admonished himself for leaving such an explicit message; he should have been more circumspect.

Within hours, Kenya CID with a contingent of several unmarked police cars raided the curio shop. The owner was arrested and the small hoard of ivory found in the basement was confiscated. Within days other warehouses across Mombasa and along the coast were raided and sealed; the warehouse where the Arab had been executed became a focal point of the investigation after fake export invoices and shipping manifests were unearthed. Small consignments of cattle bones meant for addresses in Dubai, Abu Dhabi, Bombay and Yemen were neatly stacked in a corner for imminent despatch to gelatine manufacturers – all these were seized and examined; the ivory was hidden in special false bottom compartments of the crates.

The case officer attached to the police at Kilidini harbour called up Nyayo House in Nairobi and presented a synopsis of the confessions of the curio shop owner and other employees at the various warehouses. The audit trail fanned out to various destinations, including Dubai and the Far-East – tons of ivory had been smuggled away – tusks, sometimes broken down into smaller units and exported with false documents; ostensibly as cattle bones for the production of animal feeds and gelatine. The monetary value ran into millions of dollars; representing a massacre of elephants on an industrial scale.

Alec's BA flight landed in Nairobi on time and he was quickly whisked away through the VIP lounge and to his hotel – the Hilton in downtown Nairobi. Alec had been briefed by the FCO (Foreign & Commonwealth Office) in London and was not surprised to see two CID plain clothes officers accompanying him everywhere. It all seemed very droll and melodramatic to him but he felt reassured, nonetheless, by their presence. With organised gangs and the huge amounts of money involved, Alec reckoned that the FCO must have tipped off the British High Commission, who in turn must have set the ball rolling. Certainly, both the UK and Kenyan governments were not taking any chances. The FCO had also forwarded the HMRC report to the British High Commission in central Nairobi.

Whilst Alec was aware that the case was tied up with the illicit ivory trade, he was taken aback when the sequence of events and other background details of the secret operation were divulged. He was then told that the investigating officer wished to see him privately for operational reasons. Alec was escorted to an elevator, which he took to the top floor of the skyscraper.

As he walked down the corridor and into a well-furnished vestibule, a tall figure moved towards him. The three piece handmade suit sat well on his tall frame. Gone were the bright beads and the braids. The lower two incisors were still missing as was the half ear lobe.

The Samburu, beaming widely, gripped Alec's hand in a bone crunching handshake. The transformation from a poacher to Kenya's leading undercover maestro of espionage was, to Alec, nothing short of sensational. He felt as inadequate as his Harris Tweed jacket was in comparison to the sartorial elegance of his 'adversary'!

'Karibuni, daktari! (welcome, doctor),' the Samburu boomed. Alec was stunned into silence, having thought about Laikipia and the poachers all through his time away in London and on the flight into Nairobi. Alec's imagined villain turned out to be, not only his, but the nation's saviour. What a turn around this was and he could not have scripted a better finale even if he had intended to. The 'poacher' had morphed into a conservationist – the Samburu had been appointed by a special commission and reported directly to the President. His wide-ranging remit was to unravel the links between organised poaching gangs and the trade in illicit ivory.

It took hours to be briefed on this five-year ongoing investigation by the Kenyans; with the Samburu in charge as an undercover 'plant' in the poaching network. Its tentacles spread not only across Eastern Africa but globally to Dubai, India, and the Far East. The Samburu explained to Alec that it was important that he remained incognito as the seizure of ivory, so far, was most definitely, just the tip of the iceberg. Alec concurred and gave his to assurances to the Samburu.

Whilst the ongoing investigation was progressing well, the Kenyan authorities had not yet traced the true culprits. The curio shop owner had been identified as a link almost a year ago. Kenya CID had been tailing him; in the hope that the chain of command would be exposed. The investigation was confident that in due course the international cartel or cartels would be unravelled and exposed.

It came as a relief for Alec to be told that Musa was not involved in the illicit ivory trade. The diary retrieved from the third poacher had the curio shop owner's contact numbers and other numbers; as yet unidentified. The diary was written in Arabic. The trail had suddenly become hot and the Kenyan investigative agencies were back in business; especially the newly set up wildlife unit that specialised in preventing poaching and the illicit ivory trade. Alec recollected that Musa had taken him to the same curio shop that afternoon in Mombasa. The police had been tailing the various suspects for some time. Musa with his ostentatious life style was initially a suspect but had been exculpated after a thorough scrutiny of his finances and the business dealings of his studio.

Alec tried calling Ava on several occasions without making contact – Musa subsequently called back to convey that Ava had gone away to Zanzibar for a well-earned break and to attend a family wedding. Alec was surprised to find out that her family originated from Pemba Island; one of the larger islands of the Zanzibar Archipelago. Ava Patel, according to Musa, had fallen out with her family many years ago and had moved to Mombasa to start a new life.

A few days later, the Samburu escorted Alec through the VIP lounge at Jomo Kenyatta International Airport and on to the tarmac where his BA flight was being refuelled for the flight to London.

'Kwaheri, daktari (goodbye, doctor).' The Samburu handed over the cash that he had 'stolen' from Alec's wallet. He had not revealed to Alec the executions that he had carried out that afternoon. The two game wardens had paid a heavy price and the Samburu had exacted his revenge for their deaths under his watch.

As the BA flight ascended the blue Kenyan skies with the towering Kenyatta Conference Centre and other skyscrapers receding from view, the Samburu settled in the back seat of his chauffeur driven fully loaded and customised Range Rover Discovery – a gift from the President for his exemplary work. The Samburu had come a long way from his humble beginnings in Laikipia to cosmopolitan Nairobi; his ivory tower!!

Two months later:

Mombasa police, on a tip-off, raided a flat in the old town, not far from the harbour. The flat was vacant and had been picked clean; the occupant had fled days or weeks earlier and nothing was found. The forensics team combed the flat for clues and finally marked it down as an unspecified burglary – fingerprints lifted off did not come up as a match on the police computers. The case was left open.

Musa contacted the police when Ava failed to turn up for work. When the police realized that the address of the missing person matched the flat that they had examined recently, a senior officer decided to contact the Samburu. This was probably something more than a case of burglary or a hoax tip-off.

The Samburu arrived in Mombasa the following day and was driven straight from the airport to Musa's studio.

'Jambo.' The Samburu greeted Musa who had been forewarned of the visit. He had never met Musa previously and although Musa had been cleared previously, the missing woman's connection with Alec and Musa had to be more than a co-incidence. That gut feeling made him fly down to confront Musa face to face.

'When was the last time you saw Ava – I gather she was away on holidays?'

'Just before she left for Zanzibar. When she failed to return to work, we reported her as missing to the police – all the contact numbers that we had for Zanzibar came up as 'unavailable' or 'not switched on'. Before she left she called to indicate that she was going for a family wedding and would be back in a week or so.'

The Samburu and his team interrogated Musa for more than an hour – what he divulged more or less was corroborated by the police in Zanzibar, who had interviewed the family at the behest of Mombasa police. Musa's demeanour, on this occasion and at the previous questioning, convinced the Samburu that Musa was not implicated in any way.

It had not escaped the Samburu that the trail had gone stone cold – the murder of the Arab in Mombasa and the disappearance of the orphanage staffer and now Ava Patel. The curio shop owner and the Dubai links had not borne any tangible results. The orphanage assistant's call to the curio shop owner was deemed to be the trigger that initiated a 'domino' effect. The Samburu acknowledged that yet again the poachers and their cartels were one step ahead of the law – for now the executions and interventions had succeeded in putting the brakes on the investigation.

Out of courtesy, the Samburu contacted Alec and mentioned Ava's disappearance – knowing Alec's feelings about her, the Samburu was careful not to air his suspicions; not as yet.

A few weeks later Alec received a package at the surgery, delivered by FedEx: it contained a CD which had recordings of Makeba's hit songs and a hand-written note.

Hey Mzee,

I am passing through London – shame we

can't meet. I often look back to the brief time we spent together in Mombasa – 'Malaika', our song for that one night brings back very fond memories. One of these days, God willing, we shall meet again.'

Kwaheri and Au Revoir
'Ndege',
Your little bird

Alec had couriered the CD to the Samburu, more out of courtesy than any conviction that it may shed some light on her disappearance. Alec called him a few days later.

'Habari, did you get the CD?' Alec greeted the Samburu using one of the few Swahili words he had picked up.

'Hey, Alec! Yes, I did, it's with our forensics people, although I doubt it will throw up anything new. Since our last conversation, I am now concerned – she is still missing,' The Samburu added.

'Concerned because she is missing and hence involved?' Alec surmised.

'The pattern of behaviour is a giveaway if you think about it. We are dealing with a professional outfit – no trails or clues have been left behind. Her flat did not throw up anything – it is quite obvious that either she or someone she knew did a thorough job of 'cleansing' the place.

I visited it myself – it was spartan. No family albums or photos left behind. I wouldn't even know what she looks like but for the photograph of you two taken on the night at the beach restaurant.'

'Really? I don't recollect posing for any photographs that night. And Ava wasn't with us when Musa took me around.' Alec's tone was of surprise and puzzlement.

'We got lucky, a beach photographer, a freelancer, took photographs of the diners that night. One of the tourists must have paid the freelancer – you two were caught in the frame. Kenya CID was tailing you on my instructions and we got the details of the photographer from the restaurant manager.'

'You had me followed? Why?' Alec's truculent response brought a smile to the Samburu's visage.

'Pole, pole (go easy, chill), my friend. Don't lose your shirt. It wasn't you –quite a few Mombasa residents were under surveillance – if you recollect this is an old operation. Musa was also under surveillance at that early stage as were many others. So whilst you were in Mombasa with Musa we decided to keep tabs on Ava as well – purely because she was working for him.'

'Fair enough. You reckon her disappearance

is part of a pattern?' Alec queried.

'Maybe. The strategy goes with the territory – move your operatives around if there are risks of capture or exposure. We have had anecdotal reports of a femme fatale operating in Tanzania and Uganda – her presence in Mombasa does not surprise me. It is a common modus operandi - key personnel are moved around to set up new cells and to evade the authorities by not staying in one place. She is a pro – her sudden disappearance and the fact that the flat was 'cleansed' and the trail going cold – that worries me. Someone has gone to a lot of trouble to obfuscate us – the cartel has the resources to give her a new identity. I am sure she will pop up somewhere to reprise her role.'

'You think she is implicated and she played me to get information? And I thought it was my charisma.' Alec's pained response was poignant and the Samburu realized that his friend was still hurting and in denial. For Alec's sake, he hoped that Ava's disappearance had a plausible explanation.

'Don't be hard on yourself, that's what a honey trap is – she got close to you because of your connection to the case – your presence in Laikipia, at the burning and in Mombasa,' the Samburu consoled the older man.

'Honey trap? You guys knew that I spent the

night with her at my hotel and then at her flat?'

'The taxi that you took was an unmarked police car – the hotel manager had been briefed. He steered you to the car when you came down from your room. You were also taken to the airport by us – just to ensure you got back safely.'

'I don't get it – what could be her motivation?' Alec pondered loudly after a brief silence; still in denial about Ava's complicity.

'Who knows – the trail goes cold in Zanzibar. All we know is that she comes from a very prosperous family – her ancestors were probably Khoja Kutchi sailors from Gujarat in India, some of them settled in Zanzibar – the Kutch area was known for its dhows and the Khoja and Gujarati communities have been sailing the monsoon winds for centuries. Her great grandfather was a prosperous businessman with several properties and clove plantations. Ava fell out with her family and moved out of Zanzibar almost a decade ago. She seems to be a 'pariah', an outcast – the family have no idea where she is; nor do they want to know. It's an honour thing – maybe it was her Western ethos and lifestyle that violated the conservative values of her family and the Zanzibari community at large. They weren't even aware that she had returned to Stone Town recently. Although Musa paid her a fairly decent wage, there was no way Ava could afford to own a property – in fact, even renting in that part of town would be beyond her means. She must have had other sources of income. She certainly did not get any help from her estranged family. Maybe she was on the cartel's payroll? All we have is circumstantial evidence, no proof,' the Samburu expounded to assuage Alec's feelings.

'What happens to your investigation – with her missing and the trail going cold?' Alec asked.

'Well although we do not have any convictions as yet, the poaching activity has almost stopped dead in its tracks. This cessation of poaching more or less confirms my suspicions that a powerful, omnipotent cartel is controlling the poaching operations in Kenya and maybe in Tanzania and Uganda. Over the years the cartel must have muscled in and ejected the small time criminals, thereby creating a de facto monopoly. We are more than certain that no governmental agency is involved nor are there any links with local businessmen – all the evidence points to a concerted effort by external forces to plunder our natural wealth. The thrust of our investigation is now focused on the sponsors, especially the consortium that underwrote the event – their international remit affords them all the opportunities.'

'You reckon that the deaths so far and her disappearance are connected and that's what stalled the operation?' Alec asked. 'Figures. Keeping a low profile until the furore dies down.'

'Yes it looks that way. It seems that she has been re-deployed elsewhere for now. I am sure she will resurface in due course. The lull is only a temporary respite – the operation has probably shifted to greener pastures – Uganda or Tanzania. The survival of our elephant populations is a joint venture with our friends in Uganda and Tanzania – there is a fervent political will now to stop this carnage. For your sake I hope she contacts you soon and is able to exonerate herself,' the Samburu concluded.

'You are persisting with your line of enquiry, that an international cartel is involved?' Alec was expressing his doubts about achieving a resolution to the poaching problem, certainly not in the near future.

'Of course, we have the assurances from all three nations and I have carte blanche to do as I see fit. The instructions from all three Presidents are explicit – this decimation of our wildlife has to stop. The economic ramifications for us are huge as all of us are so dependent on tourism – our survival is intricately linked to the survival of our wildlife.' The Samburu paused and continued in a more optimistic tone.

'Next time we will get lucky, so we have to persist in our endeavours. To stop the carnage and plunder we have to catch the culprits. Your accidental role in exposing the illicit trade has helped open a new line of enquiry. We are pretty much certain that the company that executed the event is at the centre of this scam. Musa's film on the day is an accurate visual record – alas, nothing of any significance has emerged from that short film.'

Alec and the Samburu ended their call after almost an hour with a promise to keep in touch. A pensive Alec buzzed his secretary to send in the next patient; his work was now his sanctuary.

A few months later, the Kenyan press carried a few lines about an unidentified body of a buibui-clad female found in the creek across from Mombasa town. The only reason the UK press carried the news was because a British family on holiday in Mombasa were the first to sight the floating body and report it to the police.

A few days later, the Samburu called Alec with the sad news.

'It was her, my friend, I am sorry – the female found floating in the Tudor Creek not too far from the old harbour. We had DNA samples from your night out at the beach restaurant –

lipstick and saliva left behind on the wine glass. The restaurant manager had bagged the glass for us. It was a bit of a break considering that her flat did not yield any DNA samples.'

'That's a bit much isn't it? Not even a strand of hair in the shower or a clipped nail in the flat?' Alec interrupted.

'Exactly – the absence of any trail proves my suspicion that a professional outfit was sent in to 'sanitize' the flat,' the Samburu said.

Alec was saddened at the way it had ended – no conclusive proof of her involvement; only circumstantial evidence.

'Alec, are you there?' the Samburu was aware of Alec's emotional conflict.

'Yes, sorry. You took me by surprise. I was, I am convinced that she would have exonerated herself had she survived this ordeal.'

'There is more I am afraid – she was executed, probably on the mainland and the body then dumped at sea. The post-mortem report also mentions a recent tattoo across the back of her right shoulder which exhibited signs of contact dermatitis; probably an allergic reaction to the dye used. The tattoo read: 'Mzee's Malaika'.

'I know you had mentioned the live band and you guys dancing to the Miriam Makeba song. The tattoo was a declaration, a cryptic message for you?' the Samburu enquired.

'Maybe; when I couriered you the CD, I did not enclose her note. Now that you mention it – maybe there was a message in there about her intentions. Let me send you the note.'

'Pole, pole, my friend, go easy. My profound sympathy, I know you liked her,' the Samburu commiserated noting the hint of melancholy and despair in Alec's voice as he ended the call.

Back in Nairobi, the Samburu understood. Her masters must have known about her intentions to quit and acted to safeguard their interests, their 'ivory towers'!

Alec found her note and re-read it:

'...One of these days, God willing, we shall meet again...'

The Talking Newspaper

Maxine Bisset, a UK trained trauma surgeon, landed in Kigali, Rwanda, in January 1994. She was a volunteer doctor for a British-Rwandan medical charity.

On the flight, she spent considerable time going through the charity's induction protocols, just as the BA captain announced that they would be landing at Kigali airport in a couple of hours – strong tailwinds had trimmed almost half an hour of flight time.

Maxine noted the historical and political nuances of the region's (Rwanda, Zaire and Burundi) Hutu and Tutsi diaspora. Historically, the Hutu-Tutsi power struggle for dominance, played out across Rwanda's eight 'kingdoms', partially ended with unification in 1900. The Germans and then the Belgians, colonised the country. The Belgians, eventually, granted independence to Rwanda in 1962.

As so happens in Africa, independence, more often than not, intensifies the tribal power struggle – the conflict festers for years to come. The Belgians had groomed the Tutsis, a minority tribe, to be the 'chosen ones' and, in the process, antagonised the majority Hutu tribe. The wedge had been driven, inexorably, and led to a protracted internecine war between the two tribes. The seeds of jealousy, sown decades ago, soon germinated into unwanted weeds of ethnic tension and strife.

Maxine was struck by the similarity of Belgian political agenda with that of the British in India and in Kenya; playing favourites with one tribe, to the detriment of the others. Similar scenarios had unfolded in many other colonies. Divide and rule was an unsavoury recipe practised in the colonies and then left behind as a legacy that unwittingly fomented strife for generations to come.

'To the victor go the spoils', a proverb oft repeated over the centuries. As Maxine reflected on the adage, she closed the file and snuggled deeper into her seat. She felt the plane commence its gradual descent and felt the 'thud' as the undercarriage locked into place.

She always tensed up during take offs and landings and the 'thud' that she felt and heard was her cue to be on her 'panic in abeyance' mode. Despite numerous plane journeys, she always felt the same; the knot in her gut quite palpable. Why in this day and age could they not design a passenger plane that behaved like a Harrier jet with its vertical take-offs and landings, she could never figure out.

She nervously fidgeted with the tiny crucifix around her slender neck and murmured a silent prayer; more out of habit than any religious fervour. Little did she realise that she was landing, literally and metaphorically, into a morass that would change the course of Rwanda's history and her future.

Within months of her arrival, on 6th April 1994 the presidents of Rwanda and Burundi died in a plane crash whilst landing at Kigali airport. Rumours abounded and the arguments persisted for decades about the culpability of each tribe in the alleged assassination and the subsequent inferno that engulfed the country. The Hutu-Tutsi conflict raged in Rwanda and then spread to the neighbouring countries.

The chaos that ensued resulted in the slaughter of almost a million Rwandans, overwhelmingly Tutsis, in a matter of one hundred days. The mass murders with machetes and axes were largely carried out by the Hutu majority – to avenge decades of discrimination and humiliation. The bloodbath that followed was cathartic and consequently laid waste to an entire nation. Both tribes were equally complicit in the annihilation of their homeland.

7th April 1994

Maxine had just arrived at a hospital on the outskirts of Kigali and was attending to several

Tutsi patients with life threatening trauma; some had been axed in the face or head with the blades still embedded. With the shortage of trained personnel, the ad hoc triage teams struggled and sifted patients subjectively rather than following any objective criteria – many died as a result whilst waiting for a surgeon or an internist. Copious pools of blood stagnating on the ward floors – a crimson carpet that would not have gone amiss in an abattoir.

The inexorable waves of the injured and the maimed soon spilled over into every available space. The doctors, the majority of whom were foreigners, representing the various international charities, had an onerous task on their hands. The local doctors, paramedics and nurses were absconding; caught up in the racial strife. It was, in view of the vast numbers pouring in, a losing battle. The stench of death was all pervasive; a tsunami of mayhem and destruction.

Maxine, a senior A & E Registrar at Guy's Hospital in London, was more than adept at dealing with life-threatening trauma, but the relentless deluge of cases in such a short timeframe overwhelmed her and her colleagues. After working almost incessantly for hours, the thirty year old medic decided to slip out for a breather and a smoke. Sweat made rivulets of wet stains as it trickled down her body; the slight breeze out in the open did little to bring relief from the sweltering heat and humidity. Her hospital whites with the mosaic of blood stains bore testimony to the battle being waged on the wards. She could hear screams and gun shots in the distance. This was far from over, Maxine cogitated, as she lit a Dunhill and watched the smoke spiral languidly in the still air. Little did she realise that her musing, on the ongoing bloody turbulence, was going to be inadvertently prophetic.

The mindless slaughter lasted for four long months and even then it was far from over. The repercussions of that fatal plane crash would reverberate locally for years to come; whereas internationally the Western powers were tainted with the guilt of indifference. Whilst the UN and its member states dithered, Rwanda was spinning out of control in a vortex of paranoia and retribution. And Maxine was, unwittingly, in the eye of the storm.

Just as she flicked the Dunhill stub away, a Toyota Land Cruiser double cab pickup, packed with several armed militia men, screeched to a halt beside her – almost knocking her down. She was about to protest when a short, corpulent sergeant with broad prominent facial features came right up to her and barked commands that she did not understand. As she recoiled to avoid the foetid smelling spittle from spraying her face, her hesitation and confusion were misconstrued as belligerence by the sergeant. He pulled a gun on her and nudged her towards the pickup. As she was bundled into the front passenger seat, the sergeant squeezed in next to her. She realised then that her bloody hospital whites and the stethoscope around her neck probably signalled her status as a medic; making her a potential target. Someone, somewhere, needed medical intervention and she was the pawn in whatever mischief these brutes had in store for her. She shivered involuntarily as the dark intrusive thoughts ran through her mind.

She could smell the sweat stained fatigues in the confined spaces of the cab. The three dazed soldiers in the rear cab were smoking and the pungent smell of cannabis wafted across. Most of these men were fleeing the rampant carnage to avoid the lynch mobs – most, if not all, had destroyed their IDs to avoid being branded. It was a 'free for all' rush to safe havens with refugees posing as militia men and vice versa. In the confusion that prevailed, there were no guarantees for anyone, whether Hutu, Tutsi or Belgian – accosting the wrong crowd or uttering the wrong phrase or wearing the wrong uniform meant instant death.

Instinctively, she glanced at the driver's forearms clutching the steering wheel – no evidence of any hard drug use; no tell-tale puncture marks. As she pulled her white hospital coat across her bosom, she felt the sergeant and the others giving her the once-over. The sexual tension in the cab was palpable. The chatter and the laughter in the cab sounded like innuendo to her – Maxine was convinced that they were discussing her. The men in the open top at the back were singing and chanting; drug fuelled bravado to counter the fear of violence and death.

Drugs taken in conjunction with alcohol, especially the highly potent Rwandan beer made from mashed bananas – Urwagwa – usually accentuates the effects and induces a trance like state. The presence of an attractive white female coupled with intense intoxication could quite easily trigger mayhem. In an ironic way Maxine was glad a gun toting sergeant was sitting beside her, although how he would react in a riotous situation was a moot point – she could hardly expect the milk of human kindness from any of this crazy lot. She shivered involuntarily in the sweltering heat of the cab.

To break the spell, she confronted the sergeant about her 'kidnap' and reminded him that her colleagues at the hospital would soon realise that she was missing. She was certain that the sergeant understood English and, as he studiously ignored her, her trepidation mounted – she knew his silence was deliberate; contrived to intimidate and isolate her.

After hours of incessant driving, she still had no idea where they were taking her. She had noticed the roadside signs 'flagging' the Ugandan border. Sometimes the signs seemed askew and were left pointing in an opposite direction – was this a huge Hutu conspiracy to drive the Tutsis into an ambush or vice versa? She knew her paranoid thoughts were displacing all rational thought – her anxiety had been mounting with each passing hour. Kigali, her safe haven, was miles away. She was at the mercy of an unruly mob; her galloping pulse was a marker of the panic that was insidiously taking over. Stay calm, she told herself, as she caressed the crucifix for solace.

Long trails of refugees could be seen trudging in the distance. Most were fleeing to escape the rampaging Hutu militia. The Hutu militia were cunningly misusing the national ID cards as an organized and premeditated exercise to identify and segregate the Tutsis – who were then slaughtered. In some instances, the fleeing Tutsis were marched up to hastily dug mass graves and butchered or corralled into churches and houses and then set alight with kerosene. More often than not the instruments and the methods were as simple as can be – machetes and axes slicing through major arteries, or organs, or decapitation. Mutilated bodies were then disposed of in mass graves, cremated in empty churches or houses or even dumped into rivers and lakes with the sadistic refrain 'cockroaches go back to Ethiopia'. The Hutus were repeating an age old slur; a racial insult. Retaliation by the Tutsis was far from swift as the element of surprise resided with the Hutus, however, when it did happen, the response was too little, too late. The tide of vehemence had swept all before it; a nation in a crisis of its own making.

Just as Maxine had almost given up, the Toyota streaked into a school compound where there were several mutilated bodies strewn about. The eerie ululation of the women from within the school, sent shivers up and down her spine. The sergeant escorted her into the school to a secluded cordoned off area. Two sentries, with swarms of flies hovering over pools of clotted blood on the floor, kept a vigil outside the door. It was apparent that someone important needed medical care; hence her enforced presence in this ramshackle place that had the appearance of a war zone.

A man in an expensive crumpled suit lay on a makeshift bed. Blood was trickling down his bare leg and had congealed into a crimson patch on the urine-stained mattress, which had been hastily retrieved from the school dormitory. An incongruous sight as ever can be – an Armani suit amongst a sea of sweat stained battle fatigues!

Maxine's cursory visual examination pointed to a flesh wound. The soldiers had already rolled down the trousers to expose the lesion. The man was alert but did not say a word and Maxine felt his intense primal scrutiny, as she went about her examination, after donning the last pair of latex gloves that she found in her hospital apron. She was sure the gloves were not sterile but pulled them on, nonetheless, to protect herself from exposure to the patient's blood. She smiled inwardly – she wasn't even sure that she was going to survive this ordeal and here she was fretting about Hepatitis B and HIV.

He had the formidable aura and hauteur of a man used to total submission from everyone. 'Probably a warlord or a wealthy politician', Maxine surmised, as she assessed her patient's condition. Her probing gloved fingers did not elicit a sound nor did he flinch. She felt his intense gaze on her. Fortunately for the patient, the bullet had missed the femoral artery, although there was some collateral tissue damage. She rummaged through what looked like an emergency crash cart and found some basic essentials; all probably commandeered from somewhere.

The man winced involuntarily as she swabbed the wound with surgical spirit and then injected the lidocaine; preferring it to the half empty vial of ketamine hydrochloride. The deft debridement, followed by a few sutures completed the job. In the absence of catgut sutures, she improvised and used black cotton thread soaked in iodine.

'That will have to do,' she said loudly, 'until we get to a hospital.' She hoped that her loud and deliberate emphasis on the word 'hospital' would resonate with the patient, if not with the sergeant.

As there were no antibiotics, Maxine used that as an excuse to urge the sergeant to return her and the patient to a hospital where proper care could be arranged. The subterfuge failed – she was instead escorted to an adjoining room. Any chance of returning to Kigali now looked extremely forlorn. She slumped onto the stringy single bed in abject resignation; her morale dented. She assumed that the patient had either left or was still languishing somewhere – his injuries were minimal and not in any way incapacitating or life threatening.

By nightfall she was brought dough-like balls of steamed maize flour, which she recognised to be 'ugali'; served with a cold vegetable stew and a few chunks of stale bread. She had seen roadside stalls in Kigali selling this staple starch meal to indigent labourers. Maxine gingerly tasted a spoonful and quite preferred the bland taste. Famished as she was, the meal was wolfed down without any hesitation. She craved a smoke and missed her usual post prandial Dunhill – her cigarettes had gone missing in the melee that had ensued during her unceremonious exit from the hospital grounds.

Sleep was a timely succour in erasing the events of the day, although as she drifted off, lingering thoughts about her dilemma persisted. Maxine fell asleep in the foetal position, drawing comfort from the crucifix around her neck. She slept fitfully in the bed provided, sure it was riddled with bedbugs and all kinds of other nasties; the incessant buzz of the mosquitoes aggravated her discomfort.

The loud commotion in the corridor outside her room abruptly ended her disjointed slumber. The sergeant and two men noisily entered her room; the chair that she had propped against the door handle failing miserably to deter the visitation. She had recalled a clip from a movie where the pretty heroine had thwarted unauthorised entry by employing the very same ruse – just her luck that it did not work.

Even at a distance, the reek of cheap alcohol descended upon Maxine before she saw the intruders in the dim light emanating from the single bulb. Maxine, although wide awake, could not move; paralysed by her fear. As the sergeant advanced towards her, she almost missed the threat from behind. Instinctively, she lashed out at the two soldiers trying to pin her down. Maxine, galvanised by the adrenaline rush, took the inebriated intruders by surprise, slipped through their sweaty grapple and bolted towards the door.

The sergeant, who was silhouetted against the flickering light, meant to just stun her. The barrel of his gun, instead of hitting the side of her temple, thudded into her left eye. As she screamed in agony, the penetrative impact almost dislodged the left eyeball from its bony orbit. Stunned and dazed, the blow knocked the wind out of her.

Her last recollection was of the heavily accented guttural voice of the sergeant and a sharp intake of her own breath, as the needle plunged into her gluteus maximus through her flimsy cotton trousers. The heavy handed intramuscular injection barely registered – the excruciating throb in her left eye overwhelmed everything else.

Although she did not pass out immediately, the blow had stunned her. As the soldiers retreated, she heard a heated and animated exchange between the sergeant and a stranger. The accent was vastly different to the sergeant's. For a transitory moment, Maxine hoped that the new voice was that of a superior officer coming to her rescue; her knight in shining armour.

The last thing she remembered was the vial of ketamine that she had noticed in the crash tray. As she faded in and out of consciousness, she prayed that it was the ketamine that had been injected and not some street cut opioid concoction.

She vaguely felt a presence in the room and her flailing arms landing a few blows. The punch from the man to her bleeding left eye was deliberate; to inflict further pain as a tool of subjugation. Before she slipped away into an abyss of pain and deep sedation, she could hear the man's laboured breathing next to her on the rickety bed. The obscenities that rolled off uninterrupted seemed to be part of a primal pattern of atavistic behaviour; the man was goading himself to perform as he tore away the flimsy cotton trousers and her panties.

Within the hour, a solitary dishevelled figure emerged from the room and contemptuously flung a wad of American dollars in the direction of the assembled soldiers. The men all reacted guiltily, caught in the act of voyeurism. With the dollars strewn all over the chipped cement floor, the spell was broken as they all scrambled in the melee to grab as many dollars as possible. American dollars were gold dust in these difficult times and, as the soldiers succumbed to their avarice, the man slipped away into the night.

The sergeant waiting patiently outside with a small select band of soldiers, nodded to the driver beside him to proceed – his important passenger promptly fell asleep in the backseat. The solders in the open top at the rear, shared the packet of Dunhills that the man had flung at them before sliding into the back seat of the pickup.

Hours later as the Peugeot sped along the dirt track, plumes of ochre soil forming a wake, the delirious figure in the back groaned with pain. Maxine was unceremoniously dumped at the junction of the dirt track and the tarmacked section some distance from the school.

Dawn was just breaking over the horizon; the pristine feel of a new day; a far cry from the stale atrocities of the night before.

By the time she came around, the early sun was filtering through the verdant canopy of foliage. She was in a ward surrounded by patients and refugees. Her left eye and socket were bandaged up and the pain had abated somewhat. The attending French doctor informed Maxine that she had been found by a group of the fleeing refugees who had carried her to the transit medical camp.

In halting English, littered with French words, the young doctor explained that an emergency debridement procedure had been performed before bandaging the left eye. Under the circumstances it was all he could do, although, given that the deep penetrative trauma that the eye had sustained, enucleation would have to be considered. He had initiated appropriate antibiotic and analgesic therapy as an alleviating measure; the surgical option deferred until she was evacuated to Kampala or Nairobi.

An urgent evacuation request to Entebbe and onwards had been radioed. He added gently, his eyes deliberately averted, that he had to suture up the severe injuries to her genitalia– it was apparent that a frenzied sexual assault had been carried out. The young doctor indicated that he had taken swabs and blood samples for DNA evidence and for other forensic protocols. Maxine nodded her tacit approval.

She drifted off under the influence of morphine and slept through her entire stay in the camp. Maxine was not in a fit state to assess her own condition. The French doctor, knowing the risks of delaying surgical treatment or immuno-suppressive therapy tried his very best to get her to Nairobi – it took almost ten days before her long winded journey by road and air ended in a Nairobi hospital.

Maxine never quite found out why she had not been transferred to Kampala, a much closer destination with equally good medical facilities, nor why it took almost ten days to get to Nairobi – it was fortuitous that the pilot of the cargo plane, returning to Nairobi after off-loading relief supplies for the Rwandan refugees, took pity on the British doctor when he inadvertently overhead two volunteers discussing Maxine's predicament. Maxine joined the cargo of wooden pallets, bunches of recently harvested bananas and sugarcane – an unceremonious exit out of riot torn Rwanda.

The consultants all agreed that Maxine was singularly unlucky in developing the fairly rare sympathetic ophthalmia. The severe fulminating inflammation that flared up in her normal right eye was triggered by the penetrative injury to her left eye. The enucleation, removal of her damaged left eye, was performed to try and arrest the auto-immune reaction that was effectively damaging her sight in the normal right eye. They initiated appropriate immuno-suppressive therapy to counteract the autoimmune reaction that the trauma had triggered.

Maxine remained in hospital for almost a month before medical repatriation to the UK. She had flown out as a doctor, full of vigour and vision, and had returned as a patient with an uncertain future.

Whilst convalescing in Nairobi, Maxine had refreshed her knowledge of the condition as she had never come across a case of sympathetic ophthalmia despite the many cases of optical trauma that she had encountered at Guy's – traumatic eye injuries as a result of violent knife crimes or car accidents.

Maxine was discharged from the Nairobi hospital with a very poor prognosis – the vision in her normal right eye severely compromised and her visual acuity under threat. Fortunately, she had tested negative for HIV and other STDs.

Years Later: The Shravan Project: a charity for the visually impaired in South London.

Maxine's tragic and inadvertent involvement in Rwanda's political upheaval left her almost blind. She also discovered, to her shock, that her rape ordeal was not over – her pregnancy test had come up positive. With all that had transpired in the last few months, her visual impairment pushed her over the edge into clinical depression; the pregnancy added further emotional upheaval. The vortex of emotions was like a deluge; whirlpools that were drowning her – her composure of control and order replaced by disarray and chaos. Maxine's medical background became her biggest enemy – she knew for sure that she was going blind.

The Shravan Project in conjunction with the Talking Newspaper Federation and its partnership with the Royal National Institute for the Blind formatted an audio version of the newsletter for its members with impaired vision. The printed newsletter went out monthly to its members and an audio version was downloaded onto USB sticks and distributed to sight impaired members – the memory sticks could then be 'played' by using special USB memory stick players or by plugging into a computer.

Interviews, book readings, current affairs and myriad other news were all recorded on site at Shravan's offices, where a mini recording studio had been assembled over the years. Volunteers and amateur radio enthusiasts teamed up regularly to put together an audio clip. The media team would then edit and finalise the audio clip before despatch to all the members on the subscription list.

When Maxine had to give up work after the deterioration in her visual acuity, she was put in touch with the Shravan Project for advice and other support services. She was subsequently referred to the local council offices for an assessment of her welfare needs based on her visual impairment. In due course the Rehabilitation Officer for the Visually Impaired (ROVI) at the council's Sensory Impairment Team issued a 'certificate of visual impairment' (CVI). This was done after liaising with her ophthalmic consultant and the optician – the certificate is used as evidence of visual impairment, which then forms the basis for accessing welfare benefits and other support services.

Maxine's CVI indicated a 'sight impairment (partial blindness)' rating, which in time, because of her poor prognosis, would be downgraded to 'severely sight impaired' (totally blind). She had finally accepted that her working life was virtually over and that she faced an uncertain future – financially and socially.

Psychologically she went through the entire gamut of emotions, an emotional rollercoaster ride, with highs and lows of 'I am fine, I will cope', 'this can't be happening' and 'oh God, what am I going to do?' Maxine was in self-denial. She was plagued by recurrent episodes of depression and anxiety and was comforted, to some extent, by the presence and support of her boyfriend, Adam. However, the initial resilience shown by him did not last long once the finality of her looming blindness dawned on him – he was plagued by his own demons.

He was having second thoughts about their relationship and, unknown to Maxine, had sought refuge in the arms of an old flame. Whilst he was battling with this guilt of forsaking Maxine in her hour of need, the news of her pregnancy and her obstinate refusal to consider abortion became the thin edge of the wedge; the chasm between them widened.

The postnatal depression that followed the birth of a son was the final straw. They parted soon after. Maxine knew that she would not be able to cope on her own; her diminished vision and Adam's change of heart meant that looking after a baby would be nigh on impossible.

Despite knowing that she was just delaying the inevitable, she prevaricated for weeks and weeks; very much unsure of herself.

Ultimately, reason prevailed and with great reluctance, she capitulated and initiated the process of adoption. Her only regret was that, under a different set of circumstances, bringing up a baby would have been the perfect antidote to her emotional and physical crises.

Although there were brief relationships with men after Adam's premature departure from her life, none of them survived the collective burden of her impaired vision and the emotional scars of her Rwandan trauma. As her sight progressively deteriorated, she became more and more diffident and reclusive. Her subconscious decision to remain single modulated her behaviour towards men – almost shunning all contact with them. It was a stroke of good fortune that her timely enrolment with Shravan gave her intent and a focus – almost a renaissance although initially she was just going through the motions. In due course, the charity and the 'Shravan brigade' would become the cynosure of her life.

She immersed herself in the various activities that the Shravan Project offered – yoga, meditation and ballroom dancing filled the void.

The staff, the volunteers and members who all supported her during this trying phase became her 'surrogate' family. With her visual acuity diminishing by the day she subscribed to the monthly audio version of the newsletter. It was something to look forward to and kept her in the loop. More importantly, it opened doors to a vast array of audio books and magazines.

1994 Kigali

Arthur Berg, whose birth almost ushered in Rwanda's independence, was a third generation Rwandan of Belgian origin. Although the family had lived in Rwanda for generations, all of them retained their Belgian citizenship – the fear that one day they may have to quit and return to Belgium was an irrational thought that many Belgians harboured. There was a marked dichotomy in this emotion and the thought processes – the older generations more worried that the shifting sands of political agenda may lead to repatriation; the youngsters more open to accepting Rwanda as their birth country and refusing to consider a return to the land of their forefathers.

Arthur had, like many Belgians born in Rwanda, completed his tertiary education in Belgium and had graduated from Ghent

University with a degree in Pharmacy. Upon his return to Kigali, he had initially worked as a hospital pharmacist, however, disillusionment soon set in at the lack of career progression – the Spartan working conditions and the meagre wages proving to be disincentives. The altruistic vision of contributing to the welfare of the poor and the needy soon stumbled at the threshold of economic practicality – the remuneration fell far short of the kind of lifestyle he had envisaged for himself. He knew immediately that self-employment was his only way out.

Once he had married Keza, his Tutsi girlfriend, who had a distinguished lineage stretching back to the original 'eight kingdoms', he took the plunge and set up a pharmaceutical distribution and wholesaling unit with the investment capital borrowed from both sets of parents. He was hoping that his pharmacy background would create an instant rapport with the small independent pharmacies which were ignored by the big pharma groups – niche marketing to penetrate a very competitive market. He had intuitively spotted a gap in the market and had achieved sales far beyond his ultra conservative projections – the bread and butter enterprise had transformed, within a short period, into a feast fit for gluttons. He was doing exceptionally and was already planning on expanding into neighbouring Zaire and Burundi – for now he had deferred expansion for a year, pending the birth of their first child.

He was, on that fateful day, visiting a pharmacist in Butare and was in the midst of a marketing presentation when they were interrupted by the raucous commotion outside. All the neighbouring shops were pulling down their shutters on hearing about the rumours of the riots and looting flaring up in the outskirts of Butare.

The news of the kidnap and murder of the Queen, Rosalie Gicanda, turned out to be the tipping point that set Butare ablaze. Arthur, visibly perturbed and agitated, decided to dash back to Kigali before Butare went into some kind of a lockdown. The riots that followed Queen Gicanda's murder almost trapped Arthur in the maelstrom that was unleashed.

As he drove back to Kigali, the thought of his pregnant wife stranded in the predominantly Tutsi enclave that they resided in made him sick with worry – all he could imagine were Hutu mobs rampaging through the neighbourhood. He prayed that Keza and the servants had the foresight to stay indoors and out of sight. His other worrying thought was that a Tutsi married to a Belgian was an obvious target for the rampaging Hutu mobs.

Within the hour his worst fears were crystallising into grim reality – the suburbs were deserted and in some cases houses and offices had been torched; the acrid smell of burning tyres masking the smell of burning flesh. As soon as he entered the quiet boulevard of detached houses, he noticed the devastation; the deserted look even more intimidating – usually the cul-de-sac that they lived in would be alive with boisterous children playing or cycling around. He was greeted with pin drop silence; not even a whimper as he double parked and ran into the house.

As he barged in, the eerie silence in the house and the absence of his canine welcoming party told its own tale – normally the two Doberman Pinchers would be all over him with woofs of welcome. The Hutu and Tutsi servants, the cook and the maid, were sprawled across the ground floor. The maid had been the focus of a ferocious attack, probably with a machete; the cook had died a slow painful death – his ribcage crushed with hammer blows. There were pools of blood on the mosaic flooring; Romulus, the older Doberman, had probably died defending the servants; his lifeless bloody body spread-eagled over the maid.

As he bolted upstairs, he saw the bloody footmarks on the stairs and on the landing; the

85

mahogany bannisters smudged with blood trails. He found his wife sprawled on the bed with a machete embedded in her pelvis; eviscerating her and the foetus. Their marital bed was soaked with blood and amniotic fluid. Remus, the younger Doberman, had been decapitated with a single clean blow – the head resting on the bed; the headless body had been flung across the room and lay in the far corner, a tangled mass of flesh and blood.

Arthur sank to his knees, stunned by the sheer brutality of the attack. He wept inconsolably as he held his dead wife's hand. It was then that he noticed the white cartilage and the exposed bone. The ring finger had been chopped off – the mangled bony stump still oozing blood; their wedding ring, Keza's pride and joy, carried away like a trophy. The looters had, in their haste, preferred to chop off her ring finger rather than pull the ring free.

Within hours he had managed to garner enough information from the neighbours, their servants and gardeners, who had somehow survived the killings, to realise that his wife had been targeted as a Tutsi married to a Belgian. Her pregnancy was a further impetus for the deliberate act of butchery – even unborn children of pregnant Tutsi women were not spared. He found enough white bedsheets in the laundry room – covered all of them including Romulus and Remus, the two dogs. He resisted an overpowering urge to give them a decent burial in the garden – he wanted to showcase the brutality that had taken place in his absence. He wanted the authorities to document the atrocities that had taken place in his house, in his neighbourhood and in his Rwanda. Deep down he knew that no one cared – he and his family had just become a mere statistic of the ongoing genocide.

This was the eternal paradox of Africa – the breath-taking beauty and untapped wealth; all denuded and exposed by tribal conflicts and political chicanery. The garden of Eden transformed beyond recognition in the twinkling of an eye.

Looking at the scattered shrouded figures, he knew that although he probably needed to flee, he had one dreaded final task to complete – he ran upstairs and carried the shrouded figures of his wife and unborn child and the older Doberman downstairs. He gently positioned the five shrouded figures in a linear manner with Romulus and Remus guarding each flank. Arthur prayed that the wolverine spirits of Romulus and Remus, both named after the twin Roman brothers who founded Rome, would somehow thwart any further atrocities on his dead family.

He cried as he wrote name tags for each shroud; 'Keza and Athena' – Athena for his unborn daughter. He picked some white roses from the garden and placed his floral tributes, roughly fashioned as wreaths, at the feet of each – it was his fervent wish that, if and when this insanity ended, the authorities would punish those responsible.

After retrieving the Bible from his study, he tried, with sobs catching his breath, reading the last rites – he had no idea what to read so quietly said the Lord's Prayer. With one last look, he tucked the Bible into the rucksack that he had packed with a few clothes, and walked out of the house that had become an impromptu family tomb – and out of Rwanda for good.

Arthur drove the short distance to his office and warehouse and discovered the premises had been ransacked. The looters had stolen whatever they could lay their hands on including his drug stocks and cash. The Class 1 drugs and the anaesthetics would command a premium price on the black market; especially the ketamine that he had imported for the wildlife veterinarians. He had the presence of mind to retrieve and pack some of these expensive and valuable drugs – ketamine, lidocaine, morphine, antibiotics; his barter currency for emergencies and for his safe passage out of Rwanda. He abandoned his car once he was clear of the mayhem – a Belgian in a brand new car would be an easy target for a mob hell bent on retribution. His personal exodus had truly begun.

Arthur managed to hitch a lift with a small band of Belgians heading towards the border who filled him in on the latest word-of-mouth news; ten Belgian soldiers had been killed and the UN forces were withdrawing to safety. The world watched whilst Rwanda combusted.

They took refuge in a school as dusk descended. Arthur noticed a group of soldiers who seemed to be escorting a white doctor. For a night they shared the same fragile sanctuary that the school afforded. The next morning the doctor and the group had already left.

The memory of that perilous journey to safety was still etched in his mind. In a matter of months, between April and July 1994, thousands of Rwandans had been butchered. He wondered how many Tutsi women, like Keza, had been attacked – probably hundreds and thousands of Tutsi women who were systematically raped by the specially appointed rape squads. There were rumours that HIV positive Hutu patients were deliberately released from hospitals to join these squads;

their only remit was the rape of Tutsi women, to infect the women and their future progeny. Two million Rwandans were displaced and sought refuge, mainly in Zaire and Burundi. Arthur had, unwittingly, become an integral part of that exodus.

As he made his tortuous and time consuming way to Nairobi, via Uganda, he came across hundreds of Rwandans who had survived the genocide and were stranded in refugee camps. Amongst this migrating diaspora, many impostors evaded the clutches of the law by posing as refugees. He heard accounts of opportunistic looting and arson – there were reports that the affluent suburbs were stripped bare; whatever that could be stolen was pilfered. The demarcation between victims and perpetrators, in the utter chaos that prevailed, was blurred – culprits and rioters fled posing as refugees. With the breakdown in law and order and the porous borders, fleets of hijacked or stolen vehicles laden with pilfered bounty disappeared out of Rwanda.

Over the next two decades, after settling in the UK, Arthur worked his way up the management hierarchy of a small privately held chain of pharmacies. He had led a very reclusive life and had invested wisely. His penchant for the stock markets earned him enough every year to face retirement without any qualms. Providentially, he was offered a generous redundancy package when the pharmacies were sold to a national chain – Arthur took the redundancy package and retired. He was content with his financial status – at peace with his world and his solitary existence.

He joined the Shravan Project as a volunteer to keep himself active and mentally occupied. Every Tuesday afternoon he helped out at the offices of the charity; a bona fide member of the 'Shravan Brigade' – a nickname for all the volunteers and staff. This was a pro tem arrangement as he had not decided whether to return to Antwerp.

As part of his induction process, Arthur was invited to a twenty minute slot on the 'talking newspaper' – to be interviewed by the Volunteer Co-Ordinator, Peter Jansen. They had met previously to plan the agenda for the short interview. He had been requested to choose a favourite song – to be played on air as his choice of music for the audio edition.

As the song, 'Bridge over Troubled Water' by Simon and Garfunkel faded out, Peter did a couple of dummy runs for the sound recordist. Shortly after, Peter launched into the interview once the 'thumbs up' sign was given.

'Good morning, members, this is Peter

bringing you the latest edition of the 'Talking Newspaper'. Before we discuss the dates of the forthcoming events and launch into this edition allow me to introduce our new volunteer. Good morning, Arthur and welcome to The Shravan Project.'

'Morning, Peter,' replied Arthur in an authoritative voice with a strong Flemish accent.

'For the benefit of our listeners could you please elaborate on your background and how you came about to volunteer for Shravan?' Peter continued.

'I have always lived in South London since I arrived from Belgium, following the Rwandan genocide. After working as a pharmacist for several years, I took voluntary redundancy recently. I am hoping that volunteering with Shravan will help me maintain a routine. Keep me out of mischief,' Arthur added facetiously.

The interview lasted for about fifteen minutes and Peter then wrapped up the audio recording with the mention of all the other routine news that the printed version would have. The audio tailed off with the Simon and Garfunkel song.

As the two were descending from the sound studio, Arthur briefly queried, 'I get that déjà vu feeling; have we met before?'.

'Don't reckon we have. There must be a twin floating about'? Peter quipped. 'I have lived in

Antwerp previously though.'

Before they could continue, Peter was called away to the phone. Arthur looked very pensive as he walked towards the train station; he just could not shake off that déjà vu feeling.

Maxine had been busy with her ophthalmology appointments at the Moorfields Eye Unit at St George's Hospital in South London. It was days before she switched on the Bluetooth device to listen to the audio clip that had arrived in the post.

As the Simon and Garfunkel song faded away, her ears perked up on hearing a familiar voice from the distant past. Her brow furrowed as she listened to the whole interview with intense and studied concentration. The accent was distinct, familiar and foreboding but she struggled to place it.

With mounting anxiety, she listened to the audio clip repeatedly before she made the connection – her ordeal in the school that fateful night in Rwanda! The man with the distinctive Flemish accent; the one who had continued with his obscene monologue whilst assaulting her! The thought numbed her – the haunting flashbacks of that period in the school, the assault and her journey out of Rwanda were still very vivid and painful.

She felt the tears brimming over and she could not shake off the sense of foreboding. As the chain of intrusive thoughts cascaded through her disturbed mind, Maxine panicked and almost passed out – the near fainting spell caused by the diminished oxygen intake, triggered by panting and hyperventilation. She knew the drill so retrieved a paper bag from the kitchen and went through her remedial breathing exercise. Gradually as she breathed in and out of a paper bag the carbon dioxide balance corrected itself. Once her breathing had assumed a normal rhythm, she triggered the alarm – the ADT alarm operator listened to the distressed pleas for help and set in motion a regulated response. The police and the ambulance arrived simultaneously; their strident sirens piercing the serenity of the residential area.

Maxine was admitted to the 'triage ward' initially for observation. Once the A & E registrar had delved into her long history of depression, psychosis and anxiety attacks, she was transferred to a psychiatric ward for appropriate anti-psychotic therapy. The full blown depression brought back thoughts of self-harm and suicide.

With a lot of care and appropriate medication, she recovered enough to be discharged after spending a fortnight in hospital. Due to her previous history of chronic depression and her mental fragility, the community rehabilitation team initiated a care plan and also referred her to several support services – she joined the Shravan Project and started taking part in yoga and other activities.

The police had arrested Arthur based on Maxine's testimony. He was interviewed under caution in the presence of an appointed solicitor. Within a few hours, as there was no compelling prima facie evidence to charge him, DCI Hamish Bruce released Arthur, under investigation. Bruce was not convinced that Arthur was their man – maybe Maxine, with her long history of panic attacks and depression, had got her wires mixed.

As the case hinged mainly on Maxine's recognition of the perpetrator's accent, Bruce and Detective Constable Judy Danner called on Maxine at her flat to interview her again. This was after consent was sought and given by Maxine – he made sure that a Shravan volunteer was in attendance to avoid any claims of overzealous police tactics.

'My apologies for the intrusion,' Bruce said to Maxine as they took their seats. The Shravan volunteer, Maureen, sat unobtrusively in one of the other vacant chairs in the room.

'If I may take you back to that night in Rwanda, do you recollect if anyone else was present? That is apart from the perpetrator with the Flemish accent'? Bruce sat directly opposite Maxine and spoke succinctly and tried to avoid gesticulating too much. His demeanour was tentative as he was unsure how clearly Maxine could see him.

Maxine could just about see movements made by Detective Constable Danner, as she readied to make notes. She turned towards Bruce, his voice guiding her to face the blurred image of the DCI.

'Initially there were two or three other people and the sergeant. As you may be aware, I was injected with something, most probably ketamine – I remember seeing a vial in the tray earlier when I attended to the patient. As ketamine has a rapid onset of action, I was probably sedated by the time the assault started. I am not sure but I felt I was alone with him just as the obscene verbal onslaught started. And certainly, the accent has stayed with me all these years.' Maxine's shivered involuntarily at the traumatic memory and her lips trembled as she verbalised her thoughts.

'And you don't recollect anything about the perpetrator – a physical description would help?' The DCI probed, hoping that a clue may emerge.

'No, I was fading in and out consciousness and the light wasn't too good either. I must have drifted off at some stage, do not remember anything. Sorry.'

They discussed the sequence of events again whilst Constable Danner meticulously took notes. It became quite evident that with Maxine's state of sedation and the inadequate lighting in the room, she would not have a physical description of the rapist; the distinctive accent was the only piece of circumstantial evidence that identified the perpetrator.

They left soon after, convinced that Maxine was not going to be of any further help. Bruce went back to the files and the list of volunteers and staff present on the day Arthur was interviewed by the Talking Newspaper team – the connecting links were the culprit's presence in Rwanda and the Flemish accent.

'Maybe,' Bruce said to himself, 'Maxine was overwrought and over reacting?' He studied the list of staff and volunteers at the charity on the day and the list of people interviewed by his team.

His brow furrowed in irritation as he buzzed Constable Danner on the intercom.

'Judy, could you please come into my office

for a moment?'

As Judy sat down, he handed her the two lists. 'How come Peter Jansen was not interviewed? I notice all the staff and volunteers have been except him?' the superior officer queried, trying very hard to keep the edge out of his voice.

'He was on holiday, I am sure,' Judy said, flicking back the pages of the file notes. As she was desperately trying to find the right page, Bruce interrupted.

'Never mind, please call him in ASAP,' the DCI said in a much calmer voice. Judy Danner was a conscientious assistant and rarely erred. Bruce regretted his brusque manner earlier; she had the makings of a good detective.

A week later, Peter was interviewed at the local police station.

Bruce looked up from the case file – Peter had just taken his seat and had responded to Constable Danner's introductory greeting.

'Do I detect a hint of a Flemish accent?' Bruce began, having heard Peter's cheery greeting. 'It sounds Flemish and yet do I detect other nuances?' the DCI enquired, raising an eyebrow.

'I suppose it's the Yiddish inflection, I'm Jewish,' Peter countered.

As DCI Bruce looked at him inquisitively, Peter continued. 'After having lived over here and abroad for very many years, I wasn't aware that my Flemish-Yiddish accent was that pronounced or discernible,' Peter parried.

'What about Rwanda – have you lived there? Any direct link to pharmaceuticals?' Bruce continued.

'I fled Kigali, like most refugees, during the trouble there in 1994. I have lived and worked, in what I term, the triangle – Rwanda-Burundi-Zaire – as an export-import trade consultant. My role was mainly as an intermediary for Antwerp based companies involved in exporting to the triangle or importing from it. None of the companies I represented back then were pharma companies.' Peter replied.

'Only Antwerp based companies – because of your roots there?' DCI Bruce asked.

'More or less, although I did have a few clients in the UK and some Indian ones based in Mumbai and Surat,' Peter elaborated.

'You were caught up in the evacuation process after the rioting in Kigali and elsewhere?' DCI Bruce asked. He wasn't quite sure where Surat was.

'Yes, if you can call it evacuation, it was more a frantic dash to a safe haven. There was a total collapse in the law and order situation, so it was very much a case of every man for himself,' Peter explained.

'You said 'represented', so you no longer

work? And I would have thought you'd settle in Antwerp to stay close to the family, your roots?'

'Yes, 'represented' but no longer now. I retired when I came over here. Don't have any family back home in Antwerp. My parents died a few years ago, so there was nothing in Antwerp to draw me back.'

'Thank you for coming in. We will contact you if need be.' DCI Bruce got up and signalled to Constable Danner, who had been taking notes, to escort Peter out.

No access to ketamine, Bruce reflected as the pair retreated. Although with the chaos that followed the riots, ketamine or any other date rape drug would be easy to come by. Bruce reasoned that Arthur too had access to ketamine as a practising pharmacist. All that they had, so far, was circumstantial evidence and unless something positive came up, Maxine's rapist would evade the police. He had developed a profound empathy for Maxine – a doctor reduced to being redundant; all the skill and knowledge and the years of personal sacrifice laid waste by an act of violent self-gratification by a criminal. His resolve to track down this despicable man was steadfast.

DCI Bruce had the uneasy feeling that he had not delved aggressively enough into Peter's background and neither had Peter volunteered any additional information. On the other hand, apart from the accent, there was nothing untoward in his testimony or behaviour to warrant any suspicion. Nothing to tie him to that fateful night in the school.

A few days later, almost on a whim, he flew to Antwerp to see for himself the city that Peter and Arthur hailed from. He spent a day there and caught the late night flight back to London. As he sipped his glass of wine on the return flight, Bruce recapitulated on his day in Antwerp by flicking through his brief notes:

'Antwerp – a multi-cultural city, dubbed the 'diamond capital of the world', with one hundred and seventy nationalities; the diamond trade was the domain of just four nationalities: Jews, Indians, Lebanese and Armenians. Eighty per cent of the Jews worked in the 'diamond quarter' and Yiddish was historically the language of the Antwerp exchange. The Indians, predominantly Gujaratis from Surat, controlled two thirds of the diamond trade in Antwerp.

Bruce paused as he took a sip of the excellent Merlot and read aloud 'SURAT' – Peter had mentioned Surat but had not mentioned diamonds. And yet the 'triangle' was known for its carbon deposits in the form of diamonds.

He read on: 'A majority of the documented and un-documented consignments of rough diamonds are polished in Surat; constituting ninety per cent of the world's rough diamonds. The diamonds are 'cut' and given the finishing touches, sorted into smaller parcels and then transported to Mumbai, the world's largest diamond exchange. By the time the diamonds are exported - the country of origin and how and where the gems were mined – the audit or paper trail becomes convoluted. If the origin of the diamond is not known or even 'lost' by the time the Kimberley Process certificate is issued, then the diamonds could be from anywhere. Conflict or blood diamonds entering the supply chain – lines blurred between legal and illegal.'

DCI Bruce finished reading his notes and said to himself, 'Peter was linked to Surat and the triangle – Burundi-Rwanda-Zaire. Diamonds, that was it – blood diamonds from the triangle, smuggled out to Mumbai and to Surat? As DCI Bruce prepared to disembark at Heathrow Airport, his gut feeling was that he was on the right track.

Bruce, banking on the dictum 'follow the money' carried out some checks on Arthur – as a registered pharmacist the audit 'footprint' was easy to verify. Even his Rwanda profile, despite the loss of records, was fairly easy to corroborate and confirm – there were several pharmaceutical export orders filled by various export houses in the UK and Europe; consignments sent to Kigali for an import company registered as 'Gihanga Pharmaceuticals Ltd', named after an ancient Tutsi king. Arthur had picked the name 'Gihanga' in honour of his wife's Tutsi ancestry. The paper trail, export-import documents, had Arthur's signatures and a registered Kigali address.

DCI Bruce's checks on Peter Jansen failed to establish any connection with any consultancy or export company based in the Rwanda-Burundi-Zaire area. He did however find connections in Antwerp with several Indian diamond merchants – mainly retainers and fees paid for marketing services rather than any invoices or contract notes for diamond stock purchases or sales.

On a hunch, Bruce decided to contact Interpol – he was aware that in the Bosnian genocide proceedings, Interpol's Fugitive Investigative Support agency had played a vital role in tracking down offenders. Interpol also maintained a DNA database in collaboration with its one hundred and ninety member countries – maybe ICTR (the International Criminal Tribunal on Rwanda) would have something similar in place, Bruce surmised.

As hunches go, it turned out to be a good one

– the Interpol Rwanda Genocide Fugitive Project had pursued and tracked down several culprits. ICTR had branded rape as a form of genocide especially as so many Tutsi women had been systematically raped and killed. The DNA samples held on the ICTR database amounted to hundreds and thousands of unidentified suspects. The UK sample of Peter's DNA came up as a perfect match on the ICTR database – DNA samples lodged by the French doctor from the transit medical camp where Maxine was initially treated. It was amazing that in all the chaos and disruption that followed the genocide, basic protocols were executed and had survived – the French doctor's fastidious adherence to medico-legal jurisprudence was exemplary; the protocols had survived the genocide.

Armed with Interpol's confirmation, DCI Bruce managed to get a warrant to search Peter's house – a large cache of diamonds and bundles of cash were recovered, as were several hard drives – an audit trail that pointed to a life of criminal activity. A small amount of cocaine was also retrieved.

Serendipity played a crucial role in Peter's extradition to Arusha and his trial for rape – not only Maxine's rape but scores of Tutsi women's as well. Peter and his entourage of accomplices had raped and pillaged as they escaped from

Kigali to Dar-es-Salaam; a swath of sexual violence and gratuitous gratification. Peter then flew off to Antwerp.

Peter's DNA also came up a match on the UK National DNA database – his previous drink drive convictions meant that his DNA had been retained. And crucially, a de facto paternity test came up positive – the fact that Peter turned out to be the biological father of Maxine's son placed Peter in Rwanda on the night of Maxine's rape.

Months later, after liaison between Scotland Yard, Interpol and the ICTR, Peter was identified as the patient whom Maxine had briefly treated at the school – the fibrous scar of that thigh injury quite distinct. After bribing the sergeant, Peter had barged into Maxine's room and raped her. He made good his escape after the assault with the connivance of the sergeant and his band of followers; paid off with diamonds – the rest of his substantial haul of blood diamonds, accumulated over the years, was smuggled out as he fled Rwanda.

Peter, as it turned out, had been involved in smuggling blood diamonds from Burundi, Zaire and Rwanda for many years. His Antwerp connections aided and abetted him in his nefarious trade. The smuggling operations and the vast amounts of cash generated, fed Peter's wayward lifestyle of drugs, alcoholism and easy women.

He had moved to the UK after the international outcry and extensive coverage given to 'conflict diamonds' – he had scaled down his operations substantially in order to evade the law – he came off the radar.

Eventually, Peter was extradited to Arusha, ICTR's headquarters in Tanzania, to stand trial for rape and genocide.

A year later Maxine married Arthur, a man who had become a confidant and a close friend. DCI Bruce was the best man and Detective Constable Danner the maid of honour.

The long and tortuous investigation that led to Peter's extradition had drawn the two tortured souls together – a perfect 'bridge' to combat the sounds of silence that existed in their respective lives; lives that were marred by an act of God – the plane crash and the subsequent genocide that ripped the heart out of Rwanda.

Soon after they returned from their honeymoon, Maxine cancelled her subscription to the Talking Newspaper – she had Arthur, her very own personal newsreader with a very sexy foreign accent.

Green Fingers

Bryan clutched his Brazilian passport as he prepared to go through immigration at Gatwick Airport. His Air Portugal flight was not yet listed on the departure lounge terminals. Subconsciously Bryan was giving in to his fears about being stopped by immigration officials; the last few months had taken their toll on a man haunted by his demons.

He tried to mask his anxiety as he approached the immigration desk and was fortunate that he evaded the scrutiny of the experts, who were short staffed and unable to cope with the buzzing mass of humanity on its annual Easter exodus to warm exotic destinations.

On a less busy day, his deliberate and conscious efforts to camouflage his heightened state would in itself be a dead giveaway. The adrenaline rush stimulating the sweat glands, the constantly shifting gaze and the mopping of the brow would have been a flashing beacon to the practised eye of the trained airport personnel.

He breathed a sigh of relief as the immigration official barely looked at his passport and waved him through after stamping it. He made his way through the various checkpoints with a sense of relief; his anxiety dissipating as he progressed through to the duty free area.

He had no intention of returning to the UK – his own personal Brexit was underway; he prayed that he would be able to see his wife in Lisbon – otherwise his exit would be extended all the way to Rio de Janeiro, Brazil.

Some Years Ago: Rocinha, Rio de Janeiro

Bryan's birth and upbringing in Rocinha, the largest favela in Brazil, and his subsequent escape from the drug fuelled environment was an act of chance or fate, call it what you may. He was one of the lucky ones, the chosen one, to get away from the clutches of poverty and crime.

The years of impecunious struggle in the large Oliveira family, sustained by his mother's cleaning job, were soul destroying and character building at the same time. Adversity taught the teenaged Bryan that the will to fight against his circumstances was his only recourse, and probably saved him from a life associated with cocaine use and drug dealing.

There were minor skirmishes with the police which fortunately did not lead to criminal outcomes, although the drug lords tried their best to seduce him into their world of crime and complicity. Bryan's juvenile aberrations remained aberrations and nothing more; criminal convictions at bay. Many before him had succumbed to the poverty of the favelas and then taken the soft and easy option of a crime laden career. For many impoverished youngsters in rural Brazil, the migration to the cities and eventually to the favelas was almost predestined – the drug centric way of life becomes a compulsion once dreams perish and reality sinks in.

The rural-urban migration created imbalances and urban ghettos, which then became fertile grounds for the drug lords to exploit. The drug trade begins and ends in misery – the 'mules' at one end and the addicts at the other – the middle 'kingdom' populated by the shakers and the pushers who feast on the spoils of crime.

It was pure chance that one morning the fourteen year old Bryan escorted his mother to her cleaning job at a mansion in the wealthy suburb of Sao Conrado. His mother was pregnant with her seventh child and had been suffering from morning sickness so Bryan was drafted in as a chaperone. The mansion, palatial by any standards, belonged to one of the biggest and most affluent drug lords of Brazil.

Good fortune struck again whilst they were at the mansion. On seeing Bryan whiling his time away in the landscaped gardens, the drug lord casually asked the teenager to mow the lawn whilst he waited for his mum to complete her chores. The contracted gardener had called off sick. The promise of a handsome tip overcame any reservations that Bryan may have had; the US dollars on offer, instead of the Brazilian Real, piqued his curiosity.

That was his baptism into gardening. He kept doing the odd gardening jobs for the same drug lord and his friends and their friends; a 'domino' effect was created. Eventually, the self-taught Bryan, with the benevolence of his employer turned mentor, set up his own gardening and landscaping company.

His application and diligence soon bore fruit and a virtuous cycle was initiated – as word spread of his green finger touch, his enterprise prospered. In a short span of five years, Bryan was running a landscaping company that employed well over twenty people. His client list included the high spenders riding the economic boom that Brazil was going through. Bryan's ascent out of the abject poverty of the favela to a middleclass neighbourhood, with all the trappings of a successful business, bore testimony to his tenacity and enterprise.

His gardening career baptised and sustained by the patronage of the drug lord, whom he facetiously called Padrinho (The Godfather). Bryan had watched the Hollywood blockbuster a dozen times. For him Padrinho was more than a mentor – he became a father figure and filled a void in his life. Bryan's real father was a petty criminal – more in prison than out of it. On each 'outing' he would spend time in the favela and leave as soon as a new baby was on the way.

By the time the 2015-2017 Brazilian financial crisis imploded which eventually led to the impeachment of its first female president, Bryan had been married to Evita for several years. They had a ten year old son and any thoughts of having another baby, in the aftermath of the financial meltdown, were deferred – their foresight was well placed as Bryan's company, 'Green Fingers', was on the brink of collapse as work dried up.

The high rollers with huge, cheap loans and big houses to maintain were the first to be hit – most of Bryan clients went bankrupt in the financial Armageddon that unravelled. The domino effect eventually caught up with Bryan and he had to wind up his operations.

With no formal training or experience of any other trade, Bryan's family subsisted on the meagre earnings of Evita, his Portuguese wife – not enough to sustain the prosperous lifestyle that Bryan and the family had grown so accustomed to. The writing was on the wall – he would have to move the family back to the favela to keep his head above water. The thought filled him with dread. Evita's upbringing in salubrious Lisbon ill prepared her for the deprivations that followed. The family was barely coping – the psychological impact of an uncertain financial future was testing the bonds of cohesion.

London: 2016-2017

Evita and their son were compelled, by the downturn in their fortunes, to return to Lisbon and the sanctuary that her parents offered whilst Bryan tried to get back on his feet. Her Portuguese passport also gave her access to the greater employment opportunities that the UK presented – Portugal was a constituent part of the European Union (EU). Evita eventually moved to South London and promptly landed a job, as a receptionist, with an agricultural company specialising in herbicides and biological control systems.

Within a month she moved into a small flat in Mitcham, Surrey. In due course Bryan joined the family – his immigration status defined by his wife's Portuguese/EU status. Evita managed to find Bryan a temporary job in the marketing and sales department of the herbicide company where she worked. Whilst Bryan's gardening expertise stood him in good stead, his poor grasp of English became an impediment for a permanent position. After several extensions to his temporary contract, the management had to let him go – language skills had become an issue.

His voluntary resignation from the company turned out to be a blessing in disguise – he once again turned to gardening and landscaping jobs. It was hard, backbreaking menial work that rarely met the national minimum wage criteria in the face of an oversupply of low skilled manual workers from the EU. Unscrupulous employers took undue advantage of desperate workers like Bryan, stuck in the rut of statutory minimum wages. He had come full circle and was starting afresh – right at the bottom.

His perseverance and his faith in his abilities kept him going. He was gradually building up his contacts as his ambition was to re-invent himself as a landscape gardener. There were plenty of opportunities for ambitious workers – he was content, for now, to do the low paid menial jobs whilst he kept his head down.

His serendipitous association with the Smiths led to regular gardening work at their suburban Surrey home. Bryan was hoping that this was his renaissance; the rebirth of his landscaping company. The déjà vu feeling was heightened when the Smiths offered him a regular contract to maintain their enormous garden. The wages were meagre but the cash-in-hand agreement was attractive – Mrs Smith was quite adept at exploiting someone's misfortune to her benefit.

The Smiths had been let down by Bill, their regular gardener, who, in their opinion, was getting too big for his boots – Bill had not shown up for almost a month. His absence was compounded by his faux pas – Bill had forgotten to forewarn Mrs Smith of his whereabouts.

Mrs Smith had cannily hinted to Bryan that she could, as a favour, recommend him to her wide circle of friends. Taking his cue from her, Bryan promptly reduced his weekly contract rate for her and they shook hands on the deal. Mrs Smith, who fancied herself as a wheeler dealer, smiled coyly as she bid adieu to her new gardener. 'It works every time,' she mused, 'dangling the carrot never fails.'

Eventually, after an absence of six weeks, Bill turned up without notice. As he waited for Mrs Smith to answer the door, he noticed what he had been afraid of – the front garden looked immaculate and he was certain that the rear larger garden would be the same. 'The old biddy has taken on someone to do her bidding,' Bill reflected, his heart sinking at the thought of losing her contract and scores of others – her family and friends.

'Morning, Mrs Smith,' Bill tried to be as cheerful as he could as an irate looking Mrs Smith answered the door. The scornful look on her face forewarned him and he launched into an apologetic explanation about being stranded in Cumbria.

'Stop right there,' she chimed in. 'You couldn't phone? The last time we were there, the phones were still working in the Lake District. Anyway, I have engaged someone and he has done a darn sight better job in your absence.' she waved expansively at the front lawn.

'I am sorry, truly, but my mother took ill and was admitted to hospital. You are my first call – I drove back last night. Surely, we have known each other for years and hopefully I can make amends – how about I do your garden for free for the first month? And—'

Before Bill could remonstrate further, Mrs Smith interrupted, 'He's doing my garden for free for the first month and then at half your extortionate rate thereafter. To think that I have been paying you double his rate for the last five years is galling.'

With that she slammed the door on him. A crestfallen Bill got into his open top Suzuki van and stopped a few doors away for his next job. On completing the job, he managed to glean that a new Mediterranean looking gardener had started doing the Smiths. The news that a foreign looking chappie had stolen his regular work did nothing to uplift Bill's spirits. He had a gnawing feeling that his drinking spree and going AWOL for six weeks was somehow going to come back and bite him on the backside. He was paying a heavy price for his unprofessional behaviour.

And bite him, it did. It soon unravelled that the Brazilian had gradually stolen, over a short period, all of the contracts he had acquired courtesy of Mrs Smith. To his dismay, he had also lost a hefty chunk of his regulars; all cultivated over a number of years. Bill, in his agitated frame of mind, did not consider the domino effect that was soon to hit him dearly.

'Damn Mrs Smith,' he cursed, as he realized that his laisse faire attitude had cost him a big chunk of his regular work. He still wondered how anyone could survive on such low rates; the new gardener was undercutting him by a considerable margin.

He had gleaned all the information from Barbara, the local publican down the road. The Brazilian was a regular there – the pub, where tongues wagged once the alcohol had taken effect, was his best bet, Bill pondered.

Bill reckoned he had done the right thing by

voting for Brexit – he had had enough of these foreigners taking work away from the likes of him. Bill was meticulous and ensured that he declared most of his income so that the business operated legitimately; unlike these cowboys who were probably moonlighting whilst collecting dole money. He had half a mind to report the maverick to the immigration authorities.

The Smiths had driven a hard bargain with Bryan, who had capitulated and gone over the top in securing all future leads. The Smiths could easily afford to pay a higher rate – their index linked Civil Service pensions notwithstanding but the lure of a good bargain enthralled the lady of the house.

Mrs Smith's love for a good deal was predicated on exploiting Bryan's ignorance of his rights and of the complex immigration rules. Evita had applied for a UK residence card and despite her assurances that there were no grounds for deportation, Bryan had developed a phobia about the UK Border Agency knocking their front door down – it was a recurring intrusive thought. Brian was petrified of the Home Office and its immigration officers.

Mrs Smith's domineering demeanour with Bryan was not unusual – Mr Smith had been at the receiving end of her abrasive tone for decades. He felt for Bryan but was powerless to intervene – his daily round of golf would be compromised if he took sides against his wife. His passive acceptance of her will had set the tone – all men were weak and indecisive was her mantra. And she had been practising the same mantra for years, at the expense of all the men in her life – Bryan just happened to be the latest unlucky recruit to her regime of bullying and excessive control.

Mrs Smith quickly realized that Bryan was desperate for work and could be manipulated at will. She, as promised, ensured that Bryan took over virtually all of Bill's contracts. Her only condition, initially, was that Bryan did all her gardening work for free; her quid pro quo opening gambit.

Gradually, as Bryan's workload increased, Mrs Smith turned the screws even further – all new contacts that came off her and her entourage would attract a back hander for her. Like a Ponzi scheme, Mrs Smith benefitted from all the work that was generated – she was at the top of the Ponzi pyramid and collected her dues without any guilt. Her greed blinded her to the needs of others – Bryan was working twice the number of hours with precious little to show for it.

Although Bryan was financially more stable, the extra work that he was taking on entailed that he had to employ a young Polish lad to take on the extra workload. He knew despite the extra work he was taking on, the discounts and the backhanders to Mrs Smith were paring his margins which were wafer thin anyway – he frequently wondered whether he would be better off earning a minimum wage rather than being a puppet of her ladyship and her penny pinching friends.

He wished he could somehow undo the mess but with Evita's pregnancy, they could ill afford to lose a regular income, however meagre. Bryan had been sucked into a vortex of fear and manipulation; a tangled web spun by Mrs Smith and her friends. He knew at some stage the law of diminishing returns was going to catch up with him.

With the Brazilian fiasco very much in his mind, Bryan tried to renegotiate not only his gratis work for the Smiths but also his other contracts. All he was hoping for was that the Smiths paid his legitimate labour costs so that he wasn't out of pocket. He revised his rates for all the other contracts to bolster his earnings.

Mrs Smith refused, point blank, to entertain any such notion – she argued that Bryan was flourishing on the basis of her connections and networking. She had no objections to Bryan renegotiating the contracts with the others as long as she got her commission. Mrs Smith's vicelike control over his work and finances was beginning to worry Bryan.

The end result was that Bryan, whilst gaining a slightly revised rate from the others, the witches of suburbia as he called them, was saddled with the Smith's contract on a gratis basis and paying her a backhander. In retrospect, after doing his quarterly books, he wished he had not bothered – he was no better off, working that much harder and was now indebted to Mrs Smith for almost all of his contracts.

He was in an invidious position – for he feared, as Mrs Smith had threatened in the past, that if he pushed too hard, the Queen witch would undo everything and he would lose his bread and butter clients. She kept reminding him that Bill had visited her on several occasions and had reduced his rates to win her over – she was playing one against the other. The threat was oft repeated.

Whilst Bryan was astute enough to deduce that Mrs Smith was blackmailing him into submission, he did not have the gumption to call her bluff. He had always been self-sufficient and the thought of depending on Evita was unbearable.

His time away from Evita and his son were

also taking its toll – by the time he got in she and her son would have retired for the night. This was now the norm and he barely saw his family except on Sundays. As both were devout Catholics, Sunday church and their lunch afterwards were the only moments he spent with them or shared with them at home. The family was drifting apart and he was powerless to do anything.

Two momentous events precipitated further strife in Bryan's life – the EU referendum and the birth of his second son. The joy of becoming a father again was only diminished by the clouds of uncertainty that prevailed generally – the vitriol of the Brexit campaign and the political sabre rattling and rhetoric created an air of suspicion bordering on xenophobia. Bryan's anxiety had just grown exponentially.

The looming threat of tightening immigration criteria and the impact on jobs and the economy seemed real – for the first time Bryan felt the latent animosity that simmered, just under the surface, when he stepped into a bar or a restaurant; even some of his clients made derogatory remarks about foreigners 'milking the system'. The worry was that the venom was spreading insidiously, almost subliminally via the relentless discussions in the media and on political platforms.

Bryan, instinctively, recognised the array of social signals that were out there. His years of struggle in the favela had taught him an important precept; when the rule of the jungle overrides the rule of law then trouble is not too far behind. He was one of the fortunate ones who had managed to escape the favela – to now capitulate and go under would negate all that he had achieved. It would be dire if, despite his hard work, he had to return to Brazil and, God forbid, to the favela.

Bryan had not qualified for permanent settled status as yet – his status was dependent on his wife's presence in the UK. The manner in which the Brexit scenario was unfolding, Evita feared that their immigration status could be impacted. It seemed to Bryan that no one was prepared to accost the elephant in the room – the fate of the EU citizens once Brexit was executed. It suited the politicians to mouth pithy sound bites that sounded great on the telly – all noise and no substance; confusion reigned supreme.

Bryan was none the wiser once he had discussed his and Evita's immigration status with Mrs Smith – he knew that she had worked at the Home Office, UK Visas and Immigration offices in Croydon and had boasted frequently that she had access to the echelons at Lunar House.

Mrs Smith, after launching into long-winded discourses on what was wrong with the immigration policies, advised Bryan to let things settle down – Article 50 had just been triggered so it would take a considerable amount of time before the future gelled into place. She advised Bryan to stay put with the family and not even embark on an overseas holiday – no guarantee that they could gain re-entry. The recent contentious US ban on immigrants from certain countries was a moot point. Whilst he was led to believe that such a scenario would never unfold in the UK, Bryan, going by the Brazilian political shenanigans, had a healthy disrespect of all politicians – 'never-say-never' was probably prudent; political expediency always won.

His local pub was run by an attractive divorcee, Barbara Gardner, who was an avowed 'remainer' and vehemently opposed the very concept of Brexit. She tried to console Bryan, who in moments of dark despair would pour his heart out to her – she had faith in Mrs May. She was sure that the right decisions will be taken to satisfy the party and the electorate. As she correctly pointed out to Bryan – with so many Brits settled in the EU countries, no one wanted a tit for tat scenario, resulting in a border crossing of epic proportions.

Bryan had a soft corner for her as she was a

good listener and exhibited a great deal of empathy. Her flirty demeanour, which was part of her remit as a publican, appealed to the troubled Bryan. He was starved of female companionship and the excitement of the chase invigorated his flagging male libido. Her larger than life vivacious persona was the antithesis of Evita's personality. Evita's world of relentless household chores, working and tending to the family left precious little time for anything else; not even for Bryan. Barbara had unwittingly walked into that void.

Not that all the political posturing made an iota of difference to the beleaguered Bryan – he was tense and worried and with that came the danger of acting irrationally or seeking the high of a thrill. The comforting and the oomph of Barbara's practised flirting enamoured Bryan – he was inherently attracted. And with a few pints in his belly, Barbara assumed the softer nuances of an empathetic old flame rather than the femme fatale that she really was; it was her USP to keep the pub's coffers full. Bryan smiled as he left and got into his beat up Fiesta. Her winsome smile and the prodigious cleavage that her low cut blouses displayed endeared her to Bryan and, indeed, to all her male customers. He thought about her as he drove home – very much inebriated.

As he was parking the car just outside their flat, the 'ping' on his mobile announced a text message. It was from Barbara assuring him that it would all be 'ok in the end and that the political 'ping pong' games should not darken his thoughts about the future, LOL xxx'.

He liked that – the symbolic kisses and the concern. She was a good sort; Bryan remembered the other texts that she had sent – birthday wishes, Christmas greetings, a few saucy jokes...if only he were footloose and fancy free.

Bryan obviously, in his lonely world full of Brexit and work stress, did not think for a second that Barbara might be an old hand at keeping her customers hooked – pie in the sky routine that she had mastered to exquisite perfection; an organ grinder par excellence. The way to a man's heart is through the stomach, more so if the stomach is full of the pints of the elixir of life. Barbara had mastered the art of flattery and Bryan was a gullible pawn.

A Few Months Later

With the relentless emotional turmoil of the birth of their second son and his increased reliance on alcohol to cope with the pressures of juggling their precarious finances, Bryan was getting lax with his work. His pit stop at his favourite watering hole and chatting to Barbara became almost mandatory, a daily routine. The alcohol fix was a panacea for the constant bickering that Evita indulged in.

On a couple of occasions, he had missed his fixed appointment with Mrs Smith and he had committed the same error as Bill had – Bryan forgot to apologise or to reschedule. Mrs Smith was livid on having her garden ignored and even more so when similar lapses were reported by others in her group. She was annoyed that Bryan was taking everything for granted. It did not occur to her that Bryan was finding it more and more difficult to sustain the payments – like a Ponzi scheme where the new investments can't keep pace with payments to the older clients.

All this came to a head when one late night on his return home, a furious Evita, feeling insecure and threatened by the amount of time that Bryan seemed to be spending at the pub, exploded into a diatribe of sexual innuendo. She accused him of having an affair with Barbara. She had long rued their cosy banter and Barbara's flagrantly intimate nuances, even in her presence, had reached a toxic level – when she inadvertently gained access to Barbara's texts, she erupted into a jealous incandescent rage.

She was so incensed that the demons of his

promiscuity reared their ugly head – she refused to listen to his protestations of innocence and stormed off to bed. Bryan did not have a chance of making up as she stubbornly locked him out of their marital bedroom. He spent a fitful night on the sofa.

The frigid and stony atmosphere continued for days; Bryan hoping that it would blow over in due course. 'Must be her hormones,' he consoled himself with some homespun psychotherapy. She thought the same – 'it must be a testosterone surge' that was making him chase other women.

In the maelstrom of accusations and counter accusations, his logical argument that he would hardly leave such 'tell-tale' evidence on his mobile if he was really having an affair failed to make an impression. Her fulminant scorn at the alleged betrayal blinded her – she was 'judge and jury' and there was nothing that Bryan could do or say to convince her of his innocence.

One evening when he returned to a cold unlit home, he found a note on the dining table – Evita had taken both their sons and flown to Lisbon that morning. She had spoken to her parents and they had wired her the cash for the tickets. Evita, although she had not raised the issue after that night, firmly believed that Bryan was going to walk out on her and move in with the lusciously attractive Barbara.

Illogical and irrational as it seemed to Bryan, her emotional state about his alleged infidelity had taken root and he could not convince her otherwise. Their hand to mouth existence and the uncertainty that the Brexit proposals had fomented took its toll on her disturbed mental state. Visions of Bryan serenading the voluptuous Barbara exaggerated her fears – she was heartbroken at Bryan's callous indifference to all that was unfolding in their lives; even ignoring the emotional trauma that he was inflicting on their sons.

Bryan swore under his breath as he realised the gravity of the situation – with Evita back in Portugal, his immigration status would be open to subjective interpretation. Bryan was bereft with worry and envisaged the day when the Home Office officers would knock on his door and initiate deportation protocols. In his heart he knew that he was over-reacting but the atmosphere of fear created by the Brexit debate and his ignorance about the immigration laws added to his phobia. In his disturbed state he was agitated more about his immigration status and impending expulsion than about Evita's departure to Lisbon.

With his inadequate grasp of English and his inherent lack of confidence, he shied away from lawyers and even declined to go to the Citizens Advice Bureau to seek legal advice about his immigration status. The panic, with Evita's departure, had set in and it fed on his insecurities – he was in a very lonely space where nothing made any sense. Bryan was at an all-time low.

In desperation and sick with worry he confided in Mrs Smith and in Barbara to gain some kind of an insight into his predicament. Both of them, to their credit, tried to assuage his disturbed emotional state. They did try and convince him that as he had lived and worked for almost two years and had paid all legitimate taxes, it was hardly likely that anything would change in the near future – the Brexit transition period had not even kicked in.

Whilst he believed Barbara, Mrs Smith's stance puzzled him – she must be playing some kind of a game to gain an upper hand or building her case to grass him to the immigration authorities. After all, he had heard her raving and ranting about the mess 'her country' was in due to the lax immigration policies. Brian was giving in to his paranoia that Mrs Smith was up to something to extract her 'pound of flesh'.

Meanwhile, Barbara was genuinely concerned about Bryan's mental wellbeing – the haunted and hunted look in his eyes worried her.

It would not take much to tip him over the edge. She was accustomed to men unburdening their insecurities to her but Bryan seemed obsessed and her heart went out to him, especially as his wife had abandoned him and gone back to Lisbon. Bryan was lonely and he felt 'boxed in'. He missed the comforting figure of Padrinho and his wisdom – if only he could speak to him.

It was all a huge co-incidence that in the next few days a letter arrived from Lunar House, the immigration offices in Croydon. The officer in charge had requested Bryan call and arrange a mutually convenient date for an interview. Bryan ignored the routine query and did not contact the officer.

He panicked and kept debating, in his mind, as to how Lunar House had known that Evita had left him. After much analysis, he realized that only two people knew about Evita's departure – Mrs Smith and Barbara. Surely, Barbara, the good listener, had never given any indication that she was against immigrants – she had always treated him with dignity and decorum. In fact, Bryan had convinced himself that Barbara was attracted to him as he was to her. He, very conveniently, exonerated her of any role in the debacle.

Which left only Mrs Smith as the likely villain – she must have grassed him to the immigration authorities as she had access to her old cronies and contacts at Lunar House. Bryan was convinced of her complicity in the matter.

He was disappointed and livid at her betrayal – he had not harmed her in any way; in fact, contributed to her earnings. His rancour grew as he convinced himself that Mrs Smith was adhering to her own personal Brexit agenda – to reduce the number of migrants entering or staying back. The more he dwelled on the matter, the more he convinced himself that Mrs Smith was the reason for his difficulties – it become an obsession that she had victimised him.

Bryan continued tending to Mrs Smith's garden as usual. He struggled to control his emotions but still managed to maintain a façade of civility towards her. On his last visit he went to the back of the garden and noticed, to his immense satisfaction, that the rhizome that he had planted a few weeks ago had taken root and was flourishing at a rapid rate. His handiwork pleased him and he smiled – his first smile in weeks.

Bryan was aware that in ideal conditions, Japanese Knotweed could grow almost four inches a day, a profligate growth rate that the World Conservation Union had classed as 'one of the world's worst invasive species'. In the UK,

Japanese Knotweed is classed as a controlled waste – meaning that its disposal was regulated by law and only licenced agents and appropriately licensed landfill sites can be employed to tackle the weed.

The distinctive shield-shaped leaves and the bamboo-like stems with purple speckles were a dead giveaway. Japanese Knotweed, also known as Hancock's Curse, had taken root in Mrs Smith's back garden. Bryan smiled sheepishly as he took some photographs of the weed. He looked around – the Smiths were entertaining some friends and were indoors.

Bryan's short stint at the herbicide company, where Evita had got him a temporary job, had given him access to the reports of the astounding spread of this malignant weed – he had deliberately chosen this particular plant as he was certain that the Smiths would incur great costs to eradicate the curse; it would be an exorbitantly expensive exercise. The standard herbicide 'treatment' yielded ambiguous and variable results; a laborious and time consuming eradication process. He may not have earned his just dues from her but if 'easy come, easy go' became a reality then his revenge would be greatly gratifying.

He also recollected that the unfettered growth and spread of the insidious Japanese Knotweed could lead to subsidence and structural damage to properties. Bryan was aware that the Smiths were thinking of downsizing and were keen on selling their property – his handiwork, he hoped, would make it almost impossible to sell without knocking off thousands of pounds. His retribution would be commensurate with the trauma that Mrs Smith had put him through.

Bryan recalled a few clients whose properties had been blighted by this curse and the prolonged battle some of them had with their insurance companies to get redress for the structural damage caused by subsidence. It was his fervent prayer that the weed would spread to the neighbouring properties – leaving the Smiths open to litigation for damage and for devaluation of the neighbouring properties. Serves her right, thought Bryan – she deserves it for the years of misery that he had to endure and for the uncertain future that he now faced.

He quickly collected his tools and walked out of the back garden without saying goodbye – he flew to Lisbon the next morning. He did Mrs Smith a final favour – he anonymously reported the presence of Japanese Knotweed on her property to the Environment Agency.

A few days later Mrs Smith called Bill in a state of panic and intense worry – could he come down and have look at the notice that she had received about this cursed weed? The letter stipulated that she was obliged by law to control and eradicate the weed using appropriate licensed methods.

Her neighbour, a retired chartered surveyor, had 'diagnosed' the rampant growth, spread into his garden from next door, as the much dreaded Japanese Knotweed. When she ignored his advice to do something about it, he promptly reported it to his insurance company, who put in a claim for appropriate redress. In due course, Mrs Smith received a letter from her insurers – it did not make for good reading.

When she trawled the internet and read the horrendous reports about the weed, Mrs Smith felt her heart sink – she was on the verge of tears as she dialled Bill again and left an urgent message.

Bill had been anticipating her call to re-start work at her house but this business about the Japanese Knotweed was totally out of the blue. Bill knew through Barbara that Bryan had left and he had been anticipating a 'welcome back' call from Mrs Smith. Whatever it was, it meant more work and more money.

'Barbara, a pint of Stella and please have one on me. You have earned it.' Bill smiled prodigiously as he took his place at the bar.

Without Barbara's constant flow of gossip about Bryan and his immigration status, he would still be out of pocket. Now that Mrs Smith was virtually back in his fold, he had no doubts that his business would recover from the damage inflicted by Bryan.

As the cold beer smoothed its way down his parched throat, Bill realised that it was a stroke of genius on his part to tip off the immigration authorities – in one fell swoop he had got rid of his competitor. The panic in Mrs Smith's messages meant that he could inveigle back into her good books and win back all his lost contracts.

Although he had never come across Japanese Knotweed previously, he was astute enough to spot an opportunity – this could be a great side line to his landscaping activity – an extra stream of revenue treating and eradicating the plant. He smiled knowingly as he recollected reading something in one of the gardening monthlies about this 'terrorist of weeds' and the allusion to a certain Mr Hancock who had first imported the exotica as an ornamental plant – his notoriety sealed for posterity as the weed was dubbed 'Hancock's Curse'.

'This could be a nice little earner,' Bill said to himself as he gleefully toasted Barbara; his unwitting 'mole' who had kept him abreast of

Bryan and Evita's break-up and Bryan's eventual flight out of the UK.

Any twinges of regret that he might have experienced at his obnoxious behaviour in hastening Bryan's premature departure were soon quenched as the Stella hit the right spots at the back of his throat. The sight of the luscious Barbara beaming at him, from behind the bar, relegated any thoughts of Bryan, the Home Office or Brexit to the past. For now at least, as he savoured his beer, his thoughts were on Hancock and his 'curse' and how he was going to benefit from a curse.

Bill's anonymous call to the Home Office was in due course processed and the matter referred to Lunar House in Croydon. When the case officer collated and assessed the immigration file he dismissed the matter as a 'crank call' – the Oliveira family's papers were in order. There was a copy of a routine letter on file, updating the Home Office records with regard to current address and contact numbers.

Sao Conrado, Rio de Janeiro

Bryan, a few weeks after his return from London, was waiting for Padrinho in the palatial home that he so remembered from his youth – the benevolent drug lord who had treated his mother with dignity and respect and had started him on his gardening career. The Padrinho epithet had stuck and the drug lord had quite liked Bryan's sense of humour. He had been chuffed when he had received a Christmas card from Bryan, a year before his departure from the UK, which had a photograph of a stallion with the head missing.

'Hi Bryan,' Padrinho boomed as he entered the study where Bryan was waiting twiddling his thumbs. 'Come on, let's take a walk in the garden – it looks much better since you stopped working on it.' Padrinho guffawed at his own joke.

Bryan smiled at the attempted levity – Padrinho had not been pleased when Bryan had wound up his gardening company after the financial crisis and had sounded out the older man about his plans to emigrate to the UK. The older man had formed a bond with Bryan and had wanted him to stay back and join him in running one of his pitches in the Rocinha, an offer that Bryan had refused out of hand. He had left for London shortly after that final meeting.

'Why now? You have always refused to join me, so what has changed?' Padrinho queried, referring to Bryan's call a few days ago about the possibility of a job.

'As you are aware, I have lost everything – my

business and my family. Evita refused to let me see my sons when I stopped over in Lisbon. I was even prepared to stay back in Lisbon to re-start our life together.'

'Why didn't you get in touch? Europe is a big market for us – I could easily have sorted something for you out there?'

'That was then, this is now. I have tried to use my 'green finger' touch the legitimate way and all I got was strife. When I saw my mother still working her fingers off cleaning for people, despite the ravages of TB that she has contracted, it made my mind up. I'll work for you if the offer is still open,' Bryan said in anticipation of a sympathetic response from the older man.

'Are you sure? Once you start with me, there is no going back – remember the headless stallion in 'The Godfather'?' Although Padrinho said it with a huge smile, Bryan noticed the cold look in his eyes – the smile on the lips never reached the eyes; the reptilian stare quite telling in its intensity.

'Absolutely, no turning back – I need the money for her treatment and who knows, maybe for my sons? I am hoping I can be a part of their future again,' Bryan remarked trying to envisage his sons as young adults in Lisbon.

Medellin, Colombia

As Bryan waved farewell to Padrinho, who had just completed a short stay and was on his way back to Rio de Janeiro, he went back to his truck and unloaded the vats of precursor chemicals that his farm hands would use – kerosene, sulfuric acid, sodium carbonate, hydrochloric acid, potassium permanganate and acetone. It was a three step process to convert coca leaves to coca base and to cocaine hydrochloride, a labour intensive enterprise. Labour was cheap and he had no shortage of applicants – farm hands in Colombia were a dime a dozen. He had empathy for these poor and desperate men – all of them trying to earn a decent living; just as he had tried in the UK.

That was almost a year ago – Padrinho had wanted his man on the ground to learn the ropes before putting him in charge of an operation that had started some years ago. The drug lord had direct links to the coca farms in Colombia from where cocaine was moved into Brazil and the favelas. He had big plans to move into Europe, his rivals were doing it and it was time he stepped up and upped his game. Bryan would head, very soon, his operation in Medellin. He needed a trustworthy person like Bryan to be his eyes and ears in Colombia.

Bryan, as he fingered the green coca leaves, was transported back to South London where he had briefly caressed the leaves of the Japanese Knotweed in Mrs Smith's back garden – it seemed eons ago as he fondly thought of Evita, his sons and the brief interlude of a normal life that they had shared until the Brexit referendum. And Mrs Smith had turned everything on its head. He still blamed Mrs Smith for the loss of his family and his exit from the UK.

His only regret about his present life was that he had eventually become a part of the drug trade and the misery that it caused all over the world. He had, in his youth, seen the devastation that cocaine caused – the drug addicts in the favelas and the breakdown of the family structure already steeped in poverty and suffering. He went through the same thoughts every time he harvested the coca leaves – grown and cultivated by him in this dusty corner of Colombia. He shrugged, dismissing the guilt and wiped his 'green fingers' on the dirty rag that smelled of kerosene and acetone.

'C'est la vie,' he murmured as he got back to work.

Many Years Later: Lisbon, Portugal

Evita Oliveira, as she hurried towards the mobile van stationed in Praca do Comercio, spotted the queue of patients, all drug users, waiting for their turn to collect free methadone and other drug treatments. She had joined a charity to help out at the square when her first born, Pedro, had almost died of a drug overdose. He had been drug free for months until a recent relapse into drug use. Evita could not see him in the queue of patients and prayed that he would present himself later on and collect his treatment dose. She was glad that she was part of the treatment scheme – at least that way she could keep an eye on her first born.

Portugal, unlike most other countries, had rolled out drug treatment programmes nationwide to give out free methadone and other opioids – drug use was considered a disease rather than a criminal activity. The Portuguese authorities had seen a recent spurt in the smuggling of cocaine into Portugal – the government had doubled its budget for the drug treatment programmes.

A few days later she read reports in one of the national newspapers of the internecine drug wars between the various cartels in Colombia. A small paragraph buried in the full page report mentioned that the Medellin drug cartels had gone through a catharsis – she felt a tight knot form in the pit of her stomach when she read that a new order had gained ascendency in Medellin, a cartel headed by 'O Padrinho' (the Godfather) and a man known as Green Fingers. For a moment Evita was transported back to Rio De Janeiro and the happy times that they shared- before Brexit Britain and before Bryan the skilled green fingered gardener became Bryan the 'Green Fingers' drug lord!

She had deliberately contrived to shield her sons from Bryan – and yet the drugs peddled by him were probably available half way across the world in Lisbon and coursing through Pedro's veins.

Barbara was pleased to see Bill come in and take his regular place at the bar. She promptly poured a Stella and slid the pint towards him. 'Have this is one on me Bill. I just signed the papers.'

'What papers? Marry me if you are divorcing your partner.' Bill retorted flirtatiously.

'I've sold the lease,' Barbara continued with a dismissive wave, 'to a consortium. They want to convert this into an Indian gastro-pub. Kenyan Indian cuisine, I am told. A curry restaurant.'

'Oh, good. I like curry,' Bill said and added

apologetically as an afterthought, 'will miss you though! When?'

'Not yet so keep it to yourself. It's going to be called 'The Friday Club' – they have already appointed a young Indian chef who I gather was on Masterchef recently.'

'Sudden isn't it? Don't tell me you too are spooked by the moribund and relentless Brexit discussions?'

'I am fed up. Can't find the staff. My kitchen team are all going back to Poland and Bulgaria. All are worried about the uncertainty that hangs over all of us. When this group made me an offer I could not refuse, I knew the time had come to quit. I own the property so will still live in the flat above. You'll still see me around. What about you, aren't you worried? Your gardening business has had problems. Remember Bryan undercutting you?'

Bill shot Barbara a venomous look. He had rued the day when too much Stella had 'empowered' him to make a play for the comely publican. He had boasted, in his stupor, about grassing Bryan to the immigration authorities. Even in his inebriated state he had known, from her pained look, that it was a faux-paus at best – he knew about Barbara's soft spot for the beleaguered Bryan. His jealousy had got the better of him. Bill retreated towards a group of friends.

Just then Barbara's mobile rang and she smiled wryly at the caller's timing. Bryan had kept in touch and Barbara had set the record straight that it was Bill and not Mrs Smith who had meddled and grassed him.

'Hi. Did you tell him?' Bryan asked. He was sitting in the mansion that belonged to his 'Godfather' and was now his. His mentor had died a year ago and Bryan had taken over the business. He had returned to Rio.

'No, not yet. I will before the night is over – he's here. We signed the papers – I had a call from the solicitor's.' Barbara said.

Mrs Smith had been astounded that a foreign buyer was prepared to pay the full asking price after the Japanese Knotweed debacle. The house had been on the market for two years and was virtually unsaleable because of the pending subsidence claim. Bryan had been very contrite about the whole episode and had promised to make amends and come good. Barbara was pleased that Bryan had kept his word and bought the Smith's house. The Smiths were retiring to Portugal – away from the Brexit endgame and the incessant bickering about a second referendum.

Bryan had offered Barbara a job – to handle the legal process of setting up a gardening and landscaping company called 'Green Fingers' which was going to be managed by the Polish lad who used to work for Bryan. Barbara's job would be to handle the finances and the back office.

Green Fingers was going to be competing with Bill's clients – and this time he would get it right. The revenge would be swift and sweet – he was determined to annihilate Bill and buy the business on the cheap. Bryan's plan was to eventually 'gift' the landscaping business to Barbara. At least that would give him an excuse to keep tabs on his 'luscious Barbara'!

Later that evening when she told Bill about 'Green Fingers' setting up business in his backyard, he almost dismissed the idea - 'beer fuelled' bravado that would come back to haunt him.

Barbara smiled and murmured under her breath, 'Wait till the Stella wears off!'

She was still smiling as she dialled the number. 'I'll take the job.'

Many miles away Green Fingers counted the days on his fingers and beamed – the 'fly' had just walked into his web!

Cold Dish

The Brahmin priest, resplendent in his saffron dhoti, blessed the new born child and his exultant parents. His gaze was drawn, almost by an innate reflex, to the neonate's lower body and his eyes, as if a switch had been flicked, lit up.

His smile widened as it dawned on him that his services had been more than adequately remunerated and, as his thoughts drifted to that torrid afternoon in the temple, he wondered whether it was his hard work or Shiva's blessings that such munificence had been granted to him, especially after the tribulations of the last few months.

Many Months Earlier

The bi-weekly state transport bus from Bhuj disgorged its passengers in the rapidly fading light of dusk. The journey had taken over three hours traversing a desert terrain that left a thin layer of dust and sand residue in the bus and on the passengers. One of the last to disembark, the Brahmin moved with great deliberation, in part due to an imperceptible limp and more so in trepidation at the prospect of starting anew as an acolyte at the main temple.

He had compromised his position as an

upcoming priest in the town of Bhuj and must now pay the price of his folly by starting afresh in a village he had, until a few days ago, never heard of. His only consolation was that the village afforded anonymity and although he was perturbed at the significant demotion in his status, he needed the space to recover his poise – he must bury the past and start afresh.

The near six foot figure towered above all and his pale, fair complexion was barely tanned by the blazing heat of the dry summer. His athletic and imposing Adonis-like persona belied the roots of his profession. In a different milieu, he could easily have been mistaken for a Bollywood star. The forlorn figure, as he moved towards the temple, bemoaned the vicissitudes of his fate and wondered whether he had inadvertently earned Shiva's wrath for his misdemeanours – the Gods punishing one of their messengers on earth?

Even in the fading light, he could discern the imposing façade of the temple in the distance, festooned with lamps. The faint acrid aroma of burning ghee became more pronounced as he progressed towards his destination. The vibrant and reverberating tones of the temple bells foretold the impending nocturnal surge of devotees assembling for the closing puja (prayer ritual) of the day. The temple bells, sounds of familiarity, aided in calming his nerves; as did his silent rendition of his mantras. The thin patina of sweat on his brow was the only manifestation of his inner turmoil on the fast approaching encounter with his future employers – the temple hierarchy of priests headed by the Raj Pandit (high priest).

The young porter, barely reaching the priest's waist, carried the Brahmin's bundle of hastily packed possessions delicately balanced on his head, as they approached the main square after meandering through the sand logged residential lanes. The open courtyards of most homes, some with cows being prepared for the evening milking, were filled with the pungent smoke of cow dung fuelled fires and the warm glow of lanterns as the evening shadows lengthened. Young children played the last of their games of the fading day as women, some with their faces veiled by their saris, prepared the evening meal on the open fires. In most cases, the prepubescent daughters joined their mothers in the evening rituals of cooking, milking the cows and arranging the beds in the courtyards or on the terraces.

The village of Bhog, like many such villages dotted across Gujarat and, indeed, India, was a microcosm of the Indian subcontinent – an agrarian economy and a mixture of different social groups. Bhog was also a trading outpost to the market town of Bhuj. The thriving village comprised of a main square, the hub, and a labyrinth of several dusty residential lanes. Sturdy brick built houses with tiled roofs nestled with lesser ramshackle dwellings, representing the patent disparity between the haves and the have nots. Most dwellings were lit by oil lanterns, easily identified by the dull yellow glow that an incomplete combustion invariably produces as compared to the more affluent homes aglow with bright fluorescent light that the expensive pressurised paraffin Petromax lamps emitted.

A few of the traders and farmers had cars and tractors parked outside their homes as an ostentatious exhibition of their wealth. The Rajputs, a warrior class and second in the hierarchy behind the Brahmins in the four-caste Indian system, showed off their regal lineage by shunning these modern contraptions and opting for stallions; an equine badge of machismo. The Rajputs with their Marwari and Kathiawari stallions tethered outside their homes, used the thoroughbreds to showcase their royal status whilst the Massey Fergusson tractors and Jeeps parked outside the homes of the business elite represented the nouveau riche; both were a minority in a village that was inhabited mostly by impoverished farmers and migrant labourers.

The Brahmins, by virtue of their exalted and learned status, were virtually demigods and Sanskrit, the language of the Gods, was their forte. These upper caste clans, especially the temple priests, wielded immense power and influence – their knowledge of the Indian scriptures enabled them to use religion as an instrument of guidance and control. The Brahmins, mostly active as professional priests, were the 'messengers of the Gods' on earth and their counsel sought at every stage of life; from the cradle to the grave.

On the outer periphery of Bhog were verdant fields which sustained the cultivation of cotton, peanuts and other myriad crops; typical of the flourishing agrarian economy. Most of these farms belonged to large landowners, the Patels, who were mostly absentee farmers. The indentured labourers, employed on barely subsistence wages, were mostly impecunious immigrants from the states of Bihar and Utter Pradesh – by far the poorest and most populous states within the Indian Union.

The Kutch, in the state of Gujarat, and its border communities were still reeling under the legacy of the cathartic upheaval that the partition of India, following independence, had engendered. The stigma and the trauma of one of the largest migrations in the history of mankind still festered under the veneer of communal harmony. Religion and faith, in these times of adversity, became the binding forces for the predominantly Hindu inhabitants of the village – every nuance of the village life was orchestrated by the Brahmin priests; omnipotent and supreme.

It was amidst this vibrant community that the Brahmin priest arrived with an optimism that only youth exhibits; before the cynicism of age and impending mortality take precedence. He was fleeing from his past and hoped that this new beginning would usher in a calmer and prosperous chapter in his life.

Probesh Chaturvedi, the acolyte, recruited by the Raj pandit and the coterie of pujaris (priests) that managed the main temple, had adapted quite well to the temple hierarchy, however, acceptance by the majority would take time, especially as Probesh was a bachelor. The pujaris all had their living quarters at the rear of the temple with ample room for spouses and families. He was the only bachelor in the midst of a very family oriented, close knit community of temple priests.

The males, accustomed to the cosy interaction with other married pujaris were irked by the Raj pandit's unilateral decision to engage a bachelor. The recruitment and arrival of the dashing priest had not gone down well with the males; the females were all aflutter. Even before Probesh could prove his mettle, the knives were out for him. However, as he was the Raj pandit's protégé, their resentment was held in abeyance – for now.

The main temple, with its imposing marble and granite façade, housed a pantheon of Gods from Ram, Krishna, Ganesh to Shiva and a myriad other minor gods and goddesses. With its larger than life façade, the temple dominated the village square, accommodating all the gods that one could wish to worship; the devotees flocked to its doors in droves. The temple's revenue was prodigious, a cash-cow, and with it came the authority and domination that wealth imparts. As the temple was one of the largest employers and an important cog in the economic framework of the village, the Raj pandit and his pujaris reigned supreme. Their hold on Bhog and the surrounding villages was absolute – they could make or break any individual or organisation.

There was a much smaller decrepit Shiva temple on the outskirts, perched on a small hill. It nestled amongst a grove of overgrown banyan trees – some trees so overgrown that a couple of them could be accessed from the temple terrace. The temple overlooked a nearby lake and the 'dhobi ghat' (laundry site), used by the village women to wash their clothes and sometimes swim and bathe in. A motley crowd of cows and buffaloes shared the watery retreat, especially in the hot summer months.

The Shiva temple was run by a solitary old Brahmin priest who lived, in a self-contained house within earshot of the temple. The two structures shared a common courtyard with a freshwater well demarcating the outer boundary of the temple. The two huge overgrown banyan trees, next to the well, afforded respite from the blazing sun in the summer months and shelter from the heavy monsoon rains. The temple terrace, overrun by the branches of the larger of the two trees, afforded an uninterrupted view of the small lake and the dhobi ghat nearby.

Many years ago, just after the priest had taken charge of the Shiva temple, he had bought a small plot of land, a stone's throw away from the temple, on which he built his two bedroom single-storey house. The land on which the temple was sited belonged to a religious trust.

In retrospect, the old priest's bold decision to invest his life's savings in buying the land and erecting a house turned out to be a blessing in disguise – he was not beholden to anyone for a roof over his head. Each day, after the final puja of the night, he would secure the temple doors and walk across to his quarters to prepare the evening meal or even walk the short distance to the lake for a refreshing swim. The old priest was king of his castle, unlike the priests at the main temple – they were all employees; subject to the rules of their contracts with the temple hierarchy.

With the passing of years, the entire Shiva complex had fallen into disuse primarily due to the rivalry between the two temples. The Raj pandit and the older Brahmin were old adversaries. The sheer numbers of devotees it attracted meant that the main temple was cash generative and financially dominant. The Shiva temple suffered as a consequence; the reduced attendance figures and the consequent decline in revenue were the harbingers that the old Brahmin recognised. He was resigned to this ever decreasing income and the dilapidation that the edifice exhibited. His only solace, in his old age, was that even if the temple fell into disuse, he had a roof over his head and would not be rendered homeless. The closure of the temple was a strong possibility unless he could rejuvenate his operations – a younger energetic priest, a new broom, was needed to revive the temple's fortunes. Meanwhile, the Raj pandit bided his time – he knew that the old priest was on his last legs.

Probesh's arrival, as a newcomer, had sparked a lot of speculation – for a young priest to move to a village temple was unheard of, especially as he was migrating from a big town like Bhuj. The married priests, sensing a cover-up, were quick to assume the worst and added fuel to the fire for their own ulterior motives – if they could fan the flames of suspicion then there was still a chance of ejecting the pesky bachelor.

There had always been a cloud of suspicion of a turbulent past and rumours abounded that Probesh's illicit liaisons with female devotees had become a modus operandi to feed his compulsive behaviour. No one really knew for sure but there were persistent allegations that Probesh had either fled an adulterous alliance or was exiled by an overzealous putative father-in-law who did not see any future for his only daughter married to an indigent priest. The fact that the priest had a physical disability, a club foot, made the grounds for rejection very compelling.

His detractors attributed his physical disability to divine retribution for past misdemeanours; whilst others cited a family history of inherited defects. The affliction had manifested and persisted through several generations. His grandfather and his father, as immediate ancestors, had both fallen victim to the trait. Probesh had obviously inherited not only the ancestral profession, but the physical handicap as well.

His affliction was probably the reason why Probesh remained a bachelor, despite his Adonis-like stature and his erudition. His mastery of Sanskrit and the title of a pandit (learned Brahmin) at such a young age presaged a bright future. However, the club foot had become a millstone; retarding his professional and social progress. Probesh's prospects, despite his hard work and professional ethos, had been impeded by the diffidence generated by his physical handicap – the lack of confidence held him back more than the club foot. He had always felt that his earnings were not commensurate with his abilities – his current earnings were a huge disappointment to him. At the rate that he was going, it would take years before he could afford a wife and a family that he so yearned for.

His perfunctory analysis of the temple finances vis-à-vis the hordes of devotees that attended did not stand up to financial scrutiny. More so, if one took into account the fact that there was a higher ratio of the affluent attending; signs of a booming economy. His dissatisfaction became even more pronounced when he took account of the prosperity that his married colleagues seemed to be enjoying. Whilst he had implicit trust in the Raj pandit, his mentor, he suspected that the other pujaris probably had a hand in hampering his progress. On more than one occasion he had sensed that they had been bad-mouthing him, sometimes to other devotees as well.

He started auditing, on the quiet, the daily attendance and the potential revenue that he estimated to be a true picture of the temple's earnings. Probesh was convinced that his share of the spoils was being misappropriated by an unfair system based on arbitrary criteria. It had also come to his notice that all the lucrative outside work seemed to go to a select few; his share of the private work was almost a pittance. This discriminatory practice confirmed his suspicions that he was being side-lined.

Despite the poor wages and the limited amount of extra work that the temple allocated to him, Probesh had managed to cope by re-doubling his marketing efforts – he had a band of loyal devotees who engaged him to do the odd puja – birthdays, funerals, etc. and recommended him to others. He was gradually building a rapport with certain sections of the community, although he realised that the real earnings bonanza was with the affluent traders who did not mind paying above the going rate.

However, the seeds of doubt soon germinated and magnified into all kinds of imaginary conspiracy theories. This sense of betrayal festered and suppurated. The 'abscess' had to be lanced before it destroyed him. In his heart he knew that unless a drastic change occurred, it was quite likely that he would remain where he was – in a rut; barely earning a pittance. The only saving grace was the roof over his head for which he did not pay any rent to the temple authorities. Almost a year had gone and his circumstances had not changed – he was still struggling, down at the very bottom of a hierarchy that was based on cronyism rather than merit.

The pressure and the frustration had been building up and eventually, in a moment of madness, he had a major verbal battle with his mentor, the Raj pandit. The tirade that followed and the outpouring of rancour and allegations did not sit well with the Raj pandit who, uncharacteristically, lost his temper as well. As neither party was prepared to compromise, Probesh, in a moment of transitory insanity, threw his job and walked out of the temple.

Although the Raj pandit had unequivocally stated his views and wished to draw a line under the conflict, a few of the pujaris saw an opportunity to settle scores by maligning Probesh. A litany of lies was maliciously circulated with the worst being that Probesh had been caught in flagrante delicto with a female devotee. It was quite evident that some of the conspirators had believed the rumours about Probesh's rather colourful past and decided that by raising the spectre of sexual impropriety, his wings could be clipped. The salacious details that were spread were relentless and vicious. It would seem that history was repeating itself and the past was again stalking the young Brahmin.

The Raj pandit, to his credit, when made aware of these rumours, took swift action to curb the gossip. He had no hesitation in reminding his pujaris that the repercussions would be far reaching if the devotees lost faith in the integrity and sanctity of the temple. The Raj pandit and, by proxy, the temple could ill afford any adverse publicity if the allegations of impropriety were even investigated, let alone proved, by the village panchayat (a governing council of elderly villagers). The conservative patrilineal society would either stop their womenfolk from entering the temple or take their custom elsewhere – the Shiva temple, although out at the periphery of town, would benefit. The thought of the old priest gloating was anathema to the Raj pandit. His 'three line whip' to his pujaris was crystal clear – fall into line or instant dismissal for anyone caught spreading rumours or innuendo about Probesh. He reminded his staff that whilst Probesh was an irritant at the moment, he could very well become the thorn in their side – best to let sleeping dogs lie.

Probesh's hasty and misconceived notion to strike out on his own came home to roost in no uncertain terms – he was homeless; his lodgings had ceased to exist. Without a roof over his head, his only viable option was to go begging bowl in hand to the only other viable option – the old Brahmin at the Shiva temple. The shelter it afforded and the distance from the scene of his alleged crimes would be a blessing in disguise – he could lick his wounds, away from public scrutiny.

Little did Probesh know that the old priest was aware of the friction that existed at the main temple and was biding his time for an opportune moment to poach Probesh – he liked the look of the young man and knew that Probesh was the answer to his prayers; the man to rejuvenate his dreams for the Shiva temple.

Whilst Probesh prevaricated, the old priest on hearing about his old adversary's difficulties despatched an emissary to Probesh – an invitation to stay with him whilst the young priest pondered his future. The 'carrot' of a job at the Shiva temple was not explicitly mentioned nor implied. The wily old priest knew that the young man's demands would far outstrip his meagre resources – therefore he had to play his cards well and make it appear as though it was a temporary favour. It was also important that the young priest's pride was not hurt.

After spending a few nights with a well-meaning devotee, Probesh pretended to spend a night out in the open, under a banyan tree next to the Shiva temple – he was hoping that he could somehow engage the old priest as if by accident. Sure enough the ruse worked – well before sunrise, as the old priest was making his way towards the lake for his morning ablutions, he saw Probesh reposed under a banyan tree. One thing led to another and Probesh spent the next few nights in the vacant second room at the old priest's house – Probesh was grateful for the temporary roof over his head. And they seemed to hit it off – Probesh, as a quid pro quo, manned the temple whilst the old man took his afternoon siesta or when he went down to the lake for his ablutions.

Within a few days, Probesh pitched a proposal to the old man – for a roof over his head, Probesh agreed to run the temple on a pro tem basis until they both decided on a mutually convenient contract. The old priest pretended to mull over the matter and then acceded. Probesh launched himself into running the temple with gusto – he was given full charge as the old priest took a back seat.

Probesh soon realized that life on the streets for an upcoming Brahmin priest was no bed of roses – it was a struggle to keep body and soul together. The relentless battle to just keep his head above water became soul destroying. His previous employer's bully-boy tactics hindered his progress – a diktat from the Raj pandit ensured that he was ostracised. It was providential that the Shiva temple became his refuge.

Most devotees, unwilling to alienate the temple authorities, shunned Probesh. Fortunately, the old Brahmin had ignored the moratorium imposed by the vindictive pujaris and assisted the youngster in his survival battle – an intrepid and magnanimous gesture. Although the old priest had a vested interest in employing the young priest, going against the Raj pandit was not a trivial matter – challenging the main temple was tantamount to open warfare; the repercussions could be immensely damaging for the Shiva temple.

*

It had been several months since his abrupt and unceremonious departure from the main temple – Probesh was grateful for the roof over his head. His pride would not allow him to compromise in any way and he decided to take on his detractors head on. Until he could break into the upper echelons of the landed gentry and the affluent middle classes, it was a fine act between subsistence and impoverishment. The real rewards would only accrue once he brought the monopoly, wielded by the omnipotent Raj pandit and his pujaris, to an end. Until that happened, it was going to be a struggle to increase the attendance at the Shiva temple and make it economically viable.

It was during this spell of abject hardship that he had a summons from a rich businessman; a local wheeler dealer and a wholesale merchant, Hari Mehta.

The Mehtas had an imposing residence, adjoining the main temple, with enough rooms to accommodate an extended family. An open yard at the front not only housed a few dairy cows but also proffered enough storage room for the season's harvests. A cement staircase, without any banisters, led to the terrace which acted as an ad hoc dormitory for the family to escape the stifling nocturnal heat. The wooden rafters in the rooms below often gave refuge to rats and snakes during the day – despite the mortal danger that cobras presented, there were very few deaths due to neurotoxin envenomation. It would almost appear that the devotees' faith in Lord Shiva somehow protected them from the cobras.

Hari, the first born of the Mehta family, lived with his elderly parents and their extended family. Hari's second wife, Menaka, a demure pretty eighteen year old, was his second chance at starting a family. Parineeti, his first, was unable to conceive after years of endeavour and, it was hoped that Menaka would offer an opportunity to safeguard Hari's lineage.

Hari's mother, the matriarch, had over the years, wrested control from her husband and was perceived to be the dominant force in the extended family; even Hari yielded to her. Her desire to have a grandson was all consuming and after years of dignified patience in the face of innuendo and gossip, her resolve finally cracked.

Parineeti's failure to conceive was the beginning of the end of Hari's first marriage – her barrenness sealed her fate. She became a pariah and a war of attrition waged by the wily matriarch, with Hari's tacit consent, eventually broke the marriage. Parineeti was coerced into returning to her parents' home in Bhuj – to face a lonely and solitary existence.

As time went by, Parineeti adapted to her new circumstances – she was young enough to quickly re-settle into her Bhuj home and reverted to her maiden surname, Vyas. Although everyone knew about the 'divorce' no one referred to it. Her parents saw to it that the first marriage was never mentioned – they had hopes that she would re-marry although the odds of that happening were next to nothing. The stigma of barrenness had stuck. Nonetheless, her parents persisted in their dream of finding a suitable second match for her. Much to Parineeti's chagrin, they actively engaged various matchmakers to find a husband for her.

Meanwhile, the matriarch quite easily found a match for Hari – he promptly remarried to fulfil the matriarch's agenda; to beget a male heir. Hari was aware of his mother's covert agenda – that of proving his virility and machismo. He knew the inherent dangers if he failed to impregnate his second wife. He and the matriarch both knew that if a pregnancy did not materialise soon enough then Hari would bear the blame and Parineeti would be exonerated. Hari was getting that déjà vu feeling; the race had begun and the clock was ticking.

After a year into the second marriage when Menaka failed to conceive, the matriarch was compelled to seek divine intervention; maybe perform an 'abhisek' (a religious ritual) to propitiate Lord Shiva. The longer Menaka's fallow period continued, the more she despaired at her son's blasé attitude – Hari was always out of town on business so she could hardly apportion blame to Menaka. The matriarch was impatient for an heir – to avoid aspersions being cast on Hari's virility. The rumour mills were already churning out salacious fodder about her son's penchant for male company or the inordinate amount of time he spent away in Bhuj or his effeminate ways. It was time to consult the Gods for divine intervention.

The Mehtas, because of their social standing and affluence, had considerable influence. The matriarch had her fingers on the pulse of the community – there was very little that bypassed her, fact or gossip. She was aware of the brouhaha that the Raj pandit and the old Brahmin priest had tried to cover up and that the new dashing priest had moved out after an acrimonious tussle.

The diktat that the Raj pandit had issued to dissuade his devotees from supporting the dissidents had, in a perverse way, opened a new line of competition. Everyone knew that with age creeping up on him, the old priest was in charge of a moribund operation which the Raj pandit had exploited to establish a monopoly. Maybe this was an opportunity to challenge the Raj pandit and the edifice of virtual dominance that he had established. It was her chance to play the kingmaker.

The matriarch, having experienced the lackadaisical and heavy-handed behaviour of the main temple saw an opportunity to flex her muscle – she wanted to cut the Raj pandit down to size by overtly challenging his diktat and supporting the young priest. With the sensitive nature of Hari's predicament, especially if Menaka failed to conceive after the rituals, she did not want the coterie of pujaris involved – the chances of a leak grew exponentially if more people were privy to intimate information; the gossip mills would have a field day.

Further, with the Raj pandit and his pujaris, she would have very little say in the religious proceedings. The new priest, with his impecunious background and his desire to succeed, would be more amenable to negotiation and even coercion. And, the biggest plus point was the fact that her will could be forced on this new comer; the Raj pandit would be an immovable force. She, after much deliberation, sent out word to the Shiva temple for a meeting to discuss an 'abhisek' (a religious ritual) that she wanted to perform to propitiate the Gods.

The thoughts of an heir and a grandson took central stage in her mind as she planned a strategy to achieve her goal with a minimum of fuss and expense.

Probesh was aware of the double edged sword that was being presented to him – if he conjured up a beneficial outcome then word would spread about his fecund touch. As long as he did his karma, the fruits would follow. Equally, any lapse on his part, would spell the demise of his embryonic career. The irony of his predicament was not lost on him; he was being coerced into pinning all his hopes on the couple conceiving. If he failed to invoke the Gods then his fate would be sealed. Probesh had no choice but to take up the gauntlet.

He referred to his 'panchang' (an almanac of auspicious dates and times) and selected a day in the lunar cycle which foretold a good result – an auspicious moment that would facilitate conception. On the day of the puja, he came well prepared with his crimson parchment bound scriptures and his paraphernalia of all things religious – turmeric, raw rice, betel leaves, incense sticks, etc.

Amidst an aura of religious fervour, incense and ghee fuelled fire, the couple sat in studious silence as the ceremony unfolded. The renditions of the Sanskrit mantras in a baritone voice, the tinkling of a hand held bell, the haze created by the burning of ghee and the incense, captured the ethos of the ceremony; the hypnotist orchestrating a trance.

The small invited audience and the matriarch watched and listened in rapt concentration as Probesh prepared some 'akshata' (uncooked rice coated with turmeric) to represent prosperity and fecundity. The yellow turmeric stained rice was sprinkled liberally over the couple as the various rites were completed. Menaka was bedecked in her bridal finery with the end of her sari draped over her head and face as a veil. She felt like a new bride on her wedding day – and behaved like one; coy and demure.

Probesh conducted the rituals with gravitas – although his curiosity was piqued by the veiled figure; he had heard that the eighteen year old was a ravishing beauty. Whilst the mantras reeled off effortlessly, all as an acquired reflex, he looked at the pot-bellied Hari and wondered how, if marriages are made in heaven, this specimen of the human race had landed such a beautiful wife? Not for him to question the Gods, the Brahmin admitted and sent a silent apology to Lord Shiva, who, as the scriptures mentioned, beheaded his own son, Ganesha, in a fit of temper. He needed all the help that he could muster and His divine intervention was the key to success.

On completion of the ceremony, Probesh was careful to collect all the grains of the coated rice off the floor. Not to be trodden on as that would incur Shiva's wrath. He also instructed her to persist with the Shiv puja every Monday. Fasting on Mondays, for the foreseeable future, was also advisable; to enhance her chances of conception.

He took pains to explain to the matriarch that if conception did not occur then the puja would need to be repeated; thereby, ensuring a repeat stream of revenue for his depleted coffers. Probesh was expecting his 'dakshina' (fees) as he gathered up his wares but the wily matriarch was nowhere to be seen. He waited in anticipation whilst the couple took the blessings of all the elders present.

As they came over to take his as well, he enquired with humility, 'Mataji (mother) has retired to her inner sanctum?'

Hari, realizing that the Brahmin was waiting to be paid, quickly signalled to the priest to hold fire as he disappeared into the house.

He came out shortly and said, 'Panditji, mother has retired for the afternoon and has requested that if you could drop in next week then she would be obliged.'

A payment in arrears was not ideal especially as he needed to replenish his dwindling finances but he was wary of squaring up to the matriarch, who had a formidable reputation of having her own way and a greater notoriety for maligning anyone who crossed her path. Reluctantly, knowing that it was a brush-off, Probesh retreated without further ado.

He dropped in on a number of occasions and on each occasion an excuse or the other was given – he came away knowing that he was being played but resisted the temptation to storm in and confront her.

When a couple of months rolled by without any news, Probesh's anxiety mounted. Probesh, bearing in mind the failure of Hari's first marriage, dreaded the worse and was convinced that Hari must be either infertile or impotent or both. He dared not even broach the subject of his outstanding fees. It was then that he knew that he would have to repeat the puja and reprise his reputation. A second failure would be catastrophic for his nascent reputation and would entail losing his promised dues; but he had no choice. He had to somehow inveigle his way back into her favour – not just for the overdue payment but as an ally who would put in a good word or two.

A second puja was performed in the absence of Hari, who was away from the marital home on business. Probesh repeated the rituals all over again, having again secured a promise of a payment. He made the puja more elaborate and took time to elucidate each Vedic mantra. Needless to say, the matriarch sat through the long winded ritual with a look of stoic resignation – her incipient fear was that history was repeating itself; Menaka had still not conceived. A sense of deep dread and déjà vu prevailed. The puja was completed and again an excuse was given – he left without any recompense; frustrated and annoyed.

Each time he pressed for a payment, the matriarch admonished Probesh for his avarice and declined to pay even a retainer. Probesh retreated without further ado; his face an inscrutable mask hiding his inner frustration. Stoic resignation seemed to be the order of the day. She wielded a lot of influence and he was unwilling to upset her for the fear of any adverse publicity.

Months passed without any news of a fruitful outcome neither was the promised payment forthcoming. The matriarch had belatedly and finally relayed that she would not pay until a positive result was forthcoming. Probesh was at the end of his tether and was deeply concerned that the matriarch may renege on her promises and may even go back to his rivals, especially as

Menaka had yet to conceive. He was in a bind and loathed her for her insensitive and aggressive behaviour.

To avert a confrontation, he convinced the matriarch that his third and his final attempt would not accrue his full fees; a 'buy one get one free' scenario. That tilted the balance in his favour and he commenced his preparations with an optimism that she would abide by the agreement. The matriarch, being very religious and superstitious, did not want to press her luck and incur the wrath of a Brahmin. The scriptures were full of the tales of retribution meted out by irate Brahmins. She could no longer defer a payment and communicated her consent for a final effort – a promise was made to pay irrespective of the end-result.

This time, however, Probesh had decided to schedule the puja at the Shiva temple in the expectation that the matriarch would not be present. In her absence the couple would be more amenable to gentle manipulation – away from the malevolent influence of the matriarch. He would have to somehow overcome her reservations about shifting the venue away from her jurisdiction, the family home.

She seemed to be convinced by his assurances that the old priest would be on site as he rarely left the temple. The omnipresence of a senior pujari swayed the argument in his favour. The usual planetary alignments were sought and the puja was scheduled a month later. Hari was strongly advised to ensure that his business commitments were deferred; his presence at the final puja was just as vital as his presence at any putative conception. The last bit delivered sotto voce and with heavy sarcasm which Probesh hoped was not missed by the matriarch – his patience was finally running out. There were times when he doubted whether Hari cared enough to facilitate conception – the matriarch was more involved in the dream of having an heir than Hari was.

An absence of regular work or a structured routine resulted in relentless boredom that compelled Probesh to while away a lot of his afternoons on the terrace of the Shiva temple, whilst the old pujari had his afternoon siesta in his room. His snores could he heard from across the courtyard – all the way to the top of the terrace. Probesh fell into the habit of stepping off the temple terrace and perching on the overhanging branch of the banyan tree to enjoy the gentle breeze that wafted across from the lake. It was a perfect vantage point to spy on the village belles bathing in the blazing sun after laundry duty. The pleasant distraction soon developed into a routine, a habit, to while away his time daydreaming and savouring the sight of the frolicking ladies; all engrossed in their watery recreation.

One such belle caught his eye, especially as she stood out amongst the motley crowd. As the area was secluded and away from preying male eyes, most of the belles frolicked with gay abandon; not worried about veiling their faces. All of them were modestly draped in their saris as they bathed in the cooling waters, their shrieks and laughter barely audible to Probesh perched precariously on a branch. On an afternoon foray into Bhuj town, he came across and bought a small pair of binoculars in a second hand shop; an investment that multiplied his pleasure many times over. He kept the instrument hidden on the terrace.

He became obsessed with this fair beauty with long jet black tresses and a voluptuous presence. He made it a point to access his usual perch and spy on this particular lady. It became a regular afternoon voyeuristic ritual, almost an obsession. So much so, that he rearranged his appointments to accommodate and indulge in his new-found post prandial titillation. He avidly looked forward to his afternoon assignation with the fair 'lady of the lake' – his epithet for the buxom beauty.

On the auspicious day of the third puja, it came as a surprise when Menaka presented herself, with her face totally veiled, in the company of her six year old nephew; a reluctant chaperone. Apparently, the matriarch was indisposed and the husband was again away on business. The young nephew had been bribed with sweets to wean him away from the village square where some of his friends congregated to play marbles, 'I spy' and other games. The promise and prospect of a swim in the lake on the way back proved too hard to resist; the youngster relented and accompanied Menaka to the Shiva temple.

Probesh was astounded that the matriarch had allowed Menaka to attend on her own. However, the alleged presence of the senior pujari and a chaperone, albeit very young, allayed her concerns. More importantly, the matriarch was worried that the celestial alignments, the auspicious time and date, may not recur soon enough – she was impatient and did not want the risk of an indefinite postponement. The advent of her grandson had been deferred for too long.

With the afternoon sun at its zenith and in full blaze, the entire village seemed to be in a collective torpor of lassitude. Even the grazing cattle were minus their shepherds, who took refuge under the cooling canopy of the leafy banyan trees. The temple's proximity to the lake did not provide any succour from the searing heat.

The senior priest had retired to his quarters across the courtyard, lost to the world in a somnolent 'do not disturb' phase. As the ritual puja progressed and was not even halfway through, the young chaperone was getting bored with the unintelligible language and the rituals; the heat from sacrosanct fire adding to his discomfort on this sweltering afternoon. The prospect of a swim, a respite from the stifling heat, was too enticing to ignore – he crept away towards the lake. He was an accomplished swimmer, so Menaka did not raise an objection when she saw him, through her veil, stealthily creep away. In a way it was better he indulged now rather than on the way back when the fading daylight would have been a deterrent – she had heard rumours of the area being haunted by aggrieved spirits; her nervousness would have been compounded by the lack of adult company. Her nephew, in his youthful insouciance, would have sniggered at the suggestion of ghosts and spirits.

The puja was completed without any hitches. The young wife bent down to pay her respects to the pujari and as she regained an upright position, the veil slipped back. To her mortification, her head, the luxuriant flowing hair and her face, became totally exposed. As she hastily rearranged her sari and her veil, the Brahmin saw a startled face; the crimson blush suffusing and gaining in intensity as she realized that the Brahmin was transfixed and staring at her open mouthed.

For a split second, the young Brahmin lost his poise as it dawned on him that Menaka was his 'lady of the lake' – the same enticing apparition that he had been spying on; the buxom target of his voyeuristic fantasy. His alluring post-prandial fantasy in the flesh!

Probesh was so totally unprepared for this tantalising vision in front of him that he froze momentarily. With images of his afternoon voyeurism flashing through his mind and in his haste to turn away from such glorious temptation, he lost his balance, as he stepped onto a brass urn, and unwittingly grabbed her to avoid falling over backwards. She lost her balance as well – a pile of arms, legs and intertwined torsos ensued on the floor. The ardour of the body contact, her proximity and the sweet fragrance of the roses adorning her hair all added to his arousal. The long distance binoculars views of her beauty, from his perch on the tree, had captivated him and now, so up-close, her touch left him breathless and bewitched.

His hypnotic eyes and the attractive physique mesmerised her as she hastily averted her gaze and stood up. Her attempts to recompose herself were in vain as she felt his piercing eyes on her and blushed profusely; his towering presence adding to her confusion. Despite her inhibitions, she was drawn to him. She held his piercing gaze for several moments and then lowered her eyes; signifying her submission. Menaka, almost under a magic spell, took his proffered hand as he guided her out of the temple.

She followed him, lamb to slaughter, as he gently exited the temple, past the well in the courtyard and towards the house. The stertorious snores of the old Brahmin could be heard out in the courtyard and in the adjoining room, through the thin plywood partition, as the couple crept into Probesh's room and settled on the narrow bed. In the throes of their passion, they were oblivious to the habitual nasal cacophony emanating from the room next door.

After what seemed an eternity, Menaka emerged from the house with her head and face suitably covered. She rushed off instinctively towards the lake to retrieve her nephew and make her way home. Probesh emerged soon after, hastily rearranging his dhoti, to go down to the lake for his ablutions and to prepare for the evening puja. The tepid waters of the lake did little to staunch the afterglow of his serendipitous encounter.

With the village lights twinkling in the distance as dusk drew closer, Probesh started his preparations for the evening puja. It then dawned on him that the matriarch's absence may well have been pre-planned, to avoid settling his dues. He had forgotten all about the dakshina. She had again prevailed in not parting with her money. In any case, he decided to stay away from the matriarch and Menaka for the time being, until his guilt had abated. The spirit had to regain ascendancy over the flesh; he had to regain his poise before he could face the matriarch. Dare he demand his fees after what had just transpired, Probesh wondered.

After an inordinate period of total silence from the Mehta family, Probesh decided to pay the matriarch a visit. His fervour had diminished and he was confident that his demeanour would not betray what had transpired. His pulse quickened when he saw Menaka tending to the tethered dairy cattle. This was the first time he had caught a glimpse of her as she had deliberately kept away from the dhobi ghat and the Shiva temple. Menaka was quick to veil her head and face as she saw the approaching priest. The matriarch reclined on a bed nearby.

Despite his doubts and the matriarch's previous feigned indifference, a part payment was made with a promise of a full settlement once the baby was born. His quick glance at the young wife milking one of the cows confirmed his perfunctory earlier appraisal; she was indeed carrying a child. Menaka meanwhile fought the temptation to look anywhere but at the milking urn. Her blushes deepened as she too thought about that afternoon and the snores of the old priest in the adjoining room. She drew her sari across her exposed midriff to cover her burgeoning girth; covering the heir of the Mehta family secure in his uterine and amniotic refuge.

A few months later

Probesh was jubilant on receiving word that he was to perform a puja to welcome the new addition to the Mehta family. His endeavours and patience had borne a result and he was now more sanguine about his future. His gait had a natural bounce to it; all was well with the world. The prospect of a final settlement of his long overdue fees brought a smile to his handsome visage. His joy doubled at the thought that this 'breakthrough' could lead to more word of mouth recommendations and more work.

Probesh blessed the neonate and his beaming parents. And as his gaze lingered over the torso and strayed to the feet of the firstborn, his heart missed a beat as he recognised the club foot. The thin cotton blanket, which had slipped off, was meant to cover the affliction but as he stared at the baby's foot the implications of the revelation dawned on him.

He walked away, with trepidation; his emotions in an upheaval. The anxiety soon gave way to a nascent smile – the sight of his son, in the flesh; proof of his virility. He prayed that his son would not have to undergo the same tribulations as he had encountered. The joy of his birth was tinged with a twinge of empathy and pain.

He mouthed a silent prayer, 'Oh Lord, please protect my son from evil spirits and shower him with your blessings.'

His dhoti had no pockets so Probesh clutched the crumpled notes of cash, his dues finally settled, with gusto, as he left the family celebrations. As he passed the main temple, his thoughts turned to the matriarch and her wily ways. She had manipulated him into a state of impotent rage, however, his pleasure at outsmarting her, albeit unwittingly, was immense. 'Retribution can be so sweet,' he muttered as he walked across the square and towards the Shiva temple.

It had been more than two months since the birth and Probesh's disappearance from the village. The old priest had contacted the matriarch and the main temple when Probesh failed to return to the Shiva temple after the celebrations at the Mehta residence. No one had seen or heard of him. The police made cursory enquiries and had given up as an FIR (first information report) had not been filed. The old pujari bemoaned his fate – just when things were returning to a semblance of normality, his protégé had disappeared without warning.

A local reporter filed an extended piece with his editor, hoping that it may turn out to be a scoop and materialise into columns of print. The editor thought otherwise and printed a few lines on the penultimate page of the Bhuj Chronicle; buried amongst the classifieds. The disappearance of a priest was hardly significant as most priests were very peripatetic and led a nomadic life. Just as Probesh's arrival in Bhog had sparked rumours, his inexplicable departure initially sparked speculation and gossip but the furore soon died down. Only the main temple and the Shiva temple acknowledged his absence – the former with glee and the latter with regret.

Parineeti fidgeted with the wedding ring that sparkled on her ring finger, as she read the brief item about the missing priest in the Bhuj Chronicle. Her smile was mirrored in her soft brown eyes as she looked at Probesh reclining next to her on the double bed. A sigh of content escaped her pouting lips. She had reclaimed her lover after so many tribulations – their relationship had started in Bhuj and was prematurely ended when her father had refused to accept Probesh's proposal of marriage.

Her mind recalled the heartbreak she went through when her father had rejected Probesh's marriage proposal on the grounds of his uncertain future; the club foot added fuel to the fire. She had been besotted with the dashing priest and they had begun a clandestine relationship. When she discovered that she was carrying his child, Probesh approached her father and proposed marriage with all sincerity. To his horror, Parineet's father rejected his offer of marriage and sent Parineeti away to her grandparents. He was sacked from the temple for bringing it into disrepute and was threatened with violence if he did not quit town immediately – by the thugs engaged by Parineeti's father.

When Probesh fled Bhuj fearing for his safety, Parineeti's world crashed around her. She was refused permission to return to Bhuj and was coerced into having an abortion – an unwed mother would spark a scandal and bring shame on the family.

After a few months, despite her vehement protests, she was forced to marry Hari – her father had known the family for years. In due course, when she failed to conceive, the matriarch started a war of attrition – she blamed Parineeti for the repeated failure to conceive. The machinations of the matriarch eventually led to the calamitous accusations of barrenness and her enforced return to her parents' home. Hari had been complicit, all along, by his silence and by giving the matriarch a licence to railroad her out of Bhog.

Just before her imminent departure to Bhuj, she bumped into Probesh at the Shiva temple – the old flames of passion and love were resurrected. Over a series of clandestine meetings at the Shiva temple, they relived the old magic. When she divulged to him that she had been forced to abort their unborn child and marry Hari, he saw the pain in her eyes. In that instance, he promised her that he would return to Bhuj and marry her – once he had avenged the pain and heartache that the matriarch and Hari had visited upon her.

Although at that stage he had no idea how he

was going to achieve his objectives, as luck would have it he was fortuitously appointed to perform the pujas for Hari and Menaka. Over the course of time the plan gradually firmed up in his mind.

His only regret was that Menaka, his lovely infatuation, was drawn into the act of retribution; although unwittingly her position in the Mehta family was secure with the birth of an heir. The matriarch had her grandson and her heir, so Menaka was safe from her vitriol. Hari's virility, with the birth of a son, was established and sacrosanct.

That day, after the celebrations at the Mehta residence, he went back to the Shiva temple, knowing that the old priest would be having his afternoon siesta, packed his meagre possessions and caught the bus to Bhuj.

On the bus, whilst he was busy making plans for his impending marriage to Parineeti and their future together, he suddenly realised that he had to come up with a plausible retribution story – he dare not divulge that he was already a father by virtue of the act of retribution perpetrated on the matriarch and Hari.

As he drifted off to sleep, his only hope was that maybe she would not raise the topic – the joy of their reunion driving all such mundane thoughts out of her pretty little head.

'In fact,' Probesh said to himself, 'maybe, a better ploy would be to keep the little woman busy – a new arrival, the patter of tiny feet would be the perfect foil!' For that plan of action he did not need any mantras or divine intervention – for sure.

Nine months later when Parineeti gave birth to their son, the first thing he noticed was the club foot. Again his joy was tinged with regret; both his sons were affected.

Meanwhile, Parineet's elation, as she held her son to her bosom, was complete – Probesh was back in her life and the birth of a son was justifiable vindication of all that the matriarch and Hari had put her through.

She beamed at her new born son as the neonate burped on having had his feed. She sighed as she smiled at Probesh and muttered, '...revenge is indeed a dish best served cold.'

Just before she lapsed into a blissful sleep, she remembered something that had been bothering her, something she had forgotten in the joy of becoming pregnant and the birth of their son ...ah yes, she must ask Probesh what retribution he had dispensed on the old witch and her son.

Sisterly Love

The throb of the powerful engine of the 350cc Royal Enfield motorbike, pulsating between his straddling thighs, was almost orgasmic. The pillion rider's soft presence and proximity, as she held on firmly, did little to calm his racing mind. His emotional ambiguity towards her, the whirlwind of emotions, made him uneasy – he prayed that he was doing the right thing.

As the powerful thrust of the engine propelled the couple towards their destination in the early hours, both of them were immersed in their deep thoughts of what the future held in store; one in trepidation and the other in anticipation.

She had dreamt and waited for this moment for so long that the distinct whiff of his aftershave and the throb of the engine tethered her to reality – it wasn't a dream; this was real. She nestled closer as the bike accelerated away, reassured by his physical presence, 'This is it,' she reflected, 'no turning back now. The Rubicon has been crossed; the die cast!'

An avid fan of the Bard of Avon, her allusion to Julius Caesar's crossing of the Rubicon river which precipitated the Roman Civil War was exactly what she did not want – a 'war' with her family because of her 'point of no return' actions. She clung on dearly as she whispered a silent prayer to the Gods.

The Air India flight AI 415 to Singapore via Kuala Lumpur was scheduled to land at KL airport on time. The lady had moved away to a vacant seat further up the aisle after her heated argument with her companion. She had to isolate herself from him to think things through – it was going to be a long flight battling with her emotions; their fierce argument had abruptly brought her to her senses.

The Flight Purser – tall, handsome and smartly attired in his Air India cabin crew uniform, located the seat number and moved towards an elegantly dressed attractive woman, sitting on her own – her eyes red rimmed and her subtle make-up smudged by her tears. He had noticed her grace and elegance at the AI boarding gate just as he, along with his cabin crew, went past the throng of waiting passengers.

'Ma'am, my colleague informs me that you wish to speak to me? How may I help?' the soft spoken purser enquired in a discreet manner, unsure of the situation. The look of pain on her chiselled face was all the more noticeable as she tried in vain to mask her patently visible turmoil.

'May I have a quick word?' she enquired as she looked up at the Flight Purser, who was in charge of the cabin crew that operated the Boeing 707 flight from Bombay to Singapore via Madras and KL.

'Ma'am, do I know you?' the purser asked, surprised that the lady had asked for him by his first name.

'No, your friend in Bangalore, Roy, had mentioned you when he found out that we were flying with AI – he used to rent our flat in Bangalore. Apparently you two go back a few years?' she asked in a soft subdued tone.

'Yes, we were at college together. How is he? I haven't been to Bangalore for a while. Is he well?' the purser queried, waiting for confirmation that she was not just dropping names to pull a favour. The last time he had spoken to his friend was just after his knee injury.

He was now intrigued and wondered how his friend was connected with this glamorous lady who looked years younger than the early forties that he surmised her age to be. He also noted the use of the plural 'we' – and yet she was sitting alone. He was almost certain that she had been accompanied by a male companion when they boarded the plane at Madras – her beautiful features and her striking resemblance to a South Indian Bollywood star had drawn attention from the passengers and crew alike. She looked even more attractive at close quarters – despite the worry lines on her face.

'Roy moved away a few months ago – into a ground floor flat after he sustained an injury at a training session in the nets. The injury made it difficult to negotiate the stairs to the flat on the terrace. The last time we bumped into each other was on Brigade Road – he was still using a walking stick to hobble around,' she replied.

The purser broke into an engaging smile, the lady had come through the 'interrogation' – she did know his friend in Bangalore. He noticed the red rimmed eyes and the slumped shoulders; her body language reflecting an inner turmoil. He listened patiently and with empathy as she tried to be brief without getting personal.

As she finished, trying desperately not to break into tears, he was relieved that it wasn't the in-flight service that she had concerns or complaints about – he ran a tight ship and would not want any lapses on his watch.

'Ma'am, I don't see any difficulty – please don't worry. This is off-season and I know the return flight AI 413 to Madras isn't full. You should not have any problem booking your return flight. Once we land at KL, I will call up the AI counter and put in a word. As you are aware this flight terminates in Singapore, otherwise I would have personally escorted you to the AI counter. Have a safe flight back.'

With that the purser went back to the galley wondering why she was flying straight back – leaving the lonely figure to fret about the mess that she had to resolve back in Bangalore.

She flew back alone to Madras on the next available Air India flight.

A few months earlier

Krish saw the rickety Vespa auto-rickshaw, spewing dark obnoxious plumes of diesel fumes, splutter to an abrupt halt a few yards from his doorstep. Suzy, his elegant tenant, stepped out and rummaged in her expensive leather purse for the fare. As usual, the driver pretended to dig deep into his khaki sweat stained uniform for the one Rupee change, a ruse that never fails – Suzy graciously waived the change and walked off. The driver paused before pocketing the handsome tip from the foreigner – despite her Asiatic features he knew she was from abroad, her English accent and her clothes gave her away. His eyes followed the smartly dressed lithe figure as she disappeared from sight, round the corner. He marvelled at her glowing fair complexion as he kicked started the auto-rickshaw and spluttered away.

Krish Iyer's craggy face displayed a gamut of

emotions that were triggered by the sight of Suzy, a petite and pretty Malaysian Chinese student. He beamed and waved with the excitement of a teenager as he watched her tantalising amble from the auto-rickshaw towards the small family run bakery, situated in a small parade of shops round the corner. He followed the graceful swivel of her hips as she passed the dhobi (laundry) shop and then disappeared from view. 'Probably picking up some bread for their evening meal,' conjectured Krish.

Sonny and Suzy, both Malaysian foreign students, had recently rented the flat above his dilapidated ancestral property. Krish was quite taken by Suzy; call it infatuation at first sight. He was on the wrong side of forty and was at the mercy of his diminishing testosterone levels – when men behave like fawning prepubescent teenagers; all sweaty palms and palpitations at the sight of a skirt. And what a pretty sight Suzy was in her skimpy skirt, which barely reached the top of her perfectly symmetrical knees.

Foreign students and, especially, trendy short skirts, were a rarity in the Bangalore suburb of Palace Orchards in the 1970s – although in the last few years there had been a small steady influx of foreign students in the area and other contiguous suburbs due to the proximity to the neighbouring University of Biological Sciences campus. Skirts and Anglo-Indians were a fairly common sight in the cosmopolitan areas of Richmond or Langford town but not in Palace Orchards and in the older parts of bustling Bangalore. The 'garden city of India' was quite liberal and cosmopolitan in a very superficial way – at the core, the deeply religious and traditional values dictated all aspects of life; a code of conduct that defined one's caste and status in life.

He wondered, as he often did, whether she would look as ravishing in a silk sari – especially a black one which would accentuate her fair complexion. As he fell into a reverie imagining the undulating silky folds of the sari contouring her lissom figure, a blush suffused his cheeks. Krish had to make a conscious effort to pull himself back from his amorous ruminations, thankful that his wife wasn't around to witness the crimson hue of his cheeks and his overtly gauche behaviour.

He dropped everything and dashed up the open staircase to the terrace where the flat was tucked away from view. Just before he reached the terrace, he met his wife, Anjali, coming down the stairs, having just retrieved the washing from the several clothes lines criss-crossing the large open terrace.

The flat, with its rear location on the terrace, was partially hidden behind a huge water tank and, if the clothes lines had clothes hanging out, then the flat was totally sequestered; affording seclusion and privacy. However, the water reservoir hindered the free flow of air; rendering the flat extremely sultry and humid in the summer months. Fortunately, the two large French windows that had been installed as a remedial measure provided plenty of light and cross-ventilation. The flat had recently been renovated and modernised, in stark contrast to the basic amenities that existed on the ground floor where Krish and his family lived.

Krish had dashed up the stairs to the terrace hoping to catch a glimpse of Suzy or indulge in his fetish of caressing her clothes that she hung out to dry every morning – at times, if the opportunity afforded itself, he would spend almost half an hour up there running his fingers through her clothes. The look and feel of them, especially the skirts and the Malaysian Batik sarongs, gave him a vicarious thrill.

Apart from Anglo-Indian women, he had not come across anyone in that type of alluring attire. The ultra-conservative middle-class society that he had grown up in frowned upon the exposed flesh that skirts invariably flaunted. He had yet to get over the novelty of Suzy sporting her array of brightly coloured pleated skirts; the expanse of exposed flesh captivated and enthralled him.

The sight of his wife broke his titillating reverie. Before a crestfallen Krish could say anything, Suzy came up the stairs with her shopping and dashed past Krish and Anjali. She smiled and nodded as she nimbly squeezed past them. Such an attractive smile, Krish reflected, as the gentle brush of her hips against his thigh set his pulse racing. His bespectacled eyes avidly followed the skimpily dressed figure advance towards the flat, his heart 'banging' against his intercostals; almost to the rhythm of Lulu's 1969 hit melody 'Boom Bang A Bang'.

Anjali, a thunderous scowl written all over her face, watched her husband's asinine show of ardour for the slip of a girl. 'She is the same age as our daughter,' murmured Anjali, as she rapidly descended the stairs and viciously flung the washing on the wicker cane chairs in their veranda. If looks could kill, Krish would be in an advanced stage of rigor mortis.

She had never seen Krish so much as look at other women, so his aberrant behaviour was hurtful. Anjali despaired at the thought that the joint tenants were entrenched for the next eleven months on a shorthold lease – an exasperating time ahead for her to tolerate his love sick antics. She wished she could teach him a lesson or two and beat him at his own game – although she could not think of anyone within their circle to flirt with. 'Or maybe there is,' she reflected, Sonny, the budding vet and the joint tenant was quite dashing. 'Too young,' she muttered as she went into the house.

In her heyday, with her stunning figure and chiselled beautiful features, she could have made short shrift of any rival – alas, the passage of time and her thickening girth had almost relegated her from the stunning dancing diva that she had been to a housewife and a mother. Anjali was being very unkind and self-deprecatory – the passage of time had actually enhanced her beauty - like mellowed wine. She had that intangible factor that one can't quantify – charisma that some men would die for. Krish, after years of marriage, was taking Anjali for granted and was pining for an exotic, forbidden 'hamburger' when he had access to 'steak' at home; an excellent Kobe beef steak at that!

The Malaysian, petite and distractingly pretty, knew the effect she had on Indian males, especially her glowing fair complexion. Suzy, though aware of this fascination with fair complexion that Indians harboured, never quite fathomed why fair skin was deemed to be synonymous with beauty. Some of Suzy's South

Indian female classmates made her feel inadequate – their large almond shaped eyes and the perfect tanned classical features would be envied in the West. She looked distinctly anaemic compared to the dusky females around her on the campus.

She was more bemused and flattered than angry with Krish's fawning antics. Suzy had noticed the same obsession on display on the campus and at large – playing to the gallery had become her forte and she used this 'facility' to have her own way. She had become quite the consummate tease and had become addicted to this male attention. She could turn on the charm at will, like turning on a tap.

The University of Biological Sciences campus housed the Veterinary (Vetico) and Agriculture (Agrico) colleges on a single massive campus. Like two siblings, the students of the Vetico and the Agrico were constantly at loggerheads – an intense rivalry that encompassed everything. The Agricos tacitly acknowledged the cerebral superiority of the vets – only the best scores secured a place on the vet course. The vets revelled in the 'edge' that their perceived brain power seemed to bestow; especially in wooing the campus females. It gave them an even greater pleasure if the female being wooed and won over happened to be an Agrico – the pleasure quotient directly proportional to the grief it caused to the Agrico males. This incessant rivalry embraced all domains of activity, especially the wooing and courtship of the female students – the fewer the number of 'fresher' female students in the annual intake, the greater the competition. A highlight of the induction week for the campus males was the first appearance of the new batch at the campus canteen – their arrival would be avidly followed and battle lines drawn quite early on with bets on for the first Vetico or Agrico to 'date' the first fresher from the opposite camp. It had become an annual rite of initiation which the college authorities had been monitoring to avoid the excesses of 'ragging' that had become quite rampant in most universities – in some cases spiralling out of control and leading to serious harm; even suicides.

This testosterone fuelled rivalry spilled over into the sports arena as well, with inter-collegiate cricket matches between the two rivals attracting a huge number of the female students rooting for their respective college teams. The crafty ones using the cricket pavilion as a battle ground to make putative boyfriends jealous by rubbing shoulders with the opposition. The females lapped up the attention, be it from the

Veticos or the Agricos and in some cases fanned the fires that led to unintended consequences. There was nothing like a wee bit of jealousy to stir the alpha male into a state of frenzy or add a zing to a campus romance.

In most instances, the Agricos suffered in silence as the stethoscope totting vets, in their hospital whites, deliberately showing off the implements of their profession, strutted about the campus in full glory – the Agricos could hardly command the same attention from the campus females by parading in their wellies or brandishing spades.

On one very intensely emotive issue, though, the two colleges were staunchly united – a closing of the ranks against a common foe; all rivalries put aside for the common good.

The foreign students, dubbed the 'phirangi' (foreign) menace were a threat to the delicate equilibrium that existed between the trio – Vetico and Agrico males and the campus females. This fourth dimension that the foreign students represented was creating ripples and eddies; the proverbial cat amongst the pigeons.

The colleges had a huge contingent of foreign students – the Malaysians and the Iranians dominating a diverse foreign contingent that also included Iraqis, Afghani, Nepali and the East Africans.

Whilst the former were aided by the Malaysian government and Colombo Plan scholarships, the latter enjoyed the power of their petro-dollars. Iran was riding the crest of an economic boom and was awash with petro dollars. Its 'black gold' wealth paid for scores of Iranians to acquire qualifications at Indian universities – a far cheaper option for most foreign students than the exorbitantly expensive British or American degrees.

The foreigners were especially resented for the vastly inordinate influence and advantage that their wealth bestowed on them. Their 'buying power' which they used to lavish attention and gifts on their paramours fomented bitterness – the local Romeos were disadvantaged and out of their depth. The 'petro dollars' skewed the campus courtship rituals; Cupid corrupted. Whilst most of the foreign students revelled in their exalted status, the Iranians, the Iraqis and the Malaysians were head and shoulders above the rest. The 'Persian' students (Iranians and Iraqis) had an extra string to their bow – their fair skin, the 'wow' factor as far as the local females were concerned.

The foreign students enjoyed a lifestyle of privilege – a separate hostel, flash motorbikes and the pick of the prettiest females on and off campus. This dichotomy between the local and foreign students exacerbated the divisions.

The warfare between the two diverse groups raged without the university authorities becoming fully aware of the deep divisions – in most cases the matter was resolved or was taken off-campus to avoid any punitive consequences from the authorities. In a minority of cases, physical confrontations did occur but without official complaints being lodged either with the police or the college authorities. In most cases witnesses were either scared off or paid off.

At the pretext of keeping the two warring groups apart, the foreign students were housed in a separate modern newly built hostel with all the amenities of a five star hotel. The rates charged were too exorbitant for the local students – it was a very subtle way of segregating the two groups. The local students, housed in mediocre decrepit hostels, felt like pariahs in their own backyard but were unable to protest due to their impoverished circumstances – the foreign students assumed a mantle of elitism.

Sonny Reddy, a final year student on the Bachelor of Veterinary Science five year degree course was a privately funded Malaysian student – his family of GPs ran several practices in Kuala Lumpur. Suzy Chan, who was a year older, was completing a two year Master's degree in

Horticulture – she too was privately funded by her parents. Whilst some Malaysian Indian or Chinese students funded their own university education, the majority of Malaysian students were supported by scholarships from the Malaysian government or the Colombo Plan, an international organization fostering socio-economic development in the Asia-Pacific region.

Sonny and Suzy were a couple, an 'item', in the small but well-knit Foreign Students' contingent on the campus. They shared a common background, rooted in the Indian and Chinese diaspora that had migrated to Malaysia in search of a better life. Both families, after decades of thrift, education and hard work had evolved and progressed from the menial jobs on rubber and palm oil plantations to professional and managerial careers.

Sonny, before his involvement with Suzy, had been dating an extremely attractive local student who was enrolled on the Bachelor of Science (Agriculture) course at the Agrico. The attraction was mutual and everything was going well until the young lady's local male admirers got wind of her involvement with a foreign student. She was threatened with exposure. She knew that her orthodox puritanical parents would not understand and would promptly withdraw her from the course or arrange her marriage.

Sonny was threatened with violence and was roughed up on a few occasions; with threats of further dire consequences. There were several acts of intimidation against the couple – minor skirmishes which would be difficult to prove to the university authorities or to the police due to lack of evidence or credible witnesses. The low level activity against them was a deliberate strategy so as to avoid any official punitive response. It was a game of attrition that the local Romeos played quite well – they had the 'home' advantage and the resources to play a long game of attrition.

Initially the threats only made the couple more resolute and rebellious – they embarked on a very clandestine courtship; away from the campus and out of sight. The romance blossomed between the two until an inadvertent slip by a confidant was picked up by an envious male admirer. The news spread on the university grapevine and the persecutors were livid that the couple had the audacity to challenge them – an ambush was planned to teach Sonny a lesson, to drive home the message that local girls were not playthings for the rich and the wealthy. Their sense of outrage was all the more acute because the culprit was a foreigner.

Whilst returning from a rendezvous with his not so secret sweetheart, Sonny was waylaid by this vigilante group. He was severely roughed up and his motorbike badly damaged – his assailants were careful enough to avoid any physical injuries that might result in admission to a hospital or involve the police. He was threatened with further action if he did not end his friendship with the 'female from Agrico'.

The incident and the veiled threats left a deep scar on Sonny's psyche. Not only was he a foreigner but also a Vetico – Sonny realised the double indemnity that the goons were alluding to. It all happened so quickly and in the dark that he could only surmise that the goons were engaged by a jealous student or students from the Agrico.

Despite the young lady's protestations that the furore would soon die down, Sonny started having second thoughts; fear had taken root. He feared that the tremendous financial outlay and the years of hard swotting would be undone – his family would not take too kindly to the accusations that their son was squandering his chances of acquiring a decent university education. The Malaysian High Commission would also have their say as the quota of seats for Malaysians was finite and not to be wasted. The fracas with the locals and any putative expulsion from the university would be an exorbitant price to pay for a campus romance.

The thugs, not letting up on the pressure, persisted with several indirect threats – the college cricket captain inexplicably dropped Sonny from the inter-collegiate team, his lab notes and records disappeared, excreta was smeared on his new bike, the bike had potatoes pushed in the exhaust or diesel fuel poured into the petrol tank, etc. Finally, Sonny, fearing the worst, succumbed to the threats – he met the perpetrators and swore not to meet the girl anymore. He cut all ties with the girl.

Sonny, in an explicit signal to his persecutors, started dating a pretty Malaysian student – he deliberately paraded her on and off campus. Suzy, a foreign student herself and a Malaysian Chinese, was a Godsend for Sonny in his disturbed state – she was from back home and therefore free of any political or cultural baggage to contend with. The campus tormentors, aware that their antics were becoming brazen and susceptible to retribution from the authorities, quietly backed off when they realized that their threats had been effective – pleased that their guerrilla tactics had paid off. The local male admirer basked in the glory of his triumph and signalled a truce.

*

The young lady was deeply affected by the split; resentment and betrayal dominating her thoughts. The 'salt on the wound' was the realization that Sonny was openly flouting his new girlfriend– her friends had corroborated the rumours of Sonny's new love interest after several sightings of the couple zooming around on Sonny's new bike. What hurt the most was that Sonny was so blasé about their relationship that a few verbal threats had resulted in his total capitulation. She felt that she had been 'used' – the friends who had all cautioned her about these 'fly by night' foreign students turned out to be right after all. Their prophecies of doom and gloom had become a reality for her – she knew that her parents' reaction would be swift and decisive.

The jilted girl abruptly dropped out of her course and deliberately cut all links with the campus and her classmates. It later emerged that the girl's parents had somehow discovered the campus dalliance and had forced her to quit

The rumour in college was that her parents had already found a suitable match for the jilted girl.

As misfortune would have it, she was compelled out of sheer necessity to confide in her mother when she missed her periods – she was immediately packed off to her maternal grand-parents in Madras; exiled for now to the safety of her mother's home town. She feared her father and pleaded with her mother to ensure that he was kept in the dark about the pregnancy, and the pregnancy became their secret.

A few days later, she presented herself to a young gynaecologist who had just embarked on his private practice. He was deliberately chosen by her mother –the family of the consultant were trusted old friends and would respect her wishes to protect the girl's honour; her daughter's future would be blighted if the pregnancy became public knowledge. The simple procedure that he performed on the nervous young lady – a dilatation and curettage (D & C) – was memorable for him; she was his first private patient. She remained in Madras after the termination of pregnancy. The entire process was mired in secrecy – even the grandparents were not aware of the true reason for their granddaughter's sudden presence in Madras.

The constant friction with the local male students and the intense scrutiny that he was under after his entanglement with an Agrico female, instigated Sonny to consider moving off the campus. He convinced Suzy to move in with him so that they could share the expenses and pursue their courtship in peace, away from prying eyes and the campus politics.

Suzy jumped at the chance to share decent Western style accommodation – she was tired of the dingy and cramped women's hostel where she shared a room with two other students. The communal toilets and showers were a major drawback – she would finally have the luxury of not waiting in a queue to access the facilities.

The cultural orthodox milieu in the suburbs meant that an unmarried couple would find it extremely difficult to rent; especially for foreign students who suffered, unjustifiably, from a reputation of being too licentious. The landlords with families of their own loathed renting to foreigners out of fear that their liberal behaviour may set a bad example to their offspring and jeopardise their conservative way of life.

The second stumbling block was that of non-vegetarian food – most landlords would not allow meat to be cooked on their premises. This was particularly true of the upper caste Brahmins who were strictly vegetarian and considered meat eating an abomination.

Sonny and Suzy encountered both these impediments and had almost given up when, fortuitously, they were introduced to a maverick estate agent who, for a hefty fee, was prepared to represent them. The agent intuitively gathered that the couple were desperate to move away from the torment of their campus life and would pay over the odds. The carte blanche arrangement was verbally agreed and the agent sprung into immediate action. He rubbed his hands in glee at the prospect of a hefty fee that had been doubled for the 'cash rich' foreigners.

After several failed viewings, the agent found Mr Krish Iyer, an upper caste Brahmin, who was an electrical engineer and had a small flat vacant above his house. The agent, knowing that Krish had experienced difficulties with some of his previous tenants, hit the right note by extolling the virtues of letting to foreign students – they would depart on graduation and therefore not become sitting tenants. More importantly, the foreign students, courtesy of their generous scholarships and favourable exchange rates, were prepared to pay well above the market rate to secure a flat – there was a dearth of accommodation that met their criteria of en-suite Western style facilities and twenty four hours of running water.

The agent was also aware that Krish was desperate to set aside a handsome sum for his daughter's dowry and wedding expenses and would be amenable to manipulation. The canny operator, cognizant of Suzy's extroverted demeanour and sex appeal, was certain that she would make a telling impression on the landlord. The smirk on the agent's face matched the twinkle in his eyes – he could not imagine Krish resisting the wiles of this Malaysian femme fatale. He should know – he had almost become a victim. She had nearly succeeded in reducing his fees.

The estate agent had briefed both Sonny and Suzy about their modus operandi – to skirt around the issue of eating meat and to pose as siblings rather than admit that they were an unmarried cohabiting couple. He emphasized the latter point and exhorted them to bear in mind that Mr Iyer had very conservative values and had a daughter of marriageable age – he would view cohabitation as a sin and certainly a bad example for his daughter to follow or emulate. The agent stressed that if they really wanted the flat then resorting to a "white lie" was not only mandatory but the only way to secure the modernised accommodation; a rare commodity in middleclass areas in the older parts of Bangalore.

Landlords had cottoned on to the 'marvel' of drilling bore wells and building huge overhead tanks to bypass the strict water rationing that the municipal authorities enforced. Unrestricted water supply was a bargaining chip, and Suzy and Sonny were prepared to go to any length to secure the lease.

Against their better judgement and in desperation, Sonny and Suzy gave in to the agent's script – they lied about their relationship and convinced Krish that they were siblings. Suzy augmented Sonny's 'sales' pitch by wearing a skimpy skirt and a tantalising perfume, flirting without being too overt. Krish, as the agent had surmised, was bowled over and even offered to partition the single large bedroom into two small units as would be appropriate for the brother-sister joint tenancy. Fortunately for all concerned, his wife, Anjali, was away at a dance performance. The female intuition would have warned Anjali about the unfettered danger of having a fair skinned femme fatale on her patch and under her roof.

A lease was signed with the proviso that they could move in as soon as the conversion of the large single bedroom into two smaller open plan units was completed. Krish was already budgeting for the extra cash the rental would bring in and was in a hurry to have the deed signed and delivered before Anjali's return.

Suzy and Sonny soon fell into a routine of masquerading as siblings. It took some time and effort to maintain the façade – avoid holding hands or not hugging each other; shunning all physical contact in public. The landlords, Krish and Anjali, were very impressed with the well behaved and polite siblings, thereby, putting at rest Anjali's initial reservations about their very Western persona. She was a tad concerned about the young lady's bold dress sense and the reactions that short skirts might elicit from her equally conservative neighbours. This was their first long-term interaction with foreign students.

Meanwhile as the days passed, Krish's crush on Suzy grew by the day, unabated. Anjali blissfully ignorant of the havoc that Suzy was already wreaking on her husband's hormones and emotions welcomed the pair with a spontaneous gusto that belied her initial reservations. The sizeable rental income that the flat generated was a bonus after the troubles that they had encountered with some of the previous tenants – she was determined to have a grand wedding for Paree, their only daughter. The revenue from the flat was earmarked only for Paree and for her wedding extravaganza.

Krish quite envied the pair's apparent affluence and their sumptuous lifestyle. They rarely seemed to cook at home. On occasions when he had ventured up on the terrace, ostensibly to collect the washing, he had noticed, through the open French windows, the paraphernalia of an extravagant lifestyle – expensive radio and cassette players; even a small fridge, the expensive clothes and the fancy accessories that made up Suzy's make-up arsenal; he had counted no less than a dozen pairs of shoes and even a pair of high heels. The sight of the stilettos filled him with awe – he had never seen a pair before except on the silver screen. A black suede miniskirt and red stilettos would be a sight to saviour for eternity, he sighed.

The flashy new expensive Royal Enfield 'Bullet' 350cc motorbike that Sonny drove was the cynosure of his envy. Krish, despite his well-paid engineer's job at the Electricity Board, could just about afford a second-hand Lambretta scooter; powered by a puny 125cc engine. The mere throb of the powerful Enfield's engine, audible from afar, threw Krish into raptures. One day very soon, Krish promised himself. Once he had saved enough for his daughter's wedding.

The two images – the Royal Enfield and Suzy in a miniskirt with the red stilettos – merged in his fertile mind into a single recurring fantasy – with him driving the bike and Suzy on the pillion; her proximity enhanced by the alluring perfumes that she wore.

Anjali had noticed that Krish spent an inordinate amount of time on the terrace, especially when the tenants were out. A couple

214

of times she almost caught him feeling the silky texture of Suzy's clothes, drying on the clothes line. Krish had withdrawn guiltily when he saw Anjali appear in his peripheral vision and moved away towards the water tank pretending to check the water level.

Anjali was glad in a way that Paree was out of town and did not have to witness her father's prepubescent behaviour. Paree was close to her father but even closer to her – they were more like best friends than mother-daughter. Paree had always looked up to Anjali and would be chuffed if strangers remarked that she was a spitting image of Anjali or that they looked like sisters. Since an early age Paree had emulated her mother in every respect and subconsciously copied her mannerisms and deportment. As she matured she frequently wore Anjali's dazzling array of saris and even used the same make-up or borrowed her expensive perfumes.

Although Anjali missed Paree's vivacious presence, she had to somehow convince her to extend her stay in Madras – for a while longer whilst she dealt with her husband's midlife crisis.

It was a few weeks later that Krish first had an inkling that his tenants were much more than what they made out to be. There had been incidents which seemed odd at the time but he had dismissed them as sibling affection and ignored his suspicions.

All those incidents came back to haunt him on New Year's night – his dyspepsia woke him up in the middle of the night. He heard the rhythmic throb of the Royal Enfield fade and die out as the bike was parked on the forecourt, under the small banyan tree. As he peeped through the partially drawn curtains, he caught Sonny and Suzy kissing and canoodling as they went up the stairs – in a very inebriated state.

He creeped across the terrace and using the water tank as his screen waited in the shadows for Sonny and Suzy to come into view. As they switched off the fluorescent overhead light, the moonlight bathed both the beds in its luminescence.   Through the open French windows he could see that only one bed was occupied – the couple entwined on the bed, in each other's arms. The other bed was still made up and empty. Krish wondered if it had been used at all since they moved in. A stab of intense jealousy rocked him as his sight fell on Sonny – with Suzy nestled in his sleepy embrace.

Since that night, Krish had kept a constant vigil on the couple and had caught them on what he called their marital bed on several occasions. He remembered the lacy silk underwear that he had seen hanging on the clothes lines. His pulse had quickened on occasions when, on hot sultry nights, he had spied Suzy just in her panties and bra parading around the flat whilst Sonny lounged on the bed.

It gave him a vicarious pleasure on having caught Sonny and Suzy at their subterfuge and he had been pondering on how best to use that insight to his advantage – one reason why he had not divulged his findings to Anjali. His dull and monotonous nine to five existence finally had something thrilling to look forward to. His surreptitious visits to the terrace continued unabated; his crush on Suzy undimmed. The forbidden fruit was even more tantalising and he did not want this fantasy to end, not yet at least.

Meanwhile, Anjali was left in the dark about the Sonny-Suzy relationship – it was in Krish's interest to shield her from his discovery that Sonny and Suzy were in a relationship and were not siblings. Krish had decided that he would reveal all to Anjali at an appropriate time – for now he enjoyed the visits to the terrace for he had a ringside seat.

Unknown to Krish, his wife had noticed the gradual change in his demeanour. After more than twenty-five years of married bliss, she did expect a waning of his passion for her but this fixation on a slip of a girl, albeit very attractive, was an exaggerated over the top reaction. Strangely enough his wayward excursions to the terrace, more often than not, induced a new vigour to their lovemaking. The resurgent interest, after years of diminishing passion, took her by surprise. Not that she was complaining but she did resent playing the surrogate to a twenty something femme fatale.

In her younger years she had attracted a fair bit of male attention and recollected her father rebutting several overtures from Bollywood producers – to cast her as a dancing diva. It pained her that Krish had not considered her feelings and was quite flagrantly embarking on this juvenile escapade with this floozy – all the years of her sacrifice as a wife and a mother reduced to nothing.

She smarted at the thought that, at the zenith of her dancing career, she had sacrificed the artistic and professional fame that was hers for the taking to marry Krish. She had completed her graduation and was on the cusp of greater achievements when the marriage proposal had come as a bolt from the blue – her parents were thrilled with Krish's professional qualifications, a Bachelor of Engineering degree from the prestigious Madras University, and his family pedigree and overwhelming credentials. More importantly, the prospective groom and his family had overlooked Anjali's dark complexion – they were more than impressed by her dusky looks and her emerging reputation as a virtuoso.

After a constant barrage of gentle coaxing to say 'yes' to the proposal, she did not have the heart to disappoint her parents and had given in. The birth of their daughter within a year put paid to any aspirations of pursuing a career in Indian classical dancing. She had initially toyed with the idea of starting a dance school but gave up when Krish objected to having a nanny look after their daughter whilst Anjali busied herself with furthering a career as an exponent of the classical Indian dance form.

Matters came to a head, one night, when Krish almost got caught on the terrace whilst watching Suzy – the sudden appearance of Anjali almost threw him. Fortunately, Suzy was alone in the flat and had just come out of the shower otherwise Anjali would have caught the couple together. Krish realised that he could no longer continue with his vicarious indulgence. He had to end this charade without Anjali knowing the true state of affairs.

After giving the matter considerable thought, Krish informed the couple, a few days later, that he expected them to move out – he would allow them to stay in the flat until they found alternate accommodation. He made it quite clear to them that had he known that they were an unmarried couple he would not have accepted them as tenants. He told them that Anjali would be furious if she found out so requested them to behave – he would use their imminent graduation as an excuse for their premature exit from the flat. The statement of intent was delivered more as a polite compromise than as a threat of eviction – despite their lying, the couple had been ideal tenants and he would be sorry to see them go. Sonny and Suzy were repentant for the obvious subterfuge – they agreed, as a mark of their contrition, to go along with Krish and not divulge anything to Anjali, to maintain the status quo.

A month later both Sonny and Suzy completed their respective degrees. Suzy's graduation was subject to the submission of her thesis and a final viva voce exam. Upsetting though it was, when she received news of her father's ill health, she jumped at the chance to get away from the strained relationship that had unfolded after Krish's ultimatum. She flew to Kuala Lumpur to be at her father's bedside – the university had granted her a two month leave of absence. She was hoping to be back soon to complete all the final protocols.

*

Paree's abrupt and unannounced return to Bangalore gave her parents a huge surprise – they were heartened to see her looking and behaving normally. It was apparent to her that her aggrieved and disappointed parents would start the process of finding a suitable match and marry her off. They were worried, not without reason, that their daughter had compromised her future, especially if word got out about her romantic escapades. Paree knew that the only way to escape the 'arranged marriage' scenario was to quickly re-join her degree course – even her parents agreed that it was vital to complete her degree so as to enhance the chances of a suitable match. She had decided to return to Bangalore so that she could re-join her degree course – the deadline for re-admittance was imminent and would expire soon.

Paree had not revealed anything about the boyfriend apart from the fact that they had parted company. It had come as a huge relief, to her concerned parents, that she had not eloped or done something silly against their wishes. They were pleased that Paree had safeguarded the family honour and had respected the religious and cultural traditions that the family abided by. They were looking forward to finding a suitable match for her, now that she was back safely in the family home and pursuing her education.

Paree was at the rear of the house, in the one bedroom outhouse that they used as a store, retrieving her books and notes, when she heard voices in the front room. She stepped out and peeked through the rear veranda and saw a young couple talking to her dad – she assumed it was the brother-sister tenants who had moved in whilst she was away in Madras.

As she moved closer, she realised with a start that it was Sonny and Suzy – she quickly fled back to the outhouse, her mind in total confusion. Seeing him again, in the flesh, had brought back the fond memories of their campus romance. All the pent up emotions came gushing back; the old wounds re-opened. She stayed in the outhouse until she was sure that they had left. She was still not over him after months of a forced exile in Madras. She had no desire to meet him or Suzy so decided to keep away from the couple. It would be difficult virtually living under the same roof but having experienced her parents' joy at her return, Paree was determined to shield them from any further shocks.

When Krish divulged casually at dinner time that Suzy had left for Malaysia to be at her father's bedside, Paree kept her emotions in check although her heart raced. Sonny was going to be alone for the foreseeable future. Her resolve was weakening as she asked, 'Did I see them in the front room with you earlier?'

'Yes, she had come to bid farewell – she has flown back to be at her father's bedside. In any case, Sonny and Suzy were going to leave, Sonny will move in with a friend until his graduation.' Krish said whilst Anjali got busy serving dinner – she had made Paree's favourite dish and did not want to discuss Suzy at her table. As far as she was concerned, she was glad to see the back of Suzy. 'Maybe Krish will start behaving as he should – the father of a grownup daughter,' Anjali muttered under her breath, relieved at Suzy's departure.

Paree tried hard to keep her emotions in check. She did not want her parents to know about Sonny – that their tenant was the boyfriend that she broke up with. Paree had great difficulty in keeping secrets from her mother but was steadfast in her resolve to keep her silence and protect the identity of her boyfriend. She feared that if she let her guard down, Anjali was astute enough to deduce Sonny's identity as the campus paramour. She had steadfastly refused to divulge any details and Anjali had finally given up trying.

Paree had not recovered from Sonny's rejection and had felt pangs of jealousy whenever she had spied Sonny with Suzy, cosily tucked behind him on the bike – a place that she had so enchantingly occupied herself a few months ago. She had reminisced about the drives to secluded spots on his bike and had missed and pined for him.

Now that Sonny had entered her life again, she was determined to give herself another chance and win him back –ready to face her father's wrath. She would stand up to her father if it came to that. She knew all about her mother's sacrifices and was resolute that she would not sacrifice her freedom and agree to an arranged marriage – she would pick her partner; not her parents.

Suzy's temporary absence and Sonny's loneliness were, truly, blessings in disguise; a chance for her to rekindle her magical relationship with him. Having made her decision to forgive and forget, Paree planned her next move meticulously – this would be her perfect opportunity to wrest Sonny away from the fair skinned Suzy. She had to act swiftly to win him back – before something adverse happened or before Suzy returned from Malaysia.

One dark tempestuous night with the heavens alight with thunder and lightning, the figure swiftly climbed the stairs and crossed the terrace

– the heavy cotton duvet over the head afforded protection from the torrential downpour. The soft turn of the duplicate key in the lock and the rustle of the sheets did not rouse Sonny from his deep sleep.

His aftershave and his manly aroma spurred her into an orchestrated ritual that was straight out of the Kama Sutra. The wiles of Eros exercised with a consummate dexterity that belied her age... Sonny, the archetypal weaker sex, did not stand a chance. He was putty in her hands.

She crept out at dawn just before the sun came up – after whispering sweet nothings in the ear of her sleeping Lothario. They would meet for lunch away from the inquisitive eyes and plan their next move. With the fires of passion satiated and her mission competed, she slipped out without making a sound. She sneaked down the stairs and returned the duplicate key to the desk in the veranda.

Sonny, awash with the passion of the night before, was still too sleepy and smiled smugly at the faint memory of his passive participation – almost like a dream, a very pleasant dream. He turned over and settled into a deep sleep that dawn sometimes induces, after a night of passion or turbulence; almost a Shakespearian recipe for a dramatic finale.

'Anjali was wonderful,' he murmured as he tossed and turned, half asleep. He had fancied the older woman the first day that they had met. Their eyes had locked momentarily before she had looked away. She must have a thing for him as well, he thought, to come in surreptitiously in the night whilst Suzy was away. He could still smell the lingering fragrance of her perfume on the pillow.

Present Day

The 350 cc bike accelerated as Anjali snuggled up to Sonny, her man. As the bike hit the main highway towards Madras, her thoughts went back to the last few weeks.

They had just eloped before her husband, Krish, realized the true impact of the events. She had convinced herself, in a convoluted manner that her husband was cheating on her with Suzy – she had no compunction for him. She was on the warpath, a woman scorned.

In total contempt of the double standards that seemed so prevalent when it came to male predatory behaviour, Anjali decided to avenge herself – if Krish could link himself with Suzy who was almost half his age, then why couldn't she harbour amorous feelings for the dashing Sonny? She had in her own emphatic way challenged the embedded distorted thinking of male domination. She had at one stroke silenced the 'moral police' and her insensitive husband. For years she had tolerated his controlling behaviour and his bigotry. In a sense she was rebelling against the tyranny of her parents who had sacrificed her ambitions and aspirations at the altar of an arranged marriage. Her time had come to be decisive and regain control of her destiny.

This elopement with Sonny was her proxy war against the stringent traditions of a bygone era. She regretted not standing her ground – she should have persisted with her budding career, her dancing. She had no sympathy for Krish and the way he had behaved, especially as she had given up her career as a professional classical dancer.

'This is my time in the sun', Anjali told herself. 'My chance to redeem and reclaim my youth.'

Sonny and Anjali had booked a flight to Kuala Lumpur. Sonny had already received an internship placement with a small animal practice and once he passed his membership exams, he could then set up his own. The first couple of years would be difficult whilst he got his practising licence but his wealthy parents had set up a trust fund from which he could draw a decent allowance – they could live quite comfortably on that. They, especially Anjali, had left everything behind to start a new life in Malaysia.

Sonny's fascination with her was for her old world charm and her mature practised demeanour. He always had a thing for the older woman, especially one so vastly different to Suzy – Anjali's ebony to Suzy's ivory.

As the Air India flight took to the skies, Anjali's thoughts turned to Suzy – her presence in Kuala Lumpur was going to be a hurdle – no more triangles, if she could help it. She would have to deal with the matter in due course – for now she was secure in the knowledge that Suzy needed to return to Bangalore to finalize her thesis and other formalities. That would give her enough time and leeway to cement her position.

'With any luck,' Anjali reminded herself, 'Suzy was going to be busy with completing her Master's. Who knows, she may have to revise her thesis and might have to spend a few additional months in Bangalore.'

With that germ of an idea incubating within the dark recesses of her devious mind, she smiled enigmatically – she was certain that if she put her resourceful mind to work, the Vice Chancellor, a silent admirer of her dancing prowess, could be called upon to ensure Suzy stayed back in Bangalore... a few extra months;

even a year... a few additional snags could always be found with her research project or her thesis. Anjali smiled indulgently – even after all these years she could still pull a few favours from her fans and the Vice Chancellor had been and still was an ardent fan.

With most of the passengers dozing in the dim lit cabin of the Airbus flight, Sonny made himself comfortable by pushing back the arm rest and snuggling up to Anjali. The fragrance of her enticing perfume was the same perfume that she had been wearing the other night when she had snuck into his bed. The memory of that tempestuous night emboldened him – a naughty thought had just popped into his young head.

As he looked around he noticed that the cabin crew were cloistered in the galley. He whispered seductively in Anjali's ear as he gently nibbled on her soft ear lobe.

'Mile High Club, what on earth are you talking about?' she whispered back. Sonny noticing the genuine puzzled look on her radiant face, whispered again to expound on what he had in mind for his wife to be. He wondered if she was feigning ignorance to annoy him or pulling his leg to tease him.

'No way,' Anjali retorted with some venom. 'No hanky panky until we are properly married. You will have to wait, my Casanova, until my feet are firmly on the ground and at the marriage registry. Not until I have the wedding ring on my finger, lover boy,' she added firmly dousing Sonny's ardour. It was Sonny's turn to look puzzled as her recent nocturnal antics flashed through his mind, as vivid as some of the erotic architectural sculptures that he had seen in abundance.

'Oh, come on, after that stormy night of passion when you snuck into my bed, you could hardly play the innocent 'touch-me-not'. You were awesome. Your perfume, your practised presence, even in the dark, was so enticing. You are wearing the same perfume and it is driving me crazy.' Sonny gushed still thinking she was having him on – goading him into arousal.

'What stormy night, stop messing about – who do you think I am? Like your floozy sister who is having an affair with Krish?' Anjali's eyes were flashing with anger. She continued, 'I have never betrayed his trust in all these years. His fling with Suzy, your sister, has changed everything for me.' Sonny saw the tears well up in her eyes.

'You did not sneak into my bed after Suzy left for KL? What about the perfume on the pillows? You were gone by the time I got up. As for Suzy, we are, we were a couple so any alleged affair with Krish is pure fantasy,' Sonny retorted. He could barely keep his temper and his voice down.

'You disgust me. Suzy is not your sister?' she almost screamed.

'Didn't Krish tell you? He caught us and we had to own up that we were not siblings. The ruse was used to get the flat. That is why we were going to leave as Krish had threatened us with eviction. Krish kept on saying that he would not have leased the flat had he known that we were a couple.' Sonny was still not sure what Anjali was playing at, still hoping that this was some kind of a game, a hoax.

Anjali was stunned – so Krish had not been having an affair. She covered her face in total disbelief and disarray.

And then she recalled – Paree had borrowed her bottle of perfume a few days ago! The campus romance and Paree's insistence on not identifying her boyfriend, the pregnancy termination, the thoughts cascaded through her mind. She turned to him aghast – that life could be so cruel.

'Paree, my daughter, you know her don't you? You are the boyfriend who jilted her – for Suzy?' she whispered, her voice reflecting the dread and the rising panic as the pieces fell into place; the jigsaw complete.

'Paree Iyer, the Agrico? I mean Agricultural College?' Sonny asked beginning to realise the

231

full import of the conversation that they were having.

The look on Anjali's face gave him the answer. Paree, his previous paramour, was Anjali's and Krish's daughter!

'You are Paree's mother!!' Sonny's voice trailed off as the significance of her nodding assent sunk in. He slumped back into his seat – he was eloping with Paree's mother to KL, to get married?

'Good God,' he lamented under his breath.

'Did you know that she had a termination after you broke off with her? Oh, God... what if she is...' Anjali's voiced trailed off. She continued in a hushed whisper, 'Paree spent the night with you – then God forbid, could she be pregnant again?' she asked looking directly at Sonny.

Sonny sat up in his seat. Suddenly there was a chill in the cabin of the Airbus. They had a long night ahead – it was a long way to KL.

The thought of catching the next flight back to Madras and how she was going to face Paree troubled Anjali. She got up, collected her things and moved to an empty seat further up the aisle – she could not bear to even look at Sonny.

Anjali buzzed for the airhostess – she needed to speak to the flight purser.

Madras

Paree walked the long corridor to the office at the end – lost in thought. Her emotions shot – this wasn't déjà vu but was actually happening.

She walked in as the nurse called her name.

'Hello, doctor. Thank you for seeing me again,' Paree said as she took her seat opposite the consultant.

The young doctor looked at her in confusion at first and then smiled –then he remembered – his first private patient. Surely, there weren't any complications on the D & C that he had performed previously? He opened her medical file and saw the GP's short referral note.

'D & C – pregnancy confirmed. Patient is seeking a termination.'

He was about to make small talk to put her at ease when he saw the pained look on the young lady's face. He ran through the standard compliance protocols and quickly completed a pelvic exam. The young lady broke down and he had to halt to let her recover.

'If you are not sure about going through with this, then by all means go away and think about it. We have some leeway so there is no urgency to perform the D & C today,' he said in a gentle assured manner.

Paree nodded and got dressed. She left still

sobbing and disconsolate. She dreaded the thought of facing her father – without Anjali she was at his mercy; his frenzied outbursts had continued well after the realization that Anjali had bolted with a younger man, her Sonny.

A Year Later: Kuala Lumpur

Paree emerged into the arrivals lounge carrying the baby, Anjali followed with their luggage trolley. They had had a bad flight – the baby had cried incessantly through most of the flight.

Anjali had, almost a year ago, flown back to Madras and to Bangalore. She was just in time to thwart a second D & C from being performed. She had convinced Sonny to return to Bangalore once his probationary period was over – Sonny and a pregnant Paree got married at the registry in Bangalore. Paree had flown back from KL a few months ago just before the birth, to be with her mother as tradition demanded.

Anjali had looked after Paree through the last months of her pregnancy – she had converted one of the rooms into a nursery at the farm that she had bought with the help of her family and a few investors. The farm housed a dance academy where she also performed occasionally.

Anjali and Krish had separated although they had not gone through a formal divorce. Krish was hoping that Anjali would change her mind about divorcing him and return to the marital home. He lived alone in the rambling house in Palace Orchards.

Michelle emerged from Mr Jacob Braganza's office just behind Double Road and almost ran to the main road. The dim street lights flickering in the dusk barely made the uneven and crookedly aligned asphalt pavement discernible – she stumbled as her foot snagged on a partially dislodged slab. The dark intrusive thoughts scrambling her mind reigned supreme, anxiety affecting her motor function as she hurried along.

She flagged down and got into an auto-rickshaw that was passing by the taxi rank across from the office and almost banged her head on the garish yellow hardtop roof as she climbed in. Michelle could not help but glance at the framed photograph of Jesus Christ – a lighted incense stick wedged between the cracked glass and the wooden frame, spewing wispy whorls of smoke.

The curling spirals of jasmine incense wafted to the rear as Michelle sank into the badly upholstered seat, almost goring her thigh on the sharp end of the coiled spring poking through the worn leather upholstery. Lights and lamps were coming on as a humid and sultry twilight descended on suburban Bangalore.

She instinctively caressed the silver crucifix nestling in her cleavage; the tiny beads of sweat glistened as they coalesced into rivulets and disappeared down her sternum. The trickle of sweat barely registering in her troubled mind; her emotions stifling her as the oppressive thoughts whirled around like eddies in a pool. The driver noticed the perceptible tremor of her slender fingers as she nervously retrieved the crucifix and caressed it – the driver's gaze lingered on her ample bosom and on her chiselled attractive features. He had to force his gaze away from the rear view mirror and focus on the busy road. He heard her mouthing the Lord's Prayer.

Michelle murmured under her breath, 'Oh, Lord, forgive me for what I have just done'.

The driver reached out and 'clocked' the meter and abruptly pulled away from the kerb and into the traffic, studiously ignoring the cacophony of blaring horns behind him. Michelle was too disturbed to notice the near collision that the driver's manoeuvre almost precipitated – he steered the three wheeled death-trap in and out of the chaotic evening traffic as he sped towards Michelle's home.

A very distraught Michelle was still sobbing as the rickshaw reached Richmond Town, just behind Baldwin Girls' School. She got off a few yards short of her home, bracing and composing herself as she walked the short distance to the imposing edifice – the dark green Morris Minor was not in the driveway, she noticed with immense relief. She wanted to be alone and needed the breathing space to recover her poise and compose herself before her parents or Anita, her elder sister, came home.

Some Years Ago

Lincoln Hall was abuzz with the outgoing batches of tenth grade pupils of Baldwin Boys' and Baldwin Girls' High Schools – the students had gathered at a valedictory party for the 'graduating' students; an annual event held jointly at the boys' school before the annual board examinations in December. This was a temporary reprieve from the frenetic revision phase just before the tenth grade final exams; an important qualification of secondary education that would decide the careers and destinies of all the students.

Both institutions were private independent schools, founded in 1880 via a grant from Dean Baldwin, an American benefactor, and run by the Methodist church in India – the schools located in the posh locality of Richmond Town, Bangalore, were elitist in that the students sat the local Cambridge examinations in December rather than the state board exams in April.

Siddhartha ('Sid') Mehta and Michelle Smith were both backstage rehearsing the speeches that they were going to deliver to the outgoing tenth class school students at the 'commencement exercise' in a few days.

As a school prefect, Sid was used to occasionally speaking at the daily morning school assembly but this onerous assignment was a different kettle of fish; he had never addressed such an august assembly of guests and dignitaries. Michelle, his counterpart, a pretty Anglo-Indian teenager, seemed unflappable and raring to go; elocution and public speaking were her forte.

Sid admired her from a distance, too shy to address her directly and a little bit overawed by the occasion and her svelte captivating persona. Her striking resemblance to Judy Geeson, the 'To Sir, With Love' star, meant that he was besotted as soon as he saw her – he had seen the Sidney Poitier hit half a dozen times just for Geeson's mesmerizing presence.

He could barely keep his eyes away from her and, as she became aware of his ingenuous scrutiny, she looked up from her speech to catch him gaping at her – although she smiled at him to put him at ease, his discomfiture was apparent and palpable. He looked away guiltily, chiding himself for gawking at her.

The speeches and the function, a few days later, went smoothly despite Sid's unfounded concerns; only the Baldwin girls in the front row noticed the slight tremor that was manifestly visible as he held the long banner-like scroll – at the end of his delivery he was relieved to hand over the scroll to the outgoing tenth class representative, who then reciprocated with his farewell speech to the incoming batch. Michelle, sitting in the front row, avidly watched Sid as he conquered his nerves and delivered a pitch perfect speech, the hand tremors notwithstanding. The evening in the Lincoln Hall came to a fitting close with a motivational speech by an American guest of honour – the official finale of the evening.

The anticlimactic feel to the evening was saved by the party continuing at a venue close to the school – the entire entourage moved to a nearby restaurant. The evening's party was a gift from Sid's parents to the graduating batches – the restaurant and banqueting hall belonged to the Mehta family, part of the family owned hotel and catering business.

Sid and Michelle were paired again as the festivities ended with some party games and an impromptu dance. Whilst Michelle, a self-assured dancer, whizzed through her steps with an effortless grace, Sid's unease was apparent for all to see. His proximity to the prettiest girl, the star of the evening, and the envious focus of all his prepubescent rivals raised his anxiety to an unbearable pitch.

It was the first time that he had been this close to a girl. Before the school staff could intervene, other students joined in – in the melee that followed the dance would go down in the school's history as a one off that the staff turned a blind eye to. In the spirit of the occasion, some of the senior teachers danced with their female colleagues – as an impromptu gesture of goodwill. Their explicit transgression of school protocols was an aberration; a heat of the moment occurrence. Some of the teachers did, for a moment, regret the spontaneous participation – visualising the reprimand that was sure to follow the next day. For now, the students and their teachers enjoyed the moment of camaraderie, the imminent rupture of the teacher-student relationship held in abeyance for a night; both groups were conscious that a parting of ways was inevitable. The theme song from the movie 'To Sir, With Love' was played as a finale to the evening; a culmination of the festivities of the 'commencement exercise'. The graduation party was quintessentially an American graduation ritual that the Baldwin schools adhered to in keeping with its American roots.

The outgoing batch of Baldwin girls elbowed each other, sniggered and watched as Sid, gauche and self-conscious, tried to feign nonchalance as he danced with studied concentration; his two left feet almost tripping him up. The whiff of Michelle's intoxicating perfume and the gentle undulation of her lower back and hips under his sweaty palm added to his discomfort – he was acutely aware of the testosterone laden and envious collective gaze of his classmates; he was the rabbit caught in the dazzle of a car's headlights.

Michelle, despite the feigned haughty indifference, was quite enjoying the occasion – she had previously noticed Sid at school events and had developed a massive crush on him. She had conspired with her classmates to ensure that he was left alone so that she could home into him and monopolise him. It took all her skills of oration to convince some of her classmates to abandon their final chance to dance with Sid.

Little did they know that the Sid-Michelle 'last tango' of the school year was certainly not a 'ships passing in the night' scenario – their paths were destined to cross; their fates were intertwined.

Both of them had opted for the PCB stream (physics, chemistry and biology) in their penultimate and final years in school – with aspirations of doing medicine at university. Dropping maths, as an elective subject, and choosing biology was a logical and a foregone conclusion for him – he had always wanted to be a doctor; since the age of seven when he used to play-act as a doctor and rummage around in the small first aid box that they had at home. The smell of antiseptics, especially Dettol, had stayed with him all these years.

His flair for human biology, coupled with a pathological dislike of maths, aided the eventual decision – opting for the PCB stream was a done deal. Whilst maths was Sid's Achilles heel, Michelle opted for PCB despite her passion for maths, to emulate her sister, Anita, who was well on her way to graduating as a doctor. She idolised her sister and looked upon her as a mentor.

Admission to all degree courses was dependent entirely on the final end-of-year scores achieved in the one year Pre-University Certificate (PUC) course. For selection to the professional degree courses of medicine, dentistry or pharmacy a minimum seventy per cent PCB aggregate was paramount – anything less than that mandatory benchmark and the chances of getting into Bangalore Medical College, a state funded college, became almost impossible.

For those who failed to get into a state college, all was not lost; not yet. These candidates had an option to gain admission to Church supported private institutions like the Lobo Medical College and other colleges of similar ilk. The selection process for these colleges was based entirely on the scores achieved in the entrance exam conducted independently by these institutions.

Invariably, the demand for places far outstripped the supply – for most PCB students a place on the medical course at the Lobo Medical College was considered to be a privilege; a sign of outstanding academic achievement. The medical college was run by a trust set up by a Kenya based Goan philanthropist, Anton Lobo. The trust's primary objective was to enhance the number of Goan students taking up medicine, especially from East Africa. There was a special quota for ethnic Goans – the trust hoped that the disparity that existed between different communities would be redressed by this affirmative action. It also aspired to level the playing field for the poorer sections of the community by emphasising merit over money.

Finally, the third and soft option for aspiring medics, who did not quite make the grade, was to acquire a medical seat on the open market –

there were several private medical colleges all over India who charged a capitation fee, euphemistically called a 'donation', to facilitate entry. This option, by and large, was the preserve of the wealthy who could afford the exorbitant sums so that their charges could become doctors. Unfortunately, this open market option placed a huge burden on a minority of students who, despite having the academic ability, missed the boat by a few marks. For those students, their fate depended on the benevolence of family or friends or on private financiers to secure a seat. Only a few managed to overcome the huge handicap of raising astronomical sums of money without any collateral – these applicants were the truly blessed ones.

With demand far exceeding the supply, in most cases, the third option was the line of least resistance – that is, if one had the money or the facility to beg, borrow or steal, then a medical seat was there for the taking. Sid had already rejected the third option – he wanted to get into med school on his own merits.

It seemed as if fate was throwing Michelle and Sid together – their paths crisscrossing again as they both ended up in the same college and in the same class – the Pre-University Course (PUC).

Their excellent tenth year results meant that both of them whizzed past the interviewing panel to land a seat at All Saints College – there were sixty students in the PCB stream. Michelle was amongst a very small number of female students and whilst there were other students from the private independent schools, the majority were from the state schools.

Sid had an extra string to his bow, an 'edge' that would have aided him to gain admission – his cricketing credentials. The college had an enviable reputation of winning the inter-collegiate cricket tournament for the last several years and was known to favour applicants with a cricket track record. Fortunately, Sid did not have to bank on his cricketing accomplishments – his academic scores got him in without any difficulty.

It became very clear from the outset that Michelle and Sid were soulmates. They both lived in close proximity to the college and they fell into a routine of arriving and leaving together. The small group of students from the convent schools soon gravitated towards a cohesive cohort who virtually mingled within their own – a class within a class which excluded the others.

Their common educational background was a bond that drew them closer – the cloistered upbringing became a comfort zone, a haven amidst the chaos that college represented. Both realised that this was the real world – they had been, whilst at school, 'big frogs in a small pond'; now in college they were 'small frogs in a big pond'. The transition from school to college was fraught with difficulties; survival of the fittest became a mundane reality – not just a Darwinian concept.

Sid's family, a Hindu-Parsi fusion, were restaurateurs from Bombay and the joint family – brothers, cousins, uncles – ran a chain of Irani restaurants. Sid was the exception – his cousins had all joined the family enterprise after completing school or PUC. He was the youngest and had managed to escape the clutches of the commercial world as envisaged by his family; his sights were set on a challenging academic route.

The joint family all lived in a sprawling double fronted house, with a small swimming pool, just off Richmond Road. Anyone peering through the ornate metal gates that guarded the palatial property and beyond the well-tended front lawn would have no doubts about the extended family's pedigree of affluence. The front drive had several expensive cars, including the odd Cadillac, parked under huge colourful canopies, to protect the glossy paintwork from bird excreta and the bleaching effects of the sun. The place oozed old-world moneyed charm, enhanced by the shimmering reflections of light from the swimming pool that was almost hidden by the luxuriant foliage of the back garden. A swimming pool in the backyard was the ultimate luxury and a status symbol – a proclamation of wealth and affluence beyond the reach of most Indians.

Michelle's father, Dean Smith, had worked as a stockman almost all his life and had eventually started his own dairy farm. Dean had broken a long-held family tradition of following his forefathers into the Indian Railways as a train driver – he had decided instead, against his father's fond wishes, to go to university and study animal husbandry. Protima Smith, his dusky wife, had been a surgical nurse at the Lobo Hospital, an affiliated hospital attached to the medical college. She retired from the hospital once her elder daughter and Michelle's sister, Anita, gained entry to the medical college, courtesy of a reserved seat for children of serving hospital staff.

Dean did, however, continue the family tradition of excelling at cricket and had persisted, after retiring from first-class cricket, with playing club cricket well into his forties. Michelle and Anita had spent their early childhood living on the farm – with a motley crowd of Holstein Friesian dairy cattle, Tamworth and Landrace pigs and Merino sheep. The two girls, inseparable and almost joined at the hip, were equally at home at cricket matches – frequently dispensing cucumber sandwiches and tea or stepping in as club scorer when the occasion demanded. The girls were well liked and were a constant feature by the side of their father at most club fixtures. The cricket mad and close knit Anglo-Indian community idolised Dean as 'the best opening bat never to play for the Indian test team'.

Both the girls had always helped on the farm during school holidays until the family moved into a bungalow just behind Baldwin Girls. The Smith family had prospered and eventually had a clutch of three farms on the outskirts of Bangalore. The family were one of only a handful who had a British car – a fairly well preserved petrol green Morris Minor 1000 four door saloon.

Both Michelle and her sister were well supported by their parents and the couple had jointly decided that their girls would have the best of education – an opportunity to go to a private school and on to university. The eventual destination that Mr and Mrs Smith envisaged for their progeny was Australia, which was perceived to be much more lenient than England in terms of immigration.

The only time when Sid spent time away from Michelle was for cricket nets once a week. The college cricket team had a full schedule of tournaments, virtually all year round. In the absence of a wicketkeeper, amongst the assembled group, Sid's selection was automatic and unchallenged. In a way, this placed him in a quandary as he was called upon to keep wickets at all tournament games; a distraction that imperilled his focus – PCB played second fiddle to his cricket.

Away from their comfort zone, the one-to-one interaction that the private school teachers imparted, Sid and Michelle struggled initially to come to terms with their vastly changed circumstances. They were truly lost in the absolute anonymity that a class of sixty students thrust upon the pair – from the aura of being a school prefect or a school captain to being a mere roll number was a huge psychological downer. Most of the private school students faced this initial 'adjustment phase' in college, where the absence of the 'one to one' student-teacher interaction proved pivotal to their progress – many floundered and failed to repeat their previous academic success. The state school pupils were used to the 'one in a crowd' setting and continued as if nothing had changed;

in a way they were better prepared for the crunch year that PUC represented.

Michelle was more mature and quickly came to terms with this transition – Sid, the inveterate introvert, was homesick for the comforting rituals of Baldwins. Whilst Michelle redoubled her efforts to focus on the syllabus, Sid took refuge in his other comfort zone – cricket. Despite Michelle's admonishments, Sid ignored the perils of spending too much time in the nets and away from his text books.

Sid convinced himself and her that he was adept at managing his time – he had done it at school, so college should be no different. For the first few months, he spent more time in the cricket nets and on cricket pitches than in the college library; slowly and surely he was falling behind. Michelle, with her disciplined focus on PCB, the core subjects, was forging ahead of Sid; the disparity in their progress was patent and striking.

His only apprehension, which he hid from Michelle, was his mental block with physics – this eroded his confidence when it came to addressing the mathematical derivations and theorems that physics abounded in.

The physics syllabus was steeped in complex derivations and he frequently lost the thread when the senior lecturer, Mr Swaminathan, expounded the temperature co-efficient of resistance or the dispersion of light through prisms or Snell's law. Gradually it reached a crisis point where he switched off and the only 'force and motion' variables that interested him were those on the cricket field. By default he devoted more time to his favourite subjects, biology and chemistry; deluding himself that any deficits in physics could be counter-balanced by over-achieving in biology and chemistry.

As the average of the three core subjects was the criterion for admission to med school and not individual subject marks, Sid carried on playing cricket till the very end. The admonishments of friends and Michelle fell on deaf ears. The finals were a long way off. The whiff of raw linseed oil as he 'seasoned' the willow of his favourite bat with a soft used cricket ball more alluring than pouring over the minutiae of 'The Principles of Physics'.

Michelle had no such impediments and was cruising along splendidly; on top of her preparations of the PCB syllabus. Had she known about Sid's phobia and his reluctance to accept that physics was a weakness, she could have helped and tutored him. Sid, still glorifying in his excellent school grades, preferred to rest on his laurels; oblivious to the pitfalls ahead.

Six months before the final PUC exams, the Mysore government amended the law – only students who had lived in the state for the preceding ten years would be eligible to apply to professional courses run by the state government. Previously a five year domicile requirement had been in place – it was felt by the state admission boards that too many inter-state candidates were taking up seats on professional courses at the expense of local home-grown students. Privately funded colleges and those charging capitation fees were exempt from these restrictive and discriminatory domicile requirements.

Sid had already completed five years, the family having moved from Bombay, and the abrupt change scuppered his chances of getting into any state run professional course; which meant that he could only apply to a private institution. Sid's chances were diminishing even before he had finished PUC.

Michelle was Bangalore born and bred and whilst the domicile amendment did not affect her, the impact on Sid's chances and on their relationship was a huge worry. She was profoundly upset; Sid was more philosophical and dismissed it as a 'we'll cross the bridge when we come to it' scenario.

His family with their vast wealth assured him

that, if push came to shove, a legal challenge could be mounted – on the grounds that the policy discriminated against students from other states. Sid tried to ignore the ethical debate that raged around him; Michelle prayed that the controversy would not affect his motivation or his focus.

With Michelle egging him on, Sid redoubled his efforts and belatedly concentrated on physics. His preparations for chemistry and biology were well in hand and almost completed, so he could devote all of his revision time to concentrate on physics, his potential nemesis. And yet he continued playing cricket.

And then the other bombshell dropped.

With the PCB syllabus yet to be fully covered and with the finals fast approaching, two months to the D-Day in early March, a thunderbolt struck. Mr Swaminathan, the shy and reserved physics lecturer, left abruptly – the PCB class and Sid were left adrift.

Despite his issues with physics, Sid had bonded with the self-effacing and erudite Mr Swaminathan. His measured and confident approach had allayed Sid's fears and apprehension, so much so that he was coming to grips with his physics phobia. He had come to rely on Mr Swaminathan's patience and support – with his abrupt departure, the panic resurfaced with a vengeance.

The fallout was that Sid took an instant dislike to the board appointed locum lecturer – Mr Jacob Braganza, whose supercilious and arrogant demeanour on the very first day filled him with foreboding. Sid's panic gathered momentum; he was bereft with anxiety and the first chinks in his resolve were becoming apparent.

No one really knew the reasons for Mr Swaminathan's abrupt departure– rumours abounded about squabbles and arguments with colleagues, mysterious illnesses and even family disputes. With the distressed lecturer's demeanour fast deteriorating, bordering on hallucinations, the college authorities were duly supportive and explored various options. A short leave of absence was also offered which Mr Swaminathan flatly rejected.

When his errant behaviour descended into a regular pattern of imaginary debates and discourses – all addressed at the bust of Isaac Newton that stood guard at the entrance to the physics lab – the board of trustees were truly alarmed. Initially the board dithered and prevaricated as there were periods of remission when all seemed to be normal. In hindsight these were episodes of normality induced by appropriate medication. However, the crisis precipitated and took an adverse turn when he started hallucinating whilst delivering a lecture – the head of faculty quietly dismissed the class and led him away. The board of trustees compelled him to withdraw on an indefinite leave of absence, with an assurance that he could return to his teaching duties once he had recovered and recuperated.

The college authorities were desperate, especially as the academic year was almost over and it would be nigh on impossible to find a suitable replacement this close to the final exams. The existing staff had their own remits and no amount of re-scheduling would have bridged the breach left by Mr Swaminathan's departure. The board tried gallantly to recruit a suitable replacement but in vain. In desperation it was decided to approach the private tutors and the tutorial colleges – these prepared students exclusively for various entrance exams and for re-sits. It was felt that the 'short concentrated' coaching that these tutors provided would solve the college's predicament.

Jacob was the only contender. He and his brother Cyrus jointly owned a dozen tutorial colleges and it would seem that only a self-employed lecturer would have the flexibility to take on this task at such short notice. After a lot of haggling, he was appointed on a three month fixed contract – at an exorbitantly excessive rate.

Jacob had noticed the rising trend of private coaching and tutorials well ahead of his competitors and had, over several years built up his empire. Uncannily he recognised the demand for private tutorials as the colleges greedily admitted more and more students each year – revenue took precedence over quality. With the poor quality of teaching that had become the norm in these mediocre colleges, parents and students were forced into depending on extra tuition – Jacob and others like him took up the slack.

He had started in his front room with a couple of students once a week; now his tutorial colleges coached hundreds of aspiring ambitious students, all chasing a dream to gain entry to a professional course. His astronomical success had not gone unnoticed and his competitors, hard hit by his dubious management tactics, could only watch and marvel at his chutzpah. He was building up resentment and envy within his peer groups and within the education industry.

The brothers had arrived and were unstoppable. Ten years ago, he was a freelancer eking out a meagre living, now he was a tycoon. The younger brother Cyrus, whom Jacob's parents had adopted as a neonate, although very industrious, barely managed to cling on to

Jacob's coat tails – everyone acknowledged that Jacob was the brains behind the enterprise.

The younger brother obsequiously played second fiddle to the Pied Piper and succeeded well in hiding his resentment; knowing that he was quite dispensable – no blood ties to keep his future secure; now that the parents had passed away. The serpent of jealousy was dormant for now as Cyrus was biding his time – he daydreamed about the day when he would be in charge and Jacob would be his subordinate.

Sid was resigned to the abrupt change and continued with his one-to-one interaction with Jacob. In a perverse way, the extra physics coaching became counter-productive. Sid's difficulty with the subject was exacerbated by Jacob's supercilious behaviour – everyone knew that the lecturer had his favourites in the class and Jacob went out of his way to denigrate the ones he thought were not up to scratch. Jacob had impeccable teaching skills and his knowledge of physics was quite profound, however, his abrasive manner negated the positive qualities.

Sid bore the brunt of the lecturer's sarcasm and acerbic comments – it was no secret that Jacob detested the national obsession with cricket. Sid became an open target for his ire – it was Sid's misfortune that Jacob carried a chip on his shoulder; Jacob had been a mediocre cricketer in his youth and despite his aspirations had failed to make the grade. Jacob had always believed that he was a victim of religious discrimination and the blatant partisan politics that prevailed within the cricketing fraternity had denied him a place in the state cricket team.

Sid's success on the cricket field, as frequently reported in the local press, made him an object of Jacob's puerile jealousy. That jealousy was accentuated and reinforced when Jacob found out that Michelle and Sid were inseparable. He seethed with envy every time he saw them together.

Unknown to Michelle, Jacob and her father had played club cricket together, albeit briefly, and he had always liked what he saw in her prepubescent mannerisms whenever the young Michelle, accompanied by her sister, attended her father's cricket outings. Over the years, as the girls progressed through school, both of them had ended up in his evening classes – the parents were keen that the girls had all the help that they could provide to succeed academically. Jacob had personally taken on the task of tutoring them and he took both of them under his wing. His infatuation with the pretty duo went back to his early days as a freelancer. The fact that Jacob was a devout Christian endeared him to the family – Mr and Mrs Smith looked upon Jacob as a family member and trusted him implicitly.

The PUC finals lasted two weeks with two hour papers in physics, chemistry and biology and an hour's papers for English and a second language; Sid and Michelle had opted for French.

The PUC exams came and went in a flurry of supercharged emotions and activity. Both were confident that they had done their best. The physics paper was perceived by all as the toughest in the last few years. Sid was banking on a good score and was hoping to get as close to the target seventy per cent mark as possible. He was confident that any deficit in his physics scores would be adequately compensated by his better than average performance in the other two papers; chemistry and biology.

Whilst Michelle went away with her family, after completing the finals, for a well-deserved break in Kerala, Sid stayed back to honour his wicket keeping commitments for his cricket club. Both of them had to be free after a month to sit the entrance exam for various medical colleges including the Lobo Medical College. The long gap of several weeks in the exam schedule was irritating for most students as the momentum and continuity of preparation diminished as time went by. There were gaps in the exam schedules of all the medical colleges, with Lobo Medical College being the last of the lot.

This 'disconnect' for weeks on end was perilous for someone like Sid who was more prone to lose focus – Sid had promised Michelle that he would continue with his preparations to avoid any lapses in concentration. That was the theory, in practice he ended up devoting more and more time to cricket.

Michelle returned just before the Lobo Medical College entrance exam; rejuvenated by her holiday. She had decided to enrol in a university in Bangalore and therefore, sat only one entrance exam – Lobo's Medical College; ignoring the other med schools based in other towns in and out of the state.

Sid kept on playing cricket and played his final match two days before the final entrance exam. Whilst he had earnestly revised for this exam, Michelle's absence meant that he was left to his own devices. Without her steadfast guidance and determination, Sid was a lost cause; adrift like an untethered raft in stormy waters. He had assiduously continued with his cricket in her absence; cricket an old habit that he just could not resist.

Then disaster struck – Sid dislocated his right kneecap in the nets just before the entrance exam. On the advice of the family GP, he opted for a 'bone setter' to manually manipulate the kneecap back into its bony groove. Had he gone to an orthopaedic consultant, a plaster cast immobilization for months would have been the standard treatment. The bonesetter ensured that he was back on his feet within hours so that he could at least hobble around with the aid of a walking stick. Sid managed, in his injured state, to sit for the entrance test.

Two months later, the PUC results were announced – Michelle had secured a PCB aggregate of seventy five per cent whilst Sid fell short at sixty seven per cent. She also passed the Lobo Medical College entrance and got through her interview. She was in the favourable and envious position of having offers from both colleges – state and private. Michelle opted for the Lobo Medical College as she was very keen on following in Anita's footsteps.

Sid failed to get an offer from the Lobo Medical College and obviously fell short, by a very small margin, to achieve the benchmark seventy per cent PCB aggregate to qualify for the state college. He was disconsolate and retreated into his shell – even cricket ceased to be of any interest. He had blown his chances with his inept performance and results. Sid later found out that his low score in physics, well below sixty per cent, had been the deciding factor. His PCB aggregate dragged down by the dismal performance in physics, despite excelling in biology and chemistry, meant that he was without a medical seat. He was the exception – all the others in their close-knit group had either got into Lobo or Bangalore Medical College.

Michelle had the onerous task of commiserating and cajoling him to re-sit the PUC exam. Sid spent several days prevaricating and was caught in limbo. He dreaded the twin perils of revisiting the physics syllabus and tolerating Jacob's obnoxious persona. It had not escaped his deliberations that he may lose Michelle, more so, if he was coerced by his circumstances into abandoning medicine as a career choice. It hurt deeply that he had defaulted on their unwritten pact to pursue their common dream – the 'tandem' ride had transformed into a 'solo' one. He dreaded Michelle's company – he could not cope with the patent look of despair in her eyes; and the look of 'I told you so' that she desperately tried to mask.

He went into that stubborn dogged stance whenever Michelle raised the topic of a re-sit. Sid was paralysed by his fear of failure – failure to achieve the marks, failure to get into medicine and, God forbid, failure to hold onto his soulmate, Michelle. The constant and relentless analysis of his circumstances was paralysing his thought processes.

Call it serendipity but the chance hearing of a tirade by Jacob piqued his pride. Michelle's friends briefed him on the encounter that they and Michelle had had a few days ago at a popular restaurant on Brigade Road. Jacob had lambasted Michelle for persisting with a loser like Sid and how history was going to repeat itself if Sid resat the exam. The sarcastic digs and denigration that Jacob unleashed in the presence of Michelle and his inner circle of friends hit a raw nerve and goaded him into action.

He went to the college the very next day and registered for his re-sit. Michelle was over the moon, her elation genuine at this long overdue decision. Sid had a second chance to join her at the Lobo Medical College. She raised the crucifix that hung around her neck and kissed it repeatedly – another silent supplication added to countless mouthed previously.

Michelle's commencement of her five year medical course at the Lobo Medical College was the pinnacle of her youthful ambition – her joy knew no bounds; it was, however, tinged with the regret that Sid was not accompanying her on this new journey. She raised a fervent prayer that he would, albeit a year later, get into med school on the second attempt.

Sid had realized his folly in taking his 'eye off the ball' and was grateful for the second chance – in a very competitive environment, his aberrant behaviour had almost cost him his dream; his future. He promised himself that he would take this second chance seriously and prove himself capable of getting into medicine on his own steam. He still baulked at his family's suggestion of paying the capitation fee for a medical seat – the easy option that he had boasted all along that he would not entertain under any circumstances.

Michelle started her medical course and Sid meanwhile enrolled with a well-known evening tutorial college – not far from Michelle's med college campus on Double Road – where she would be pursuing her first year – the Pre-Professional Course (PPC).

He wasn't aware that the tutorial college that he had just joined was owned by Jacob and his brother – he had picked the tutorial college purely on its long history of successes; most of its PCB students managed to get into medicine.

After six months, the initial shock of his failure had almost dissipated; much to

Michelle's chagrin. Sid had re-started cricket, an old passion hard to deny; cricket was obviously more fun than physics.

One evening they were having a quiet dinner in a small bistro in Church Street, when Michelle voiced her concerns; her brow furrowed with a déjà vu feeling.

'Sid, you are doing it again – Ravi tells me that you have re-started your cricket nets? What if you injure your knee again – surely it's not worth the risk?' Michelle pouted, extremely annoyed.

'What's that supposed to mean? You can't expect me to have my nose buried in a physics textbook all the time – all work and no play, remember?' retorted Sid, his anger getting the better of him. He knew which way the argument was heading.

'Within a few months you take your re-sits. Surely, you can do without the distractions?' Michelle pleaded plaintively.

'I am on top of my revision, I just need that last burst of intense revision to cap it all. I haven't forgotten Jacob's tirade against me; the sarcasm and the digs. It will be pure joy to rub his nose in the dirt when I get into med school.' Sid's glib reply and the bravado irked her.

Before she could stop herself, Michelle twisted the unintended knife in an old wound, 'Why don't you confront him tomorrow? He is already aiding you – the tutorial college that you have joined belongs to him.'

It took Michelle the rest of their ruined dinner to pacify Sid, who was aghast that he had not known. It was with great difficulty that she convinced him to stay put and not switch colleges at this late juncture. The déjà vu feeling that they had been here before persisted for the rest of the evening.

'Shall I speak to Mr Braganza? Maybe he can take you in hand and offer a real one-to one? These days he just manages the office in Double Road and very rarely teaches. I can vouch for his skill – you know he helped Anita when she was preparing for her PUC and entrance exams. We go back a few years – we were the very first to join his tutorials,' Michelle explained.

'He gives me the creeps! His brother is no better – a clone of the elder brother,' Sid said, with contempt in his voice.

'Oh, come on, not that old canard again! You can't be serious, all that rubbish about the Braganza brothers and their sexual antics.' Michelle exploded without much conviction. The brothers were both inveterate bachelors, which meant that the salacious details of their affairs made the press on a regular basis.

There had been unsubstantiated reports about Jacob and his 'extra-curricular' activities;

probably initiated by his envious commercial competitors who blamed all their ills on the Braganza brothers. Their enterprise was growing by leaps and bounds – a huge commercial success which generated a lot of jealousy and rivalry. Try as they may, the rival colleges were no match for the behemoth that the Braganza enterprise had become. Their notoriety attracted the seedy side of society – the corrupt politicians and officials who were drawn by the promise of backhanders and easy money.

'Also,' she added, 'he has been in this game for years, he knows the ropes. His finger is on the pulse – he will, going by past exam papers, guess what to expect. He can definitely point you in the right direction. Why don't you concentrate on the exam rather than on the man?' Michelle demanded.

She managed to extract a promise from Sid that he would have a serious think about not rocking the boat at this late stage; a switch to another college or tutor would be suicidal. Meanwhile, without Sid's knowledge, Michelle visited Jacob at the tutorial college.

'Hello, Mr Braganza, thanks for seeing me at such short notice. As discussed, I was hoping that you would help Sid. He is not too happy with the revision and neither am I. Could you please ignore his antics and guide him? He can be an ass at times.'

'Sid's full of himself, isn't he? Are you sure he is serious about pursuing medicine? It seems to me that cricket matters more to him – I gather that he is attending the state cricket association's trials for the state B team.'

Michelle was astounded at the remark; obviously he was well informed. She assumed that Jacob had kept his contacts in the cricket world. Sid had told her that Jacob had been involved in the state association; had been an office bearer for a while until he quit, ostensibly, to concentrate on his business. The rumours about his sexual proclivities had probably soured his standing in the association and he had resigned.

'Well, no. He is fiercely passionate about medicine and besides with his knee injury he has been advised to give up cricket all together. I know he's in denial and won't give up cricket as yet. Probably reckons that even if the injury reoccurs, then he can go back to the same bonesetter and get it fixed. Maybe you could help him? He needs the extra help with physics,' Michelle pleaded.

'I might accommodate him – only on your assurance that no matter what happens you will be responsible for paying my dues? Also, I don't come cheap – are you, I mean, is he prepared to pay the price, whatever that may be?' Jacob finished with a deadpan face, stressing 'whatever' and looking Michelle straight in the eye. His gaze then hovered over her tantalising figure; her glowing fair complexion – no doubt due to her Anglo-Saxon heritage. He had always liked Michelle, better than Anita, who was more Asiatic in her appearance.

'Oh, his parents are quite well off, he can afford it,' Michelle retorted. She had missed the innuendo and the lecherous glint in his eyes as she gathered her things.

She left with a promise to drum some sense into Sid. Jacob, ever the predatory male, watched from the first floor office window as she walked across towards the taxi rank opposite. 'She has matured into a buxom beauty,' he murmured as she faded away in the crowd.

With two weeks to the re-sits, Jacob, true to his word to Michelle, took over the coaching personally – Sid was put through his paces doing only old PUC exam papers – going back several years. Each question and answer was analysed and a perfect answer formulated – 'spoon feeding' ad nauseum.

The exam format had not changed for years – four or five essay questions to be chosen from a list of six or seven options. All the tutorials followed the same revision routine – practising exam papers from previous years. The various private colleges and their entrance exams essentially followed the same format. The only draw-back for students was that the old entrance exam papers of the private colleges were not available, not in the public domain. These colleges diligently guarded their entrance tests and selection procedures to avoid any kind of external manipulation. The shroud of secrecy was a deliberate selection strategy to avoid 'leaks' of the exam papers and to avoid frivolous and malicious legal challenges.

In the final week, Jacob put Sid through the paces – previous PUC exam papers going back several years and papers from the exam boards of other states; especially from Bombay and Madras; reputedly to be the most difficult of all board exams. The strategy was to prepare Sid for all combinations and permutations - the remit was to virtually cover all eventualities and reduce guesswork.

'This format of standard essay questions going back decades and exam papers from Bombay – surely that is going over the top?' Sid exclaimed, exasperated at the mind numbing and exhaustive preparation. Bombay's papers were based on an extra academic year. Sid reckoned the extra pressure being piled on him was deliberate. He just did not trust Jacob – was he playing devious mind games to undermine him?

'Better to be prepared, you never know what the examiner might get up to. Trust me I know what I am doing,' Jacob boasted. His colleges had a singular record of successes over several years – more of his candidates got into medical colleges than any other rival tutorial college.

Two weeks later Sid sat for the PUC re-sit followed by the Lobo Medical College and other similar entrance exams.

A few months later the results were declared – he had scored seventy six per cent in his PUC re-sit; and had performed equally well in the entrance exams. Sid was shortlisted by three medical colleges and was interviewed by all three in quick succession. A month after he had been interviewed by the respective panels he received written confirmation of acceptance from two colleges – the Bangalore Medical College offer was subject to compliance with the ten year domicile stipulation.

Sid's family had taken legal advice and had been assured that the ten year domicile ruling had been successfully challenged previously by a student from Bombay. Sid's family sought and retained the same firm of lawyers and had been assured that Sid's case had greater merit due to his higher scores. Despite the risk of a 'rogue' or an adverse legal ruling the Mehta family was confident of a successful outcome. As far as they were concerned, Sid was guaranteed a place at Bangalore Medical College – it was a done deal; the arrogance of wealth and power excluding any doubts whatsoever. However, unknown to Sid, his father had already secured a place for him with an established 'capitation fee' medical college – at twice the going rate; just in case a default option had to be employed.

Michelle and Sid celebrated that evening. Michelle was elated for him but Sid was subdued and pensive.

'What's the matter? You seem distracted, anything I should be worried about? Not a new girlfriend?' Michelle asked facetiously.

'No such luck, I am stuck with you,' Sid joked. 'I haven't decided as yet whether to take up the Lobo Medical College offer. Not sure I want Jacob to start bragging that he was instrumental in getting me in. Do you realise he has already placed a full page advert boasting about his success in 'securing' the highest number of medical seats this year?'

'Why should that colour your choice? All the tutorial colleges do that every year to market themselves. Besides you have secured a seat, fair and square. Your results reflect the hard work that you have put in. What's wrong with that?'

countered Michelle, worried that Sid had changed his mind about joining her at the Lobo med campus.

She knew Sid well – if he got onto his high horse then he would go off on a tangent. If he opted for Bangalore Medical College then they would be miles apart on different campuses. Her shoulders drooped as she frowned at the thought of Sid on a different campus.

'There's another issue,' Sid said sheepishly, avoiding eye contact. 'Bangalore Medical has an enviable reputation in the sports arena – their cricket team has won every cricket tournament that the college team has participated in; local and national ones. Now that I am spoilt for choice, I might as well throw cricket into the pot.'

'So I am now playing second fiddle to your damned cricket?' Michelle retorted angrily. The fond thought that Sid would soon join her on the campus had kept her going. She was close to tears, fighting desperately to avoid a showdown with Sid. They parted without a resolution; despair and disappointment displacing the joy of the evening together.

A few days later, Sid finally made up his mind and decided to take his chances with Bangalore Medical College – despite the small risk of contentious litigation he accepted the offer;

confident that his father's legal team would deliver on their promises. He still wasn't aware of his father's default option.

Sid was relieved once the decision was made and decided to break it gently to Michelle – he knew that she would be hugely disappointed. Michelle had, after their tiff, calmed down considerably and acknowledged to herself that she was overreacting. She had a sneaking suspicion that her father would readily 'accept' Sid as a future son-in-law, despite his 'non Anglo-Indian' pedigree, if cricket was thrown into the mix – a doctor AND a cricketer would be a tough proposition to reject. She smiled as she envisaged her mum's probable reaction – another cricket aficionado to contend with at the dinner table.

'Hi, Mrs Smith, is Michelle around?' Sid asked as her mum answered the front door.

'Son, how are you? Haven't seen you for a while, the cricket season must have started?' Before Sid could respond she continued, 'She's gone to have her hair done, I think. Not sure, I'm afraid. These days, I hardly know what she's up to,' Protima protested with a hint of regret.

'Okay, please tell her I called. I have nets in a short while so will catch up with her later on,' Sid replied as he hurried off, already out of the drive on his new Java motorcycle, a present from his cousins for his imminent admission to a medical college.

'Congratulations on your excellent scores. I will pass on your message, Doctor Mehta.' She shouted as he waved his acknowledgement and sped off. He smiled at her emphasis on the 'Dr' prefix – Sid had a soft corner for Protima, despite her 'anti-cricket' stance.

Present Day

Anita, after a hard day at gynaecology clinics at the hospital, walked into a dark house wondering where everyone was – the Morris Minor was not in the driveway so she assumed that her parents were at one of their farms or had gone out socialising.

It came as a shock when she found Michelle visibly distressed and in a state of panic. Anita's protective instincts towards the younger sibling kicked in, their lives had run on parallel paths – Baldwins, All Saints College and now Lobo Medical College. The six year gap between the siblings had reinforced the bond between the sisters. Anita prided herself on 'nurturing' her younger sister through the pitfalls that she had succumbed to. Now that Michelle had embarked on a medical career, their relationship had strengthened. There was no sibling rivalry between them and never had been.

With Anita's warm and comforting presence, it did not take long for Michelle to unburden herself and make a full confession – she blurted out the details of her ordeal; she would not have opened up to her mother. Anita was horrified at the narrative that unfolded, deeply resonating with her own dark guilty secret.

She was appalled to hear how Michelle had gone to Jacob's office to settle the fees on Sid's behalf and had ended up being alone in Jacob's private office, his 'sanctum sanctorum' her own vivid memories flooded back. Anita cringed at the thought – Michelle alone and vulnerable and at the fiend's mercy. It was more than likely that Jacob had stage managed an opportunity by ensuring that Michelle would be alone in the office with him. The same ruse, the same modus operandi – the bile rose in her mouth as she envisaged Jacob in bed with Michelle.

Jacob's untrammelled passion had got the better off him – he had been drinking all afternoon; manifested by the almost empty whiskey bottle on the desk. The alcohol had worked its effects on him – as his body became more and more tolerant to the alcohol intake, the quantum needed to produce a 'kick' increased almost exponentially; he had started imbibing a vast amount of whiskey on a daily basis.

Michelle had failed to read his body language as he walked across and collapsed on the settee next to her. Before she could recover from the strong stench of alcohol, Jacob had leaned over and tried to kiss her as his hands took on a life of their own; like a child in a candy shop, Jacob, aroused by his passion, just could not decide which 'jar of sweets' to target. His clammy hands had groped with an urgency that had almost ripped Michelle's silk top away. Anita cringed visibly as Michelle continued with her rendition of the sordid episode – the tears streaming down her fair cheeks.

The touch of his sweaty hands had taken Michelle by surprise. The sheer brazenness and audacity of his assault made her recoil with repugnance – she slipped under him just as he tried to pin her down. The sound of a door slamming in the corridor had distracted Jacob for a split second – in that brief moment of indecision Michelle had pushed Jacob off-balance and had bolted out of the office. She had exited the building and had raced towards the empty taxi rank, where she had flagged an auto-rickshaw and got home.

Michelle started sobbing again and Anita quickly realised that her sister's heightened guilt feelings, anxiety and rapid breathing, almost hyperventilating, were harbingers of a panic attack.

She calmed Michelle down as much as she could and left her in the company of their house boy – with instructions to stay with her and not leave her on her own. She jumped on her Vespa and quickly drove to the local pharmacy just round the corner. Fortunately, the dispensing technician did not ask any questions as he dispensed the diazepam tablets – the white hospital apron with the 'Lobo Hospital' logo blazoned across and the stethoscope that Anita had with her obviated any awkward questions.

Anita was back in the house in ten minutes – relieved to note that her parents were still not back. She administered a loading oral dose of diazepam to calm Michelle down. She helped Michelle into her room and put her to bed; the sedative effect of the diazepam would soon kick in. She would tell her parents that Michelle had retired early.

The chilling nature of Michelle's ordeal almost broke her down as she sat in the front room sipping a glass of Merlot. It took Anita back all those years when Jacob had regularly abused her every Monday evening at the private tuition that her parents had arranged with him; the abuse only stopped once she had stopped the tutorial classes.

She had guarded her guilty secret all these years, not expecting that her silence would come back to haunt her. She had never told her parents about the sexual abuse and had always felt that she was somehow at fault for inviting such lurid attention; the fear of exposure and a scandal prevented her from speaking out. She had repressed her feelings and somehow thought that if she kept out of his way, things would fall into place. She was acutely aware that her parents considered Jacob a part of the family. She had feared that they may not believe her if she made such serious allegations against him, especially of a sexual nature.

Sure enough, in due course, Jacob lost interest in her as his sights settled on other girls. Anita had, all along, made sure that Michelle stayed out of his clutches and watched over her like a hawk. The thought that she had failed her younger sister, now that Michelle had become a target of his depravity, gnawed at her. The guilt magnified by the repercussions of her silence – she shuddered at the thought of Jacob having his way with Michelle; one victim in the family was one too many. To Anita's immense relief, Michelle had confirmed repeatedly that she had escaped just in time; Jacob had not had his way with her.

By the time her parents arrived, she had

already devised her plan and how she was going to execute it. It was time she took a stand against Jacob's sexual predation; time to, not only, exorcise her own demons but to teach the monster a lesson. A lesson that been deferred for too long. Now that Jacob had made a move on Michelle, it was imperative to stop him – before it was too late.

She had not seen or met Jacob since her tutorial days and was taken aback when on her ward rounds she had overheard the registrar discussing a case of alcoholic hepatitis. The patient turned out to be Jacob. He had been admitted for alcohol dependency.

Anita recalled incidents, going back years, when Jacob reeked of a cheap local brew called arrack, an illicit alcoholic drink. Over the years, as his success and affluence had gathered pace, he had progressed to hard spirits, especially imported Scottish whiskey. He had been discharged shortly afterwards from the rehabilitation programme and was prescribed diazepam to treat his chronic insomnia and the alcohol withdrawal symptoms. Anita had read the case notes with a sense of elation – the ogre was getting his just desserts for defiling her and countless other young girls. She smiled, almost vicariously, as she recalled the pathological and metabolic effects of chronic alcoholism and the attending chronic liver disease – 'brewer's droop', a euphemism for impotency and erectile dysfunction, was definitely poetic justice as far as she was concerned.

'He must have regressed and started drinking again,' Anita said to herself. Michelle had mentioned that Jacob frequently appeared drunk and she always saw bottles of liquor on display on his desk and around the office. Sid had, after having met the man at the Smith's, flippantly labelled Jacob a 'brewery on two legs'! Anita smiled at that recollection. She knew of Sid's mercurial temper so decided to keep him out of the loop – bad enough using Michelle as bait.

The next day there were no clinics and on the pretext of going down to the library, she went to their farm – knowing that her father would not be around as Dean was attending to an outbreak of summer mastitis in his dairy herd at the other farm. Dr Kadam, a dairy vet and a fellow cricketer, was already on his way to examine the herd – mastitis in dairy herds was greatly feared by dairy farmers as the disease drastically reduced milk production.

She went into the small barn, set aside by her dad as the calving unit and stock room, and retrieved the Burdizzo from the vast array of instruments that had accumulated over the years – calving ropes, drenchers, syringes etc. The nine-inch Burdizzo used primarily on small animals fitted quite easily into the large handbag that she had carried into the stock room. Both she and Michelle were familiar with some of the instruments, including the Burdizzo, having helped on the dairy farm regularly in their school holidays. She went back to a different pharmacy and stocked up on diazepam tablets.

Two weeks later, when Michelle had regained her poise, she, as instructed by Anita, got in touch with Jacob and apologised for her abrupt departure on that evening. She flirted outrageously with him over the phone to put him at ease; pandering to his massive ego. A 'tryst' was set up for late evening – Michelle was the bait and under Anita's coaching, Michelle had a 'cameo' to perform. Anita would accompany her on the visit and wait in the corridor outside – Jacob was not to know that Anita was involved; to avoid any suspicion.

Anita and Michelle arrived at the office by auto-rickshaw, the smog visible in the twilight, deliberately not using the Vespa. As planned, and knowing that Jacob was a creature of habit, they were certain that he would have gone through a bottle of whiskey by that hour. They were banking on Jacob's devious behaviour – he would have ensured that the office was unattended and deserted.

Michelle and Anita went up the stairs and into an empty reception. As Anita stayed behind, Michelle entered Jacob's office further along the corridor – he was sitting at his desk imbibing his whiskey, the bottle less than a quarter full. All Michelle's misgivings evaporated and her confidence surged when she noticed the inebriated state of him – the slurred speech and his unsteady gait as he excused himself and went into the en-suite toilet.

As planned and rehearsed, Michelle, donning the latex gloves that Anita had provided, retrieved a glass container from her bag. She mixed the pre-prepared powdered diazepam in the glass full of whiskey. Just as Jacob flushed the toilet and came out, Michelle handed him his drink, his lecherous stare fixated on her bosom – he hardly noticed the gloved hands.

Jacob, true to his reputation, downed almost half a glass of whiskey in a single gulp. Michelle knew that the pulverised tablets had a loading dose of diazepam in it. Whilst they made small talk, Jacob took another swig and emptied the glass – it would take approximately thirty minutes to take effect or even less due to his heavy alcohol intake. Anita had assured Michelle that all she had to do to ward off his lecherous advances was to keep him talking and at bay – the diazepam and the alcohol would do the rest.

The sedative kicked in within fifteen minutes and Michelle kept him preoccupied by seductively posing on the settee and flirting outrageously. Jacob eventually walked unsteadily towards her and dropped down next to her. Just as he leaned forward to pin Michelle down, she slipped out from under him – Jacob sprawled onto the floor and tried to get up. After a while he just gave up and managed to half sit up – propped up by the settee; almost comatose. As Michelle moved towards the door, she could hear his stertorious breathing.

She peeped into the corridor and waved Anita in – they had rehearsed the entire operation for days with almost pinpoint accuracy. Anita swiftly unbuttoned the inebriated Jacob's trousers and pulled the trousers and his underwear down to his ankles. With his girth and weight, both sisters struggled briefly to partially undress him.

As Anita looked up, Michelle, on cue, removed the Burdizzo from the handbag and slapped the instrument into Anita's gloved hand – very much like a scrub nurse slapping a scalpel into the lead surgeon's hand. She opened up the jaws of the castrator in one practised deft move and positioned herself across his legs – effectively straddling Jacob. Michelle had already swabbed the edges of the castrator with whiskey – a quick fire sterilisation process. On her signal, Michelle slipped behind Jacob and cradled him so that he was semi upright, his head resting on her chest – she braced herself for what was to come and tried to look away but could not; her eyes were riveted on Anita and the menacing shiny Burdizzo.

Michelle's apprehensive gaze was transfixed on Anita's right gloved hand as she applied the Burdizzo, locking the clamp in place. She knew from past experience of castrating male lambs, usually less than three months old, that ten to fifteen seconds of continued pressure was enough to sever the spermatic cord. Jacob groaned in his sedated state and almost jerked out of Michelle's grip. Anita quickly repeated the procedure on the right side.

She recalled her father's words and training as she viewed the near perfect castration. The pinch marks on both sides were visible, however, there was minimal bleeding on the skin – she knew that the crushed blood vessels in the cords would interrupt vital blood supply to the gonads; the procedure was aptly dubbed as a bloodless castration.

Anita smiled wickedly at the ashen faced

Michelle – the word that sprang to mind was 'impotent'; Jacob was going to be as harmless as a eunuch in a harem. He had just been emasculated for his past sins. She likened him to a thirsty man adrift in an ocean – water everywhere and not a drop to drink.

After clearing all the tell-tale signs of their presence, Michelle removed her gloves and packed them away with the Burdizzo and the whiskey glass in her bag. Michelle left Jacob's office without so much as a cursory glance at the prostrate man, who was groaning and whimpering on the floor. Anita stayed behind to wipe clean surfaces that she or Michelle might have inadvertently touched. She then removed her gloves and stuffed them in her trouser pockets.

Anita's utter disdain for the man was masked by the urgency of their withdrawal, now that their mission was complete.

As rehearsed, Michelle exited the building alone with the handbag. Anita stayed back so that they would not be seen exiting together; two Anglo-Indian women together would be easily recalled but Michelle on her own would be lost in the rush hour crowd. Both of them had also taken the precaution of wearing dark trousers rather than a skirt.

Michelle maintained her composure as she

swiftly walked across to the busy coffee house and mingled with the evening crowd gossiping over cups of steaming coffee and snacks. She was sweating as she gathered herself – all she had to do was act normal and wait for Anita to join her.

Just as Anita was about to go down the stairs, she heard the front door slam shut and the sound of footsteps – someone was coming up the stairs. For a split second she froze and almost continued down the stairs; the first instinct of 'fear-flight' actions. She paused, took a deep breath, and checked her descent in mid-stride and went back to the reception desk, pretending she had just arrived.

'Hello, can I help?' the out of breath, short man in his early forties queried from behind her.

'I was hoping to speak to someone about physics tutorials,' Anita blurted out as she turned around to face a balding stocky man. She assumed he worked there.

'I'm afraid the office is closed, I'm sure the receptionist has gone for the day. Would you mind coming back tomorrow?' the man said, looking away at the empty corridor. He had not been expecting anyone and appeared flustered at discovering Anita in the reception area.

'That is fine. I will drop in another time, thanks,' Anita remarked as she smiled weakly and hastily descended the stairs. She crossed the street and walked into the coffee house where Michelle was nervously sipping the strong freshly made 'kaapi' (coffee). They paid the bill and caught an auto-rickshaw from the taxi rank to their corner pharmacy and walked the rest of the way to their home.

'What if he calls the police and reports us?' Michelle questioned nervously as they walked back, the mental turmoil showing on her strained face.

'No chance, what man is going to broadcast to all and sundry that he was castrated by a couple of females? More importantly he would have to explain his injuries and draw attention to his lecherous activities,' Anita retorted with a confident smile. She was certain that Jacob would bear his punishment in silence – it would be their secret for the rest of their lives.

She was also convinced that Jacob would not dare involve them in any way as he would then incriminate himself. Her concern, which she did not discuss with Michelle, was directed towards the unknown man she had encountered in the corridor – that was where the danger lay. Anita assured herself that despite Michelle's fragile mental state she could contain the risks of exposure; this new threat from the unknown man could pose a serious and direct problem. Anita had instinctively got it right by not divulging the sudden appearance of the stranger to Michelle; not knowing how her sister would react in her heightened state. Anita prayed that the accidental witness would not be able to identify her – just as she wasn't aware of his identity.

Michelle gripped her bag firmly and prayed that Anita was right – that Jacob dare not advertise his ordeal to anyone. On reflection she came to the conclusion that Anita's inference had merit – Jacob would rather take that secret to his grave than disclose his castration; any disclosure would be too embarrassing to live down. He would become an object of ridicule, a eunuch in a world dominated by alpha males.

'Anita has got it right', she murmured to herself, 'Jacob's ego and machismo would prevent any such outcome.' A weight seemed to lift from her drooping shoulders as the sisters walked hand in hand towards their home.

The man entered Jacob's office on hearing the groans emanating from it and saw Jacob writhing in pain. He wondered whether the woman he had just accosted in reception had anything to do with Jacob's prostration and his semi naked state.

'Unlikely,' he said to himself as he could not imagine a wisp of a girl tackling the portly Jacob.

In that brief moment, a thought crossed his mind. He worked swiftly; almost as if the thought had been practised many a time over the years. He saw the empty bottle of whiskey on the desk – a constant feature for the last few months. He knew that Jacob had gone back to drinking and was addicted to his daily doses of diazepam – to function; to combat his chronic insomnia and depression.

He dashed down, locked the front door and turned the lights off. Back in the office he poured a glass of whiskey from a fresh bottle that he found in Jacob's well stocked mini-bar. There was a hoard of diazepam in the desk. He worked with a practised ease – took a fistful of tablets from the desk into the kitchen; crushed them using the small granite pestle and mortar. The office had a small fully equipped kitchen which was used regularly by the office staff and occasionally by a caterer to prepare food for Jacob and his distinguished guests.

It took a while for the powdered diazepam to dissolve in the pale golden hued whiskey. He then propped Jacob up against the settee. It took almost an hour to make Jacob drink the whiskey – sip by sip. It suited him – he was a patient man. He had waited a lifetime so a few more hours would not make an iota of a difference.

The small crucifix that had been mounted on

the office wall had become a shrine where Jacob prayed every morning – he lit a candle and sat down in the semi darkness to wait for Jacob to lose consciousness. It took a while; soon silence pervaded the office. It was an eerie scene – two men in a semi-darkened room; the single candle distorting the features of both men.

He left in the wee hours – a dark figure melting away in the night, not before he had deliberately planted the whiskey glass next to Jacob on the floor. He left the diazepam tablets on the desk and scattered a few next to Jacob. He wasn't quite sure why Jacob was on the floor, with his trousers and his underwear around his ankles. Lucy, the receptionist, and the other staff knew about Jacob's drinking and his addiction, so it would be easy to explain a case of heavy drinking and an accidental overdose of diazepam as the cause of death. Before he left, he went into the kitchen and washed the mortar thoroughly. The auto-rickshaw driver at the all night taxi rank was having a cup of coffee to keep awake –he saw the man walk away from the office across the road.

The silver haired professor and chief forensic pathologist, in charge of conducting the post-mortem, noticed the pinch marks on the man's scrotum which puzzled the senior pathologist.

He had seen a few bizarre things in a career spanning decades but nothing to match this case. The man had obviously died from an overdose – the toxicology results had revealed high concentrations of diazepam and alcohol. Apart from the scrotal marks, the only other unexplained conundrum was that the diazepam had two separate spectroscopic profiles – meaning that the diazepam was not from the same manufacturer. The pathologist had discussed this with the toxicology lab – the spectroscopy had been repeated and had yielded the same result.

The scrotal lesions were not significant in any way to the eventual outcome the professor had concluded. The small amount of scrotal bleeding and the presence of clots were clear indications that the man had been alive when the injury was inflicted on him.

'The bilateral and symmetrical scrotal lesions are an enigma,' the professor murmured to himself. He was flummoxed and at a loss to explain the findings – he had rechecked the police report about the presence of any implements or instruments at the crime scene.

On the spur of the moment, he dialled the number for the Veterinary College, which was located on the outskirts of Bangalore.

'Doctor Xavier, please. Professor Murthy

from the City mortuary,' he informed the operator.

The call was transferred to Dr Xavier, Associate Professor, Dept. of Veterinary Pathology, who was in the middle of a post-mortem on a racing horse, an equine case of sudden death at a nearby stud farm.

'Xavier? A few minutes of your time - pick your brain?' The senior pathologist quickly recapitulated his findings and the media hysteria about Jacob Braganza's death under suspicious circumstances. He also discussed the drug overdose and the alcohol abuse and his conclusion that the ingestion of diazepam and alcohol was the cause of death.

Professor Murthy continued, 'The conundrum is that I can't reconcile the scrotal lesions – the pinch marks on the scrotum. As both the spermatic cords have been severed, castration was the obvious intention. The victim was alive when the castration was performed.'

The older man was fastidious and anything inexplicable piqued his curiosity – he did not like loose ends. The forensic pathologist's dictum that 'dead men do tell tales' did apply, as always, except for this unexplained scrotal injury. The two spectroscopic profiles, the pathologist deduced, were a puzzle, especially as all the diazepam retrieved from the crime scene matched only one profile – from the office and from the kitchen. Either the second diazepam profile was an artefact or the diazepam was from another source or maybe the patient had bought the tablets from different pharmacies. The dead man's tale was incomplete.

'I have read the press reports about this case. Can it wait? Remember we are meeting for lunch – the board meeting?' Xavier spoke into the phone held by one of his trainee pathologists – his gloved hands were covered in equine blood.

'I'll drop in at the mortuary on my way in,' the young pathologist added as he went back to his autopsy. The local media had whipped up public hysteria as a result of the overly salacious reporting – a half-naked businessman caught with his pants down; nothing like sexual innuendo to sell newspapers.

The veterinarian had, over the years, acquired a formidable reputation for his clinical acumen and diagnoses. The two pathologists frequently consulted each other if the autopsy findings turned out to be ambiguous or unexplained; more often than not, they would eventually come up with an explanation and a definitive diagnosis.

Dr Xavier peered at the gross lesions on the scrotal skin and the dissected scrotal sac and the severed cords. The police had not divulged the scrotal injury, so the press knew nothing about the putative sexual injury.

'The severed spermatic cords prove intent – to castrate the victim. By the size of linear pinch marks, I would hazard a guess, from experience, that a castrator was used – probably a Burdizzo. It is commonly used in farm animals to facilitate a bloodless castration,' he said, looking up at the sceptical expression on his senior friend's face.

The young pathologist further expounded in a measured voice, 'A Burdizzo castrator is easy to use, most stockmen on dairy farms castrate animals without having to call in a vet. Sometimes, even experienced dairy owners carry out the procedure themselves – quite easy if one knows what to do.'

'Why though?' the professor quizzed. He skimmed through the police FIR (first information report) again. 'No mention of an instrument found at the scene.'

'Maybe it's a case of sexual revenge, a jealous girlfriend? Maybe the emasculation was performed to inflict pain, a punishment? Although the Burdizzo is easy to use whoever did this must have had help – to hold the man down, despite the sedative effects of alcohol and diazepam. It could be an envious business rival or an aggrieved cuckolded husband?' Xavier said with a shrug of his shoulders.

The press had sensationalised Jacob's rapid 'rags to riches' story and the vast number of toes that he must have stepped on to reach the pinnacle of astounding success in such a short span of time – plenty of aggrieved and jealous competitors waiting for an opportunity to bring down an unscrupulous rival. The general feeling amongst his business peers was that Jacob deserved what he got – the consensus was that poetic justice had been delivered. No tears were shed for a man reviled for his ruthless rise to the top and for his sexual reputation as a predator.

Two weeks later when Jacob's will was read and the revelation that Cyrus was the sole benefactor, the final piece of the jigsaw fell into place.

Cyrus was arrested by the Crime Branch for Jacob's murder – the vast wealth left behind by the victim established an unequivocal motive for the crime. Cyrus was unable to provide an alibi for the time frame and was known to be the last person to see Jacob alive. The coffee house owner and a driver from the taxi rank had seen Cyrus lock up the office and leave in the small hours.

The evidence that clinched his conviction was the powdered residue of diazepam found in the kitchen. Whilst the mortar had been thoroughly washed, the pestle, which had rolled onto the floor had tell-tale white residue on it – Cyrus, in the heat of the moment, had forgotten about the pestle which had rolled out of sight. He had just inadvertently left the pestle untouched. The acts of pulverising the diazepam, dissolving and administration pointed to premeditation. The disclosure that the diazepam tablets had been pulverised before ingestion had blown the suicide theory to smithereens; premeditated murder was the only logical conclusion.

Cyrus initially did not mention the woman he had accosted in the reception area – she would not have helped his case; on the contrary she would have incriminated him by confirming him as the last one to see Jacob alive. He had no alibi as he had gone straight home; he had moved into his own flat several years ago after the death of his adoptive parents. He had put up with Jacob's bullying and overbearing demeanour all these years as his parents had insisted that the family live under one roof as a joint family.

Cyrus tried a last ditch attempt to wriggle free – he told the investigators about the unknown woman that he had accosted in the corridor, trying to insinuate that Jacob was alive when he left. The police were unable to trace the mystery woman despite announcing a substantial reward

– the prosecution accused Cyrus of making things up to back up his 'not guilty' plea. The scrotal lesions remained just that – an enigma. The diazepam profiles were not investigated further and the finding was dismissed as an artefact. After months of police investigation and interviewing scores of leads, the case ground to a halt - in the absence of any new witnesses or fresh evidence Cyrus was charged and convicted.

Two months after graduating as a doctor, Anita accepted an offer of a job at a regional hospital near Sydney. No one knew about the abuse that she had suffered and neither did Michelle confide in Sid about the near assault that Jacob had perpetrated. The two siblings did not accept any culpability for Jacob's death and kept silent about their 'act of revenge'. Anita had followed the police case in the newspapers and was surprised that the man she had accosted in the lobby that evening was not only Jacob's brother but the culprit. Whilst she had exacted her revenge for the depravities that Jacob had perpetrated on her, it was a relief that he had not succeeded in 'defiling' her younger sister.

There was genuine remorse and regret that it had ended fatally for Jacob – on the contrary she was, in fact, disappointed that Cyrus' premeditated intervention had robbed her of her ultimate vengeance. She had wanted Jacob to suffer, for the rest of his life, the punitive effects of the castration. The lack of sexual desire and the feminizing effects of the emasculation would have been a fitting punishment for all the acts of sexual grooming and abuse committed over the years. She was certain that Jacob had defiled and violated scores of young girls and women – most of them having been his students.

Cyrus obviously knew the history of alcohol abuse and the dependence on sleeping pills – it was then quite simple for him to execute a fatal overdose; the death would be either construed as an accidental overdose or a suicide. Even without the diazepam administered by the siblings, the huge amount of powdered diazepam administered by Cyrus proved to be fatal.

A few years later, both Sid and Michelle joined Anita at the hospital that she worked for to commence residency training in pathology and psychiatry, respectively.

Sid had given up competitive cricket to indulge in his first passion – medicine – and graduated with distinction. Michelle had graduated a year ahead of him and had worked in the Lobo Hospital to bide time and wait for Sid to graduate.

Whilst packing for the imminent migration to Australia, Sid came across a pile of his old textbooks. He donated all his textbooks to a charity, save one.

It gave him immense pleasure to 'cremate', in the presence of family and friends, his most loathed tome - 'The Principles of Physics'. The mock ceremony was performed in the garden at the family's palatial residence. He then collected the ashes in a small brass urn and packed it away for the flight to Sydney – he hoped one day to scatter the 'ashes' on the hallowed grounds of the SCG (Sydney Cricket Ground), a venue that was fabled for the intense rivalry between England and Australia for the 'Ashes' test series.

The pleasure he experienced in attaining his very own 'ashes' victory against physics, the scourge of most PCB students, was total and absolute; second only to his achievement of suffixing 'MBBS' to his name.

Mojo Charms

My only regret, apart from the guilt, is that my son caught me "in flagrante delicto" and I have been dreading the consequences ever since. The sword of Damocles was suspended only for a day in Cicero's story; in my case, indefinitely. My son, the putative executioner, was unlikely to have heard about Damocles but the power that he wielded was just as forceful – the fear of exposure driving me round the bend.

On the other hand, if the better half had barged in instead of my son, then I could not have defended myself by using the age-old default line, 'It's not what you think, I can explain.' However, thank God for small mercies that my son made an ill-judged entry – not my wife. I was, therefore, afforded an opportunity to recover my poise and conjure up a strategy of damage limitation. We all make mistakes, some more than others, but how we deal with the consequences is what separates the chaff from the wheat. My strategy of damage limitation was far from ideal and bordered on postponing the inevitable – it suited me to stick my head in the sand. I knew I was going to be caught but for now the consequences could be deferred.

All I had to do was to buy my son's silence. Easily said than done, one might add. After all, we men must and should stick together. However, despite the stiff upper lip gambit, it dawned on me that bribing my way out, on this occasion, would be a tad difficult, bearing in mind that he has always been a mummy's boy. The umbilical cord very much still attached. That said, I had to somehow 'wean' him away from her apron strings.

My extracurricular activity had become an addiction and, despite my earnest endeavours, there was no respite from the vice-like hold it had on me. It was no surprise that my attempts were futile as I was a prisoner to one of the oldest passions known to mankind.

It had all started at an early age and had continued even after we were married. Notwithstanding the fact that my beautiful wife was a soul mate, the temptation to stray had become a compulsion; part of my male DNA. That was my excuse, although deep down I knew I was betraying the implicit trust that existed in our marriage. Our vows taken at the outset with sincerity had been diluted by the passage of time. The seven year itch had come and gone as had the fourteen year one and then, just as we were getting smug about it – it struck with a vengeance. I was, just like the rabbit caught in the glare of an oncoming car, blinded by my cravings. The profound desire to partake, to indulge, became relentless. My rationale was that I had, and still could, get away with it – the 'have the cake and eat it too' delusions.

I was not the only one caught up in this age-old passion. There are thousands, nay, millions of men entrapped all over the world; all in the same boat. Not that I was using that as an excuse to join the masses. Far from it, the herd mentality – 'lemmings over the cliff' – was the antithesis of my being. I was deluded enough to think that I could forge my own way forward.

Temptation is like a googly; any hesitation and it will bowl you over. I was bowled over by the elegant crimson, sometimes sheer black, vision that came back from my past to mesmerise me, like an old flame. Old flames are dangerous – their intensity directly proportional to the passage of time; the older the flame, the greater the risk of 'third degree' burns.

There were no grounds for straying, especially as both of us, hitherto, had remained faithful. Well, I suppose I can only presume that she has not erred; it's not just a man's prerogative to succumb to temptation. Eve led the way by proffering the apple; Adam was the lemming. The rest is history.

Some men fantasise about that illicit one night stand or a short fling. The thought in itself is exciting; doing something illicit, that is. The more risqué the activity, the greater the adrenaline rush; the thrill is directly proportional to the risk of exposure.

It is debatable whether men, being the weaker sex, are 'programmed' to commit this 'high octane, spur of the moment' type of activity. In this new age of the human genome, all mapped out, it would not be too difficult to find a gene, a marker, that 'expresses' errant behaviour. The DNA angle would be the perfect 'get out of jail' ploy if we were playing Monopoly; certainly not a good throw of dice for the real life play of monogamy. Shaggy and his hit song 'Wasn't Me' encapsulate the blasé attitude I had adopted. I had become inured to the hazard warnings that my conscience had set off.

Where there is money to be made, crime follows. Organised crime has taken centre stage by trafficking and exploiting the economies of Eastern Europe - manipulated to bring the price down. It is often the case that the wheels of commerce are lubricated by the 'oils' of avarice and exploitation. The free flow of merchandise from a borderless Europe renders the temptation quite inexpensive – affordable and freely available.

My compulsion, my habit, has led me to seek therapy to cure myself; to rid myself of the baggage of guilt and shame. The treatment failed as the psychotherapists all concurred that joint sessions with the spouse or partner would be more appropriate. I could not, obviously, go down that route without making a full and candid confession to my wife. A catch 22 situation, if ever there was one.

I could have saved myself heaps of aggravation had I listened to my inner voice and done the fair thing. Having taken several bites of the apple, my only path to salvation would be a full confession and then face the sounds of music. If life were that simple, we would all be one big happy family living in Utopia. I took, as always, the soft option of silence and persisted with my instant gratification. The passion and addiction continued with the tacit approval of my son.

My behaviour was even more complicit as I had intentionally involved my son. Fourteen year olds have limited capacity to empathise. I shudder to think what it may do to my marriage once my wife finds out; assuming that my son does sing, eventually, like a canary.

My pride was at a nadir as I plotted my strategy to bribe my son. I reckon he would understand as we had discussed the birds and the bees, and other 'now that you are in your teens, we need to talk' agenda. Nonetheless, I was at his mercy.

I admit that I let everyone down by my indiscretions and had set a bad precedent. Hopefully he would grow up to understand my frailties and forgive my lapses. Looking back, it was definitely an error of judgement on my part to even consider such a reprehensible act – 'bribing' him to buy his silence. O, what a tangled web we weave...

Despite the adverse ramifications, it had become virtually impossible to resist the temptation and I continued to surrender to my uncontrolled urges. My activity, grotesque no doubt, continued unfettered and unabated. The habit was my prison without walls.

Slim and slender, embellished by captivating colours. That's the image embedded in my scrambled mind. My roving eye was locked on the bright crimson look; like a laser guided missile honing onto a target. Every time I focused on the sheer beauty or imagined the sleek body in its entirety, my passion was reinforced. The anticipation and then the consummation of my urges left me gasping. The feel good factor; the euphoria, was enthralling; fuelled by the surging endorphins.

Sometimes the variable scents – the pheromones – are enough to entice some men. The visual and tactile impulses converted into an aphrodisiacal symphony; sensory stimulation par excellence.

Even I acknowledged that this was momentary, a mirage, and I would have to contend with the wrath of a scorned woman. The guilt piled up with the realisation that I was damaging my son's moral fibre. His future marred with emotional baggage inherited from the father. Freudian theories and their consequences took centre stage in my troubled mind. Poor Hamlet, he had no chance, just as I have none. My despair at the way I felt – totally impotent in the face of my predicament, compounded my guilt.

There were occasions when I thought that I had vanquished my urges but the subsequent abject surrender, triggered by a look or a whiff of fragrance, would be draining – the surrender somehow very deflating. At these low points, I questioned my judgement and my resolve. How on earth did I fall into the trap?

I had to bring myself up to speed on the likes and dislikes of the modern day teenager – in my day a trip to the cinema or a cricket game at Lord's would be adequate recompense for buying a youngster's silence. It soon dawned on me that buying a cache of games and a game console would be the bare minimum required. Words like Xbox, Nintendo Switch or

PlayStation4 were as alien to me as Latin or Sanskrit. I had to surreptitiously consult my friend's twelve year old to ascertain what was in and what was not. Poor boy, he erroneously thought that I was planning to give him a present for scoring a century in a school cricket tournament. Another youngster scarred by my inconsiderate behaviour.

After some prevarication, I handed my son a brand new PS4 and a cache of games thrown in for his patience. My son was ecstatic at my largess and beamed. Or was that a sneer? Even I knew that this was just a temporary stay of execution. The sword of Damocles suspended for now but for how long?

Was it my overwrought imagination that read danger in every word or look that my son exchanged? He would mention the latest adverts about Man U kits, iPods or iPads and my blood pressure would spike – each gesture or word became a threat; a ransom demand. I would, fearing imminent exposure, bargain and buy him yet more gifts – playing the golden goose to the hilt.

Chicken, more like, as I envisioned my wife applying for a decree nisi. I just could not take the chance of upsetting my son for if he spilled the beans, then all would be lost.

*

As ever to maximise their profits, the criminals started sourcing the merchandise from far and wide. European imports became the norm as a marketing strategy. In some cases, the distinct foreign look of the goods became a USP; some men found the exotic look more alluring and tempting.

There has been a huge clamour from politicians to set up an enquiry or even a commission to investigate this illicit trading activity. As with most political agendas, I knew that very little was going to be done. Political promises are made in the heat of the campaign; nothing is ever delivered. And the voters have short memories. I was safe in the knowledge that my supply chain would not be affected. What I fancied would be readily available; at a price, no doubt. I persisted with my passion buying as cheap as I had to – my bribes to my son were costing an arm and a leg and I had to somehow recoup and rebalance my budget.

A few criminals are apprehended at the altar of tokenism, just to sweeten the voting public. The few that are brought to justice barely scratch the surface of this rampant and nefarious activity. Like Hydra, cut one head off and more take its place.

My problem is compounded by the fact that I work from home and have lots of opportunities to indulge my passion. It all came to a head when I found some appalling images on my son's mobile. It looked as though he was following in my footsteps, like father, like son.

When I confronted him he gave me a look of total disbelief and more or less conveyed that the kettle can barely afford to call the pot black. Touché! I panicked and promised him a bagful of new goodies. I knew I was being callous in bribing him repeatedly but the constant fear of exposure paralysed me and prudence took a back seat. The web was getting more and more tangled, except I was losing control – I was the fly and he the spider.

I was at the end of my tether as maintaining the status quo, the constant negotiation with my son and feeding my insatiable habit, was becoming impossible to manage – something had to give. I was now consciously debating whether the benefits of buying my son's silence were worth the risks that I was taking. I was on the verge of making a full confession to my wife to end the nightmare when fate intervened.

I had just arrived at Victoria Station for a meeting with an important client when he called me – due to unavoidable circumstances he could not make it. We re-scheduled the conference for the following week and I caught the next train back.

On entering the master bedroom which also doubled as my office, I walked in on my wife and stopped short as the scene before me stunned me. The guilty look on her face said it all. She was at it as well!! Oh, ye Gods! Have mercy!

She had just showered and with her head wrapped in a towel was lounging on the marital bed. The bedsheets were all crumpled up and a couple of the pillows were strewn across the floor. A mini tsunami seemed to have passed through our bedroom. How dare she do that in our bed! I looked around for the culprit; full of pent up and impotent fury. Just then I heard the front door slam shut.

Then I noticed, belatedly, the crimson slender body of a Mojo cigarette, angled precariously on the edge of a makeshift ashtray by the bedside table. She, with great deliberation and looking straight into my eyes, sucked deep on the cigarette and then exhaled; blew a few smoke rings in my direction. Languor personified.

Her scornful grin was challenging me to protest. I thought I could shift the blame and pretend that I was the maligned party. I laid it on thick – the vows we had taken not to smoke as her dad had died of lung cancer; the example that we were supposed to set our son, etc. She just listened in silence, whilst I waited for her to remonstrate with me. I was emboldened by her silence and was about to launch into my sermon when she stopped me in my tracks by her derisory wave of dismissal.

Then she beamed and with a dead pan expression, retorted, 'Darling, drop the act. I am aware of your shenanigans and your backhanders to our son to keep mum. Ditto! Where do you think he got the mullah to sustain his sudden luxurious lifestyle or haven't you noticed? How do you think, without my monetary assistance, he could have afforded all the goodies – the visits to KFC, the expensive aftershave, his new set of golf clubs, etc.? He caught me as well – smoking in the garage months ago. Obviously, he has been blackmailing both of us.'

We had shared a penchant for the expensive Mojo cigarettes when we were courting. Handmade in the UK since 1850, the cigarettes were elegantly extra slim and came in various hues. The wife was partial to the crimson tips; I preferred the sleek black ones with gold foil filter tips; called the Black Mojo. The taste of the tobacco and the aroma were the epitome of exhilaration; crème de la crème of the ciggy world.

The cigarettes took me back to the seventies – the invigorating cricket under the blue Kenyan skies, the satisfying smoke in the club bar after a good game and the company of girlfriends and wives. The Black Mojo became a star at the bar no matter how badly I might have kept wickets or scored ducks as an opener; the sleek black cigarettes always drew attention. The females were drawn irresistibly; like moths to a candescent flame – the Mojos worked like a charm! Sometimes I 'scored' more with my smoke rings in the bar, after a game, than on the field – the life of an opening bat is fraught with difficulty; 'ducks' and 'golden ducks' come with the territory especially if the new ball is swinging.

A bit like walking a dog, especially a golden retriever, or pushing a pram with a baby - it never fails to break the ice with the ladies. The slender black tips had more pulling power, inch for inch, than a Porsche.

I should know – I pulled and married the best of them; Miss Nairobi and a merit scholar; summa cum laude. She had the brains and the beauty; whereas my nearest claim to fame was a University blue in cricket and nothing much else!

Needless to say, our penitent son has agreed to new protocols, a code of behaviour, to make amends for his moral turpitude. He has been grounded for an indefinite period – in view of our complicit involvement which initiated the chain of events we have agreed that 'parole' may be considered in due course. As a joint exercise of contrition we have decided to donate to an appropriate anti-smoking charity – as long as he donates his ill-gotten bounty to a suitable children's charity. He has promised not to smoke, ever. And he has deleted all the images of smoking related activities from his mobile phone – after we threatened him with confiscation of his mobile phone.

Meanwhile, our hidden cache of the filter tipped slims, in the distinctive packaging, is going to be 'cremated' on the barbeque next Sunday. The ashes will have a symbolic burial in the garden, presided over by our contrite son. Our collective penance as a couple will probably be abstinence; the Mojos binned, forevermore.

For a brief moment, I almost snuck out and retrieved a few packets of the 'doomed' cigarettes but then rebuked myself. The spirit should prevail, always; especially if the flesh is weak.

About The Author

Ashwin Dave was born and raised in Kenya. Following Kenya's independence from Britain in December 1963, the family moved initially to Bangalore, South India, and subsequently to London. The author is a graduate (BVSc) of Mysore Veterinary College, Bangalore, and has post-graduate qualifications (MSc) from the Royal Postgraduate Medical School, University of London.

'The Ivory Towers & Other Stories' is his debut book. The author has had a peripatetic life having embarked on several 'migrations' - the first of which started in May 1964 and the last ended when he returned to the UK in 1996. He has lived in London since 1977.

Acknowledgements

For the wonderful memories:
The Class of '68 (Baldwin Boys' High School, Bangalore)
The Class of '76 (Mysore Veterinary College, Bangalore)

My thanks go to the following people for making delivery of this debut book ever so possible – the gestation has lasted so long that I feared 'mummification' was, not only imminent, but inevitable.

H A Gopinath (Gopi), Dr Pinakin Dave, Bharat Dave, Dr Alkesh Dave, Pratap Joshi and Sumitra Iyengar.

And last, by no means the least, Nilesh Trivedi – that chance meeting in Dr A K Dave's GP surgery in Nairobi in 1978 was the start of many good things.

My apologies for leaving out so many but I would be remiss if I did not acknowledge the contribution of my serendipitous trio – they came in threes just at the right time – Mrs Nishtha Mayur Patel, Ms. Debbie Viggiano and Ms. Rebecca Emin (Gingersnap Books).

20091594R00192

Printed in Great Britain
by Amazon

The Ivory Towers and Other Stories

Ashwin Dave

ISBN: 9781728860039

Publishing managed by Gingersnap Books
Formatting and editing by Rebecca Emin
Cover design by Jonathan Temples
Proofreading by Maureen Vincent-Northam
Cover photograph by vicxmendoza